IT SOUNDED

IN MY HEAD

IT SOUNDED  IN MY HEAD

Nina Kenwood

FLATIRON
BOOKS
NEW YORK

IT SOUNDED BETTER IN MY HEAD. Copyright © 2019 by Nina Kenwood. All rights reserved. Printed in the United States of America. For information, address Flatiron Books, 120 Broadway, New York, NY 10271.

www.flatironbooks.com

Designed by Devan Norman

Library of Congress Cataloging-in-Publication Data

Names: Kenwood, Nina, author.
Title: It sounded better in my head / Nina Kenwood.
Description: First U.S. edition. | New York : Flatiron Books, 2020. | Originally published in Australia by Text Publishing Company in 2019. |
Identifiers: LCCN 2019047956 | ISBN 9781250219268 (hardcover) | ISBN 9781250219275 (ebook)
Subjects: CYAC: Dating (Social customs)—Fiction. | Body image—Fiction. | Divorce—Fiction. | Security (Psychology)—Fiction. | Australia—Fiction.
Classification: LCC PZ7.1.K50926 It 2020 | DDC [Fic]—dc23
LC record available at https://lccn.loc.gov/2019047956

Our books may be purchased in bulk for promotional, educational, or business use. Please contact your local bookseller or the Macmillan Corporate and Premium Sales Department at 1-800-221-7945, extension 5442, or by email at MacmillanSpecialMarkets@macmillan.com.

Originally published in Australia in 2019 by the Text Publishing Company

First U.S. Edition: April 2020

10 9 8 7 6 5 4 3 2 1

For Dan

IT SOUNDED

IN MY HEAD

THERE IS NO ONE TO BLAME HERE

It's Christmas Day, we've just finished playing our annual post-lunch game of Scrabble (bonus points if you play a word with a Christmas theme), and Dad says we need to talk. He's using his Bad News voice, and I figure he's either going to give me another lecture about getting my driver's license or tell me he's reactivated his Twitter account.

"Natalie, this is really hard to tell you, but we're, uh, we're separating," he says.

"Who is?"

"Your mother and I."

"Separating." The word feels strange and heavy in my mouth.

"Breaking up," Dad says, because he can never resist hammering a point home once he's made it.

Mum walks into the room then, eating an apple. She vowed fruit would be her only dessert at Christmas this year because she wants to lose two kilos before January, which makes more sense now that I know she is prepping for single life.

"You're breaking up?" My tone is friendly, giving them the

space to say, *Just kidding!* in case it's an elaborate prank, even though we are not a household that is open to pranks of any kind, most especially unfunny, emotionally scarring ones like this.

Mum looks startled at my question, and spends a long time chewing every last bit of her mouthful of apple before speaking.

No, they're not *breaking up,* present tense, verb. They have *Broken Up.* Past tense, capital letters. This isn't new information. I mean, it's new to me, but they've known for ages. Ten months, to be exact.

"What do you mean, ten *months*?" I slam my laptop shut for emphasis. I would like to pretend I was doing something profound in the moments before this life-altering conversation, but in truth I was watching a video of a cat getting scared at the sight of itself in a mirror.

Mum is rattled. This wasn't her plan, to tell me right now, like this, she says. Well, of course it wasn't her plan. It's *Christmas.*

"Remember at the start of the year, when your father went overseas?" Mum says.

"Vaguely." I want to hurry to the part of the story where they explain the fact that they lied to me for the better part of a year. Or to the part where they explain when, exactly, they stopped loving each other and how I missed it.

"Vaguely? Natalie, I was gone for a month!" Dad looks insulted. He's sitting on our old beanbag, which needs more beans, so he's awkwardly sunken right down onto the floor, with his knees almost touching his chin.

"Yes, of course I remember." He went to London and bought me an ugly tourist T-shirt with a slightly distorted picture of Prince Harry's face on it because we have a family tradition of buying each other tacky tourist items whenever we go anywhere. That T-shirt is now my second-favorite thing to wear to bed, after my green Slytherin pajamas.

"Well, we used that time apart to think about our relationship, and when your father got back we decided—mutually—that we didn't want to be romantically together anymore." Mum's eyes are shiny with emotion, but then she ruins the moment by biting into her apple again with a loud, cheerful crunch.

It's all so disgustingly civilized and casual. I can't stand it. I want screaming, tears, drama. I want someone, other than me, to feel like their chest is being stomped on by a giant.

"No one is at fault here," Dad says, which is exactly what someone at fault would say.

"And you made this decision at the end of February?" I'm still hoping that I've misunderstood this part.

"Yes," Dad says.

"Ten. Months. Ago." Saying it more slowly and loudly doesn't make it feel any more real.

"Correct." Dad nods encouragingly, like I'm grappling with a tricky math problem.

"But you've been living together all year."

"In separate bedrooms," Mum says.

"You said it was because of Dad's snoring."

"Well, it was, in part. And in part because of the separation."

"But . . . but I just bought you both matching aprons and you said they were *exactly what you wanted*."

"Well, we can still wear the aprons, sweetheart."

"No, you can't!"

There are so many reasons why this is not okay.

We might be a small family, but we're a great one. An enviable one. Take today, for example. We do a cozy, three-person Christmas so well. We have stockings with our names on them, we watch *Die Hard,* play Scrabble, eat Dad's homemade mince pies, and open our presents one at a time to great fanfare. We listen to carols, wear Santa hats, and take silly photos. And now they've gone and poured vinegar all over our sugary sweetness.

Ten months. They've been lying to me for so long I am momentarily dizzy trying to comprehend it.

"Your father and I are still friends, Natalie. *Good* friends. We are going to stay in each other's lives. We just don't want to be married anymore."

Mum seems to be under the mistaken impression that I consider their friendship a worthwhile consolation prize.

"But it doesn't make any sense. And why did you wait so long to tell me?" I wish I were hysterical and crying, but their calmness is a blanket dampening my angry fire. It's probably a part of their strategy. *Don't let her make a scene. If we stay calm, so will she. Things are only as big a deal as you let them be.* Mum, in particular, loves to throw around that last line, especially when I'm having a bad-skin day and she wants me to go outside.

Unbelievably, Mum goes to bite her apple again, but I snatch it out of her hands.

"Can you stop eating for one second, please?" I'm getting much closer to shouting.

Mum moves and sits next to me on the couch. She puts her arm around me and smooths my hair down, like I'm an animal that needs to be calmed. I want to gnash my teeth, struggle out of her grip, and run howling down the street.

"We wanted to wait until you were finished with school. We didn't want to disrupt your studies during such an important year."

My last exam was in November, and it's been almost two weeks since I received my final results. They've had plenty of time to bring this up before today.

"We love you, honey," Dad says, scooching the beanbag closer. It makes an unpleasant farting noise against the wooden floorboards, which we all pretend not to hear.

"So, you've been lying to me all year?"

"Not lying. Pretending a little. Omitting details."

"Avoiding the inevitable," Dad says.

"Your father and I have grown apart."

"We wanted to be completely sure before we told you."

"It's just one of those things."

"The guilt of not telling you has been eating us up inside."

I can tell they've rehearsed all these lines. Written them down, maybe, practiced in front of a mirror. Read it off a piece of paper like a script. *Do I look sad enough?* I imagine Mum asking Dad. *Speed it up to sound more natural,* I imagine him saying back. *And don't forget to tell her we'll still be friends.*

"No one is to blame here."

Dad has got to stop saying that if he wants me to believe it.

"We love you," Mum says.

This is no comfort. I'm their only child. They have to love me.

"Who am I going to live with?" I ask. What I mean is, *Are you at least fighting over me?*

"You can live with whoever you want," Dad says, voice bright, as though he's handing me a present.

That's not the plan, though. The plan was for me to keep living at home, in this house, in Melbourne, with both of them, when I go to university next year, and after that. I would remain here for the foreseeable future. There was no end date on our situation. That's our plan. That's been our plan from the beginning.

"I don't want to move." My voice shakes a little, and I sound whiny and pathetic instead of firm.

"Honey, no matter what happens, you'll always have a home," Mum says, which is the kind of vague wording designed to comfort but only raises more questions. No matter what happens? *What else is going to happen?*

"You'll have two homes," Dad says, in his most upbeat voice.

I don't want two homes. Who wants two homes? Home only makes sense in the singular form.

I look at them both, with their identical please-adjust-quickly-to-our-terrible-news fake smiles, and I feel a sense of dread.

This is the end of life as I know it.

MY FACE AND OTHER PROBLEMS

I was a cute child. I don't say this as a boast, but as a matter of truth. A woman once came up to my mother and asked if she had thought about getting me into child modeling.

"Your daughter would be perfect for our catalog. She's got the right look."

The woman was talking about a catalog for a chain of discount supermarkets, and the "right look" probably meant ordinary, gap-toothed, and relatable, so we're not talking high glamour, but the point is that my face was once considered photogenic. I had shiny dark hair. Chubby, unmarked cheeks. Twinkling brown eyes. (Okay, I don't know if they were ever actually twinkling, but it's certainly possible that they were, in the right light.) My favorite clothes were my purple glitter sneakers and a T-shirt with a unicorn on it. I even have a name perfectly suited for a pretty child: *Natalie*.

Then, puberty.

Puberty is treated by adults like it's a big joke. Any mention of it seems to be accompanied by humor and knowing smiles. There's talk of voices breaking and hair growing. If I thought much about it at all beforehand, I assumed I would start wearing a bra and have to figure out how a tampon works. But puberty, as it turns out, was an assault. My body changed fiercely and terribly, and I didn't know how to handle it.

I went from being a straight-up-and-down stick figure to a scribble of hips, stomach, breasts, thighs, and stretch marks. I didn't even know stretch marks were *a thing*. I truly did not know they existed until they appeared on my body. When I googled them, all the information was geared toward pregnant women. I felt like a freak, with angry red lines slashing across my hips and lower back, and down my inner thighs, like a graffitied wall.

Once, a girl from my class saw them when I was changing for PE, and she said, "What happened?" and pointed at my hip, and I said, "My cat scratched me," and she widened her eyes with horror, but she believed me because that's what my stretch marks looked like—savage claw marks from a monster cat.

But the stretch marks were nothing compared with the pimples. A regular scattering of pimples at first, and then more, and more. Then pimples that turned, almost overnight, into deep, cystic acne. Thick, hard, welt-like lumps formed under my skin on my back, shoulders, neck, and face. That's not a cool story, or a tragedy that people want to hear about. It's gross. *I was gross.* I woke up thinking that every day for a long time.

My period was heavy and really painful, and managing it felt like a full-time job. I obsessively checked my school dress, my bedsheets, my underwear, my jeans, the couch, the car seat, the train seat—anywhere there could be a hint of what was happening to me. I looked at the back of myself in any reflective surface I could find. I was paranoid about leaving a trace of evidence. The pimples on my shoulders would sometimes burst and leave stains on my top. I was messy, leaking, uncontained.

My body was a shameful disaster. I was too embarrassed to go outside unless I absolutely had to. No, it was worse than that. I was too embarrassed *to exist*. I hunched down and inward, trying to hide every part of me. I hated how much space I took up, because I got taller too. I was huge and hulking. I felt like everywhere I went, I was being seen and noticed in a way I didn't want to be seen and noticed. Even now, on my very best skin days, I'm uncomfortable with people looking at my face. Eye contact makes me feel exposed.

At thirteen, fourteen, fifteen, going to school was hard. Friday night would arrive and I would be filled with such relief. I would unclench and lie on my bed and breathe deeply and reassure myself: *I don't have to go outside or see anyone other than my parents for the next two whole days.* The outside world was a place where I was constantly on edge, waiting for someone to look at or comment on my bad skin. I always carried a book with me so I had an excuse to be looking down, and I rarely spoke up in class so that no one would have a reason to look at me directly. I grew my hair very long and let it fall over my face whenever I could. I would part it on different sides depending on which half of my face needed more covering. I avoided sitting in the brightest part of a room. I watched hundreds of hours of YouTube makeup tutorial videos.

I would never look in a mirror in the school bathrooms, because I didn't want to meet anyone's eyes, but I carried a little compact mirror in my pocket all the time so when I was alone in the toilet cubicle I could check my face slowly, carefully, and without shame and see how bad it was. I would smuggle concealer and foundation in too, and reapply it constantly throughout the day.

Acne hurts. No one talks about how painful it is. Well, no one talks about it at all. My face, my back, my shoulders, they all ached. If someone bumped me, I would flinch away. If I accidentally knocked a pimple on my face, involuntary tears would pop into my eyes. I had to slink and maneuver my way through the world, trying not to be seen, touched, or noticed at all.

Somewhere around the age of thirteen, a new personality appeared along with my pimples. Reluctant Natalie. Anxious Natalie. Bitter Natalie. Neurotic Natalie. I was never these things before, and I wasn't them, not really, but that's how people saw me, and so that's who I became.

I'm eighteen now, and sometimes I still want to stand up and scream, *This isn't really me*.

This is all a roundabout way of saying I became something of a shut-in during high school. I mean, I'm still something of a shut-in now, but I was a *pathological* shut-in for a long time.

And until my face was fixed, until I met Zach and Lucy, until I got a bit tougher, my parents were all I had.

SOMETHING OBSCENE ON
A PARK BENCH

The day after the Christmas bombshell, I go to Zach's house and walk in through the back door without knocking. I've been friends with Zach for a few years now, and I still get a secret thrill out of being allowed to walk into his house unannounced. It feels like I've unlocked the highest friendship level.

"Hello," I call out.

"Natalie." Lucy appears at the end of the hall. Lucy and Zach have been officially together for nine months, which is a very long time at our age, practically a marriage, but it's a situation I am still adjusting to. We were once a friendship group of three individuals—three equals, three devoted but platonic points of a triangle—and now we're a breathlessly in love couple (them) and a person who spends her Saturday night taking photos of the back of her head in a mirror so she can understand what it's like to see herself from behind (me).

I am forced to second-guess everything. Is it movie night like always, or am I crashing their date? If I tell one of them a secret, will they automatically tell the other? If they have a fight, do I have to pick a side straightaway, and can I change my side halfway through? How often, exactly, do they talk about me when I'm not there? (I hate the thought that they might, but I also hate the thought that they might not. I would like to be one of their top three conversation topics, but only if they are spending a significant amount of time reflecting on my sparkling personality.)

Zach appears behind Lucy, sliding in his socks. Zach is the yardstick that I measure every other guy against. Zach's mannerisms, Zach's way of doing things, Zach's voice, Zach's tallness, Zach's lankiness—he's just how boys should be, because he's the only boy I've ever really been friends with, and the best one I've met.

Lucy hurries down the hall to hug me.

"It sucks," she says. I told her about my parents last night.

Lucy is a good hugger. She's my favorite person in the world, so even just seeing her face makes me feel better.

"I'm sorry," Zach says.

"Thanks," I say. I would like to say I don't want anyone's sympathy, but I generally quite enjoy my friends feeling sorry for me, especially about this. Firstly, it means I actually have friends who care about me, which, when you know what it's like not to have any friends at all, means a lot. Secondly, "my parents are splitting up" is a refreshingly normal and acceptable problem to have, and it's far less embarrassing than an I-have-an-infected-pimple-that's-so-huge-and-disfiguring-that-it-has-sent-me-into-a-spiral-of-depression-so-I-won't-be-getting-out-of-bed-today kind of issue.

I follow Zach and Lucy farther into the house, and Zach's mother, Mariella, rushes out of the kitchen to hug me.

"Darling, how are you? Zach told me about your parents. Don't you worry for a second. Everything's going to be fine.

And don't go blaming anyone. Relationships are hard. Sal and I have almost separated at least four times over the years. It's actually a miracle we're still together."

Mariella is an oversharer.

"Mum! Please." Zach puts his arm between us, as if this can stop his mother's words.

"Run, Natalie," Zach's younger brother Anthony says as he walks past, stirring an almost overflowing glass of Milo. Zach has three brothers, and I only truly understood the necessity of jumbo tins of Milo after my first visit to his house.

I laugh, and push Zach aside for another hug from Mariella. I suspect I'm her favorite (out of Lucy and me), and that thought pleases me more than I care to admit. I'm not Zach's number one, but I can be Mariella's first pick.

Adult approval has long been my drug of choice.

Zach's house is much bigger and fancier than mine. He's richer than Lucy and me, although that's not something we would ever talk about. It's obvious, though. It kind of seeps out everywhere, from his house to the fact that his parents send all four kids to a private school to the way he always suggests we see movies at IMAX in 3-D, even bad movies that we're only seeing for a bit of fun.

In his house, they have a room they call the den, which is a word I had only ever previously encountered in American books and movies and never heard said out loud in this context before. The den has a huge TV, various game consoles, two big old leather couches, and not much else. It's the designated hangout space for all the kids, because Mariella doesn't like the boys in the good lounge room.

"Too many teenage boys in one room for too long and it gets a smell, and that smell never leaves," Mariella says. I don't know if that's true, but it *sounds* true, and if anyone would know, it's the mother of four sons. And the den does have a sort-of smell to it—a musk of deodorant, sweat, and food.

We set ourselves up in the den. Lucy sits next to me and Zach sits on the other couch. I sense this is a deliberate move on their behalf, to deemphasize their coupleness in the face of my parents' separation. The thing is, Lucy and I used to be the inseparable twosome, and Zach was the one slightly on the outside. He could never quite crack the closeness we had. Until, well, I guess he found a way.

Lucy rests her head on my shoulder. Her hair tickles my cheek.

"What's going to happen with your parents?"

"Dad is moving out."

"Wow. That's fast," Zach says.

"Well, not considering they've been broken up for almost a year. It's actually very slow."

"Where's he going to live?" Lucy asks.

"He's renting an apartment. In Port Melbourne."

I can't picture him in an apartment. It seems like something for young people. Not forty-seven-year-olds who like playing chess, cooking paella, and singing in a choir. Or maybe apartments are for exactly these kinds of people. Dad is single now. He will start online dating and I will have to sit through painful introductions to polite women who have as little interest in me as I have in them. I will have to take a photograph of Dad that he can use on the site, one that doesn't make him look like a serial killer (this is tough, because he doesn't smile in photos), and then check his dating profile for spelling mistakes, because he has no one else in his life to do these things. I can see my future unfolding before my eyes—hours spent editing the dating profiles of my parents and then consoling them when they are ghosted or, worse, scammed out of huge sums of money.

"Say what you like about my mum, but at least I know she can't keep a secret that big from me," Zach said, his mouth full of Tim Tam.

It's true. Mariella tells you more than you ever want to know about anything. Over the years, she has told us about the man she lived with before meeting Sal ("He left his toenail clippings in the sink, and if that's not a sign of a sociopath, I don't know what is"), the time she was caught shoplifting ("I was twelve and my cousin said she'd distract the salesperson for me, but she didn't, and that's why we don't go to their house at Easter to this day"), and the time she saw a ghost ("An older woman with white hair, standing at the end of our bed, but I wasn't scared because I knew her rage was toward men, so only Sal was in danger").

"My mum would never leave Dad. Or let him leave her," Lucy says. That's true too. Lucy's mother would push through fifty years of deep unhappiness before she got divorced, because divorce might be misconstrued as failure, and that word isn't in her vocabulary. That's literally her phrasing, not mine. Lucy's mother runs ten kilometers every morning before breakfast, wearing a singlet that says "Don't Stop When You're Tired, Stop When You're Done" in a very aggressive font. She works sixty hours a week managing her own business, and she started introducing Lucy to people as "my little champion debater and future lawyer" from when Lucy was about twelve, before Lucy had even joined the school debating team.

Lucy's mother is . . . a lot.

But now that my parents have dropped this breakup bombshell and performed an elaborate charade for the better part of a year, I can no longer be soothed by the idea that my mother is less damaging than Lucy's or Zach's. My one life advantage is gone. I have family issues now, along with everything else.

"I can't believe we never noticed," Lucy continues.

"I can't believe *I* didn't notice."

I can't dwell on this too much because it makes my stomach feel squirmy in the same way as when I think too hard about my existence and what will happen after I die. It was my Wizard of Oz moment—my parents pulled back the curtain, and what I saw there makes me feel sick.

"But do you notice now, in hindsight?" Zach asks.

"No. I always thought they were perfect, which means my entire idea of what constitutes a happy relationship is irreparably damaged. I need to be in some kind of pre–couple's therapy right now, heading off my own future marital problems before they start."

Zach and Lucy exchange a she's-spiraling glance that I pretend not to see.

Zach's older brother Alex walks into the room then, followed by his friend Owen Sinclair.

Alex is nineteen and has just finished his first year as an apprentice chef. He and Zach are almost eighteen months apart in age, but they were only a year apart in school, because Zach was bumped up a grade in primary school when they moved from Perth to Melbourne. That's Zach's role in his family: the Smart One, the High Achiever, the Smug Grade-Skipper. I might be an only child, but I've figured out that siblings tend to occupy roles in their family. Alex is the Irresponsible One Who Kisses All the Girls and Can Make Delicious Gnocchi from Scratch. Their two younger brothers are the Shy One with the Face You Can't Say No To (Anthony, age fifteen) and the Dinosaur-Obsessed Attention-Seeker (Glenn, age twelve).

Alex moves through the world with the effortlessness of a

well-liked firstborn son. He has a hot ex-girlfriend, a seemingly endless supply of gray V-necked T-shirts, and hundreds of people he could classify as friends. He's the kind of generically popular male that I instinctively avoid.

I don't like Alex. No, that's not true. Alex has never done anything mean to me. In fact, he once offered me the last slice of pizza, and another time he was walking through the room when Zach and I were arguing about something and he said, "Natalie's right," as he breezed past. But I still don't *trust* Alex, because he's the kind of guy a girl like me is naturally wary of. My default assumption is that he's probably thinking something negative about me.

Alex's friend Owen Sinclair is a slightly safer kind of popular guy, because he's so openly preoccupied with himself. He's not thinking bad things about you because he's thinking good things about himself. He's tall, baby-faced, and surfer blond, uncomplicated, and he seems to be clueless about anything that's not happening directly in front of his eyes. Girls love him, and he loves them back. He once did something obscene—I'm not sure exactly what—with a girl on a park bench in broad daylight. He can play the guitar and almost dunk a basketball. He sometimes wears his hair in a man bun. And his middle name is Macaulay, because his parents' favorite movie is *Home Alone*. That's everything I know, have overheard, or somehow gleaned about Owen Sinclair.

"Hey," Owen says, sitting down next to me. I'm pretty sure he's never spoken directly to Lucy or me before. I'm pretty sure I've never made eye contact with him before. Owen Sinclair is like the sun. I've never looked straight at him for more than one second.

"Hi," Lucy says.

"Hi," I say.

"What's happening?" Owen says.

"Nothing much," I say.

"Cool." Owen leans back on the couch, running his arm over the back of it so it almost, kind of, could be construed as putting his arm around me. I mean, his arm is *not* around me, but if it slipped off the couch, it—momentarily—would be.

I drop my face a little, so Owen is seeing my best angle. After two rounds of Accutane, a range of topical lotions, and finding the right brand of the Pill, my skin is a thousand times better than it was. These days, I usually have no pimples at all, and at worst there are only one or two, plus the scarring I cover up with foundation. I have lots of deep, irreparable scarring on my back, where the acne was the very worst (I don't wear backless tops, bikinis, or strapless dresses), but, all in all, my skin situation went from life-destroying to manageable to good. I forget that, though. I still think from the life-destroying perspective.

Years ago, when I was hiding in a toilet cubicle checking my face, I overheard Heather Hamilton, the girl in my year level with the most Instagram followers of anyone I know in real life, say offhandedly, "You know, if it wasn't for her terrible skin and her big nose, Natalie could be pretty," and a few girls said, "Oh yeah, you're right!" as though she'd discovered something profound. I don't care what Heather Hamilton thinks about anything, but I did care what she thought about me in that moment, because it confirmed everything I'd thought about myself. *If it wasn't for my skin* . . . everything might have been so different. I could have been someone who was confident, taking perfect selfies, going to parties, auditioning for plays, maybe even a minor YouTube celebrity . . . *I could have been so much better.* I was fourteen when Heather said that, and I still think about it. I wonder if I will think about it for the rest of my life.

(The nose I can live with. Big noses are artistic. But the world has assured me only villains and losers have acne.)

"Let's watch a movie," Owen says.

"We were about to play a game," Zach says, which is a lie, but only half a lie, because in truth playing board games is how we spend a lot of our time. Zach doesn't like Owen. I'm not even sure he likes Alex that much.

"Cool. What game?" Owen seems genuinely interested in hanging out with us. Alex looks less interested, but he's not protesting.

Lucy makes quick eye contact with me. I can tell by her face that we're both thinking the same thing: Since when have Alex and his friends ever shown any interest in spending time with us? Maybe now that we've finished high school we're automatically cooler. We're giving off the sophisticated, worldly vibe of adults. Or maybe they're just really bored.

"We're playing Resistance," Zach says.

"Can you teach us?" Owen asks, looking at Lucy and me.

"It'll take too long," Zach says.

"No, it won't. It's easy to learn," Lucy says. A series of looks have been passing between her and Zach as they argue with their eyes.

"I'll show you," I say.

Owen and Alex listen as I run through the rules, holding my hand up to silence Zach when he tries to interrupt me. Zach is a stickler for following a game's exact rules and explaining every detail.

"Okay, we've got it," says Alex, who is lying on his stomach on the couch, resting his head on a cushion. I try to look at his eyes without being obvious. Is he stoned? Maybe. He's certainly eating a lot of our Tim Tams.

"We have too many people. It's better if you have three or four," Zach says.

"You sit out, then," Alex says.

"Fuck off."

Zach and his brothers regularly swear and yell at each other with affection. I think it's affection, anyway. Siblings, especially brothers, confuse me. They can go from talking to wrestling in two seconds flat. I come from a family that has excitedly sat around and listened to the *Hamilton* musical soundtrack after dinner on a Friday night. We enjoy nature documentaries. We get excited about buying stationery. We keep our phones on silent, all of the time. I don't know what to do with all the noise, the energy, the physicality of Zach's family.

"Lucy and I will be on one team, and you three on the other," I say.

"You seem very confident," Alex says.

"You'll see," Lucy says.

They do see. Lucy and I win easily. Zach is grumpy, because Owen doesn't understand the rules and Alex doesn't care enough to try. Zach doesn't like losing, but he especially doesn't like losing through the incompetence of his fellow team members.

"Okay, another round, but we change up the teams this time," Zach says.

Zach and Lucy team up, and I join Owen and Alex. I excuse myself to go to the bathroom and look at my skin, check my teeth for food, my nose for anything that might be there. I look okay. It's hard for me to trust that this will still be the case once I'm away from the mirror, though.

"Okay, let me make the strategy decisions and we'll win," I whisper when I get back into the room and I'm sitting cross-legged on the floor.

"So what do we do?" Owen says.

"Watch and learn." I can be just a little bit bossy when I get caught up in a game.

"I understand it now. I'll be better. Let me help," Alex says, reaching for another Tim Tam.

"Okay. You tell me what move you think we should make, and I'll tell you if it's right or wrong."

"When did you get so competitive?" Alex says, shaking his head and grinning, before biting into the biscuit.

"Natalie is the most competitive person I know," Zach says, overhearing us.

"Says the guy who once told me to leave his house when I beat him at Monopoly," I say.

"Well, that's different. That's Monopoly. The worst game in the world," Zach says.

Alex laughs. "Zach once cried when I put a hotel on Park Lane," he says.

"I was six at the time," Zach says.

"You were at least ten," Alex replies.

In truth, Zach and I are probably equally competitive. When I lost motivation for studying, I would sometimes imagine him up late, still working, and I would feel renewed energy. We enjoyed pushing each other to do better. Lucy, less so. I'm pretty sure she hated every moment of our last school year.

We're currently in that strange limbo month between mid-December and mid-January when we know our final results but we don't yet know which course or university we've gotten into, which is stressful for all of us, but especially for Lucy. She changes the subject anytime we talk about it.

We all got good marks. We had to. Zach and Lucy have very concrete career aspirations; he wants to be a doctor, and she wants to be a lawyer. Extremely cliché, if you ask me (all the type-A high achievers at my school said doctor, lawyer, or engineer when asked what they want to be), but at least they have goals. They want to be *something*. They'll have real jobs. And money. I don't know what I want to be. I mostly trained myself to do well at school as an antidote to all the dark thoughts, the ones that said, *No one likes you very much,* and *You have nothing to show for your life except schoolwork,* and *You have the face of a monster.* As if each A+ could somehow offset each pimple.

I chose Australian history, literature, Australian politics, psychology, and English as my subjects to study. All areas I knew I could do well in, where I could read and write and analyze. I was boringly sensible in my choices. I avoided math and science because they're not my strengths. I dreamed of doing drama and theater, but I never had the confidence to perform—there's too much focus on your face. You have to be comfortable with someone looking at you in order to stand on a stage. So I did everything the Right Way in order to get the Right Score and now I am waiting to find out if I got into the Right University. But none of this has helped me figure out who I am or what I want to do. Do you just wake up one morning after a really good sleep and know? (I'm relying on this happening.)

I may not have a plan for my life, but I do have a plan for winning at Resistance. Under my guidance, Alex, Owen, and I are victorious—just—and Zach sulks, which makes it even sweeter. Alex insists we keep playing, because he's remembered how much he enjoys beating his brother. We play again, although Owen has clearly lost interest, and this time we lose.

"Okay, that's it, you can go now," Zach says, looking smug and packing up the pieces.

"We have to go anyway," Alex says, yawning and stretching. He's not tall, but there's something about him that seems to take up a lot of space.

"That was fun. Hey, Natalie, you should come to Benny's party with us on Friday night," Owen suddenly says to me.

Before I can react, Zach and Lucy both speak at the same time.

"Yes," Lucy says.

"No," Zach says.

Alex looks at them both. "Are you guys Natalie's friends or her parents?"

"A bit of both," I say.

I know why Zach is saying no—he thinks his brother and especially his brother's friends are not Good People, and that I will be in way over my head at their party. Both of which are probably true. Lucy is thinking that Owen is hot and he's inviting me somewhere, so I should go, and also—possibly—that she and Zach can have a guilt-free night alone. All of this is true too.

I look at Owen.

"Who's Benny?"

"Our friend. He's cool. You'll like him."

"Okay. I'll go." I say it before I can chicken out. I can't actually believe I've said these words. I don't *go* to things. I hate going to things. Most especially parties.

"Give me your number and I'll text you the details," Owen says, pulling out his phone. I can practically feel Lucy vibrating with excitement from the other couch.

I say my number out loud, twice, because I can't stand the thought that this opportunity might be lost because he mistyped a number. He sends me a text straightaway, the smiling emoji with sunglasses. That self-assured little emoji face has never looked so beautiful.

"Now you've got my number," Owen says, unnecessarily.

I am trying to ignore the fact that I find his personality a tiny bit dull. "Awesome," I say. I hate the word *awesome*. It slips out when I'm nervous.

After Alex and Owen leave, Lucy grabs me and shakes me. "You're going to a party with Owen Sinclair!"

"I know," I say.

We hold each other's arms and squeal and jump up and down, and when Zach looks disgusted, we do it again and collapse with laughter.

Mariella pokes her head into the room. "Everything all right in here?"

"Natalie is going to a party with Owen."

"Owen Sinclair?"

"Yes."

"Oh goodness." Mariella looks surprised, pleased, and worried all at once.

"See? Mum thinks it's a bad idea." Zach looks triumphant, even though normally agreeing with his mother about something like this would automatically make him change his mind.

"Don't worry. I'm not going to fall in love with him or anything," I say, even though I am already running multiple fantasies of our romance through my head. (Scene: Owen and me holding hands, walking into a cool café filled with everyone I disliked from school, who all turn their heads and stare at us. I'm wearing an amazing leather jacket and my hair is falling in gentle waves, and someone takes a perfectly lit photo of us laughing together over coffee that somehow ends up all over social media because in this scenario we're also low-level famous.)

Later that night, lying in bed, unable to sleep, I decide the best thing about agreeing to go to the party is that I am so stressed and worried about it that I have hardly any space left in my head to think about my parents.

4

PATRICK SWAYZE AND
OTHER PEOPLE'S BATHROOMS

Mum pulls up across the road from Benny's house (whoever Benny is—I'm still not entirely sure). I can hear the thump of music coming from the party. It seems very loud. I wonder if the police will turn up. Could I be arrested? I'm still getting used to the idea of going to the house of someone who doesn't live with their parents.

"You sure you're okay?" Mum asks.

I'm obviously still extremely mad at her about the separation, and even more so for lying to me for a year, but I put my anger on a temporary hold tonight so she could drive me to the party.

I'm freaking out and I need my mother.

"Of course," I say.

But I don't get out of the car. I'm so nervous I could throw up. I don't know if Owen is there yet, but I don't want to message him and ask. He said he would be there at eight. He didn't say, *I'll meet you there,* or anything. He just wrote, *We'll be there at 8,* and the address. It's eight forty-five. He must be in there. But he hasn't texted me to see where I am, so he's either not there or he's there and doesn't care that I'm not there. It's a lose-lose scenario.

"We can just go home, you know," Mum says. She has pushed me to socialize since I was ten years old, and now here I am at a party and she's trying to sabotage me.

"No, thanks." I cross my arms, so she can't see that my hands are shaking.

"You can go to parties without going to *this* party," she says.

"I'm going."

"Okay."

"In one minute."

"Okay."

We sit in silence for about thirty seconds and then I open the door, but I'm still not quite ready to get out of the car.

"'Bye, Mum."

"Call me to pick you up."

"I'll get an Uber."

"I can pick you up."

"I might . . . stay at Owen's." I haven't actually considered this possibility until the words come out of my mouth. Am I seriously planning on hooking up with Owen? Am I planning on having *sex* tonight? No. The idea is preposterous. Owen and I have had one conversation in our lives. We're unlikely to make eye contact, let alone bodily contact, let alone kiss, let alone have sex. I don't even want to have sex with him. But it feels important that Mum believes it could happen. That's the first step toward it one day actually happening—that other people look at me and think, *This person could feasibly have sex with someone.*

Also, I want to test Mum a little.

"Oh, Natalie, no, I don't think that's a good idea."

"Do I need your permission?" I'm not being snarky or rude with this question. I genuinely don't know. I turned eighteen seven weeks ago. I'm an adult. I. Am. An. Adult. I do not feel like an adult. I feel light-years away from being an adult. I mean, I'm also still a teenager, which is a relief. I always had this vision of myself doing something important during my teen years. I didn't think I would be a child prodigy, but I thought I would be something *very* close to it, and now I'm almost out of time. Before I know it, I'll be twenty-one and no one will be impressed by anything I do.

Mum purses her lips. "I suppose not. I mean, I like to know where you are. But you're eighteen, so you can technically go wherever you want."

"Technically?"

"Legally. Officially. In the eyes of the law."

"But?"

"I don't want my baby to stay at some boy's house."

"Don't call me your baby. That is gross and infantilizing."

"You get a boyfriend and now you're too good to be called baby. You'll never have Patrick Swayze with that attitude."

"Patrick Swayze is dead."

"I know, sweetie. It was a *Dirty Dancing* reference." Mum made me watch *Dirty Dancing, The Bodyguard,* and *Muriel's Wedding* when I was fourteen, in order that I would, as she put it, understand her "emotional landscape."

"I get the reference. But it was weird to mention him."

"If I can't make *Dirty Dancing* references, then end my life now, because it isn't worth living."

"He's not my boyfriend."

"What?"

"Owen. Just in case you somehow meet him and call him my boyfriend. It's not like that. At all. We're not even friends. We barely know each other. I don't think he'd recognize me if we passed each other on the street."

"Well, why on earth are you thinking about spending the night with him?" Mum says, her voice jumping about five octaves.

"Because that's what people do. Boyfriends and girlfriends aren't really a big thing anymore. People are more casual now. They just hook up whenever." One of my superpowers is pretending I know a lot more about something than I actually do.

"If boyfriends and girlfriends aren't a thing anymore, then what are Zach and Lucy doing?"

"Being old-fashioned."

"Well, there's nothing wrong with old-fashioned."

"I'm going now."

"I think you should at least wait until you know his surname."

"It's Sinclair."

"Owen Sinclair? Didn't he do something with a girl on a park bench once?"

I need to stop having conversations in front of my parents. My mother retains far too much information.

"No, you're thinking of someone else." I turn to get out of the car.

Mum reaches out and puts her hand on my arm.

"You've scared me. I don't want to let you go now."

"Mum, probably nothing is going to happen. I just wanted to clear a path in your mind in case it does."

"Clear a path in my mind?" She's smiling.

I frown at her. "Yes."

She pulls me back into the car and kisses my cheek. "Okay. Consider the path cleared."

"'Bye, Mum." I shut the car door and start crossing the road. I can hear the buzz of her window rolling down.

"'Bye, hon. Text me too. I'll be waiting up. And don't do anything you don't want to do. Don't let anyone put anything in your drink. And don't take drugs—you're not ready for that. Have fun!"

Oh my god. I hurry away before she can think of another stream of mortifying things to call out. She hasn't driven off yet, which means she's going to sit there and watch me go in.

I slow down as I approach the house, trying to look a lot more confident than I am. There are two guys I don't know sitting on the steps leading up to the front door. They glance at me as I open the gate and walk toward them but continue their conversation. Should I say hi? I should say hi. I imagine myself saying hello in my nervous, too-formal voice and I imagine them raising their eyebrows at each other and then mimicking me behind my back as I walk in. I won't say anything. That's safer. I should pretend to be on my phone. But it's too late for that now. I'm right beside them. Oh god, is one of them Benny?

I pause at the steps and maneuver awkwardly around them. They don't even look at me or stop their conversation as I brush past.

The front door is open. There's a long hallway with a stained carpet that could be gray or brown or blue—it's impossible to tell—and music. I follow the hallway, peering into empty rooms as I pass them (a messy bedroom with an unmade bed and three guitars propped against it, another bedroom with posters of people I don't know on the walls and a stack of dirty dishes on the bedside table) until I find a big lounge room where a bunch of people are sitting on couches and beanbags. There are double doors thrown open to a courtyard, and I can see more people out there, smoking and vaping. I can't see Owen. Everyone looks so much older, even though I know most of them are only a year or two ahead of me.

I hover in the doorway to the lounge room, feeling like an idiot. I spend ten agonizing seconds trying to look relaxed and normal, scanning every face desperately for Owen or Alex, and then I turn around and walk into the bathroom and lock the door.

I sit on the toilet for a while, and play on my phone until the battery goes down to 40 percent (I somehow forgot to charge it this afternoon, an amateur mistake) and then I stop, because getting through the rest of this night without a phone is an unbearable thought. I should just text Owen. He might even be here and I just didn't see him, but I can't bring myself to go back out there. How do people do it? How do they walk into a room of strangers and join conversations? And even if I could pretend I was comfortable doing that, I'm not sure this is the kind of party where that can happen. I don't have the first clue how to interact with these people, who all know each other and go to university together and are utterly comfortable in each other's presence. I'm some weird high school kid who's spent her whole life reading about parties rather than going to them.

I'm nervous-sweating now. I put bunches of toilet paper under my armpits to stop myself from getting sweat stains on my clothes. I'm wearing a cheap patterned dress I bought from a chain store that's designed to look like it might be a nineties vintage dress from an op shop. I bought it because it looked soft and floaty on the mannequin, and because it has cute buttons on the front, but it's not quite soft and floaty on me. It's itchy and doesn't sit straight over my left boob. But the buttons do look cute.

Someone knocks on the bathroom door and I say nothing. They turn the handle, find it locked, and knock again. I call out, "I'm in here. Sorry." I hear footsteps walking away.

I really, really want to call Mum to pick me up, but, no matter how grim this night gets, I won't do that.

I start looking through the bathroom cabinets because I

have nothing else to do. Painkillers. Fungal cream. Birth control pills. Toothpaste, with the cap off and a thick gloop of it on the shelf. Multivitamins. Mouthwash. Condoms. Lots of condoms. Medication that looks like antidepressants. I close the cabinet door, feeling bad for snooping.

They have a big, grungy bathtub that looks like it hasn't been cleaned in months. I put an already damp towel in the bottom and sit in the bathtub, because it seems less gross than sitting on the toilet. I can see several dark hairs clinging to the side of the bath. There's nothing more disgusting than other people's bathrooms. I sit there for what feels like a long time, but is probably two minutes, waiting for something to happen. I imagine standing up, slipping, hitting my head on the edge of the tub, and no one finding me until the next day, when it's too late to save me. That would be a very sad way to die, in the dirty bathtub of a stranger.

There's a chorus of loud shouting and laughter as a new group of people arrive, clomping down the hallway, carrying bags of clinking bottles.

"Heeeeeeyyyyyyy!"

"Yo!"

"You're finally here!"

"Bro!"

I recognize Owen's voice and I feel so much relief my body actually sags against the side of the tub.

There's more noise and then someone tries to open the bathroom door and rattles the handle.

"I hate to be rude, but there's a line of people needing to piss out here," a voice says from the other side of the door.

"Some chick has been in there for, like, half an hour," says another voice.

"We're about to start peeing in sinks out here!" a third voice chimes in.

Surely they would pee in the garden before they used the kitchen sink. People just don't think sometimes.

I stand up, not knowing what to do. I pull the toilet paper out from my armpits and flush it down the toilet. I immediately regret doing that, because now they'll think I've been *on* the toilet all this time.

I walk to the door and unlock it, opening it a crack. Six faces stare back at me. One of them is Owen's, another is Alex's, and the rest I don't know.

"Natalie!" Owen says. He looks like he is very pleased with himself for remembering my name.

Alex leans forward. "Are you okay?" he asks.

I don't think I've ever seen him look concerned before.

"Yes, I'm fine. I haven't been in here for half an hour. It's been ten minutes. I needed somewhere quiet to make a phone call. Sorry." I'm babbling, and I can feel that my face is red.

All six of them continue staring at me. I need to walk away now, but that means walking back into the party. I am frozen, unwilling to give up the safe oasis of the bathroom.

Owen steps forward, pushes the door open, and walks into the bathroom.

"Turn around," he says.

"Why?"

"I'm about to pee."

He's already standing over the toilet and unzipping his fly. I am a prudish only child who grew up with a bathroom to herself and no brothers, so there's no way I can remain in the room with a guy peeing. Also, it's not a thing a guy would do in front of a girl he wants to maybe kiss at some point, so my fantasy of hooking up with Owen Sinclair takes a further step away from the realm of possibility. Or maybe Owen is so self-assured, has lived a life of such untouchable male privilege, that he can pee in front of someone with full confidence that he could still kiss them later.

I leave the bathroom and walk about five steps before I'm at a loss where to go, again. This time there is a familiar face to bail me out. Alex is putting beers in the fridge in the kitchen. I hover nearby, forgetting all my wariness about him. No longer is he somebody I don't trust. Now he's my life jacket, my safety net, my I-will-hang-on-to-you-like-grim-death fellow partygoer.

"What were you doing in the bathroom?" he asks when he sees me.

What kind of outrageous question is that?

"I told you. Making a phone call."

"Not hiding?"

"Definitely not hiding."

"Okay. Just seemed like you might have been hiding."

"I wasn't."

"Good." He finishes putting the beers in the fridge and waves to someone across the room.

Owen walks out of the bathroom, running his hand through his hair in a way that makes it obvious he knows how great his hair is. It's weird to look at someone and know they are probably very vain and they just peed in front of you but still be attracted to them.

"Hey, having fun?" he asks me.

"Yes," I reply.

"Cool," he says, very clearly looking over my shoulder for someone better.

My heart is pounding. What happens now? Do we keep talking? Owen walks out of the kitchen and into the lounge room.

I follow him, and hover in the background. There's a free chair in the far corner, and I sit in it and smile at people, trying to catch someone's eye, trying to see an opening to say something. There's none, in part because the chair has been pushed off to the side and wedged half behind a shelf, so I'm out of the eyeline of the people chatting on the other chairs and couches.

I pull out my phone and pretend I am texting someone. I google "top ten tips for talking to people at parties" and scroll through suggestions about introducing myself with a firm-but-not-too-firm handshake (I don't know much, but this party really does not seem like the kind of party where you would shake hands with someone), asking engaging questions (it does not explain how to know if a question is engaging or not), and smiling and laughing when appropriate (which sends me into a spiral: *Maybe I've never smiled or laughed at an appropriate time in my entire life and I just didn't realize that until this moment*).

My phone battery drops to 30 percent and I reluctantly put it away. I have to keep it for emergency moments only now. Or maybe I can find a charger in the house. That could be a conversation opener, if I can figure out who Benny is and then ask him if I could borrow a charger, and then maybe we keep talking and I ask a bunch of really engaging questions and we hit it off. Maybe Benny and I will fall in love.

I walk back into the kitchen. Someone has spilled Coke all over the bench, so I grab a cloth and clean it up. I throw a few empty beer bottles in the bin and I'm contemplating the dirty dishes when Alex walks in.

"Are you cleaning? Why are you cleaning?" He's laughing.

"Just wiping up a spill," I say.

He stops laughing. "Are you sure you're okay?"

"Yes."

"You don't have to stay here, you know." Alex sits on the bench I just wiped, and I try not to be annoyed by this.

"What does that mean?"

"Parties aren't your thing."

"Who told you that?"

"You did."

"No, I didn't."

"Yeah, you did. About six months ago. You said you can't stand parties and you hate most people."

That definitely sounds like something I would say. I mean, it's kind of true, but it's also a great line for someone who is looking for an excuse not to leave her house. It's such a relief when every internet quiz I do says I'm an introvert, like I've been given written permission to avoid everyone and everything. You don't have to try now because you're an introvert, is what I take it to mean.

"I've changed my mind," I say.

"Really?"

"Yes. I love parties now. And people." I'm using my most upbeat tone.

"What brought on this turnaround?"

"I'm trying to be more open-minded. It's my New Year's resolution," I say. This is a lie. My real New Year's resolutions are to learn how to do my own eyeliner, read one hundred books, and fix all my issues (emotional, physical, mental) before I start uni.

"But it's not New Year's Eve for another four days," he says, smiling and making what I think my "top ten tips for talking to people at parties" article would call "warm eye contact."

"I'm starting early," I say, trying to maintain the eye contact, which is difficult because my heart is racing.

"Smart," he says.

Alex stops smiling, and his eyes go to someone behind me. I turn, and see that it's Vanessa Nguyen, his ex. She went to my school, a year ahead of me. Now she studies fine arts at the

Victorian College of the Arts and she has a nose piercing and a tattoo of a bird on her wrist and she's cooler than I can ever dream of being. She and Alex were on-again-off-again all through high school.

"Hey, Ness," Alex says, and his face is all tight and tense. He's still in love with her, I assume.

"Hi, Vanessa," I say, because I am trying to show Alex that I don't hate people.

"Hi," she says to me with a hint of uncertainty. I can tell she vaguely recognizes me but has no idea who I am.

"How are you?" Vanessa says to Alex.

I should leave, so they can have their awkward conversation in private, but I have nowhere to go and, also, I was here first.

"I'm good, how are you?"

"Busy. You know."

"Yeah. Are you still working at that bar?"

"Nah, I quit."

"I'm glad. That manager was sleazy."

"He was the worst. How do you two know each other?"

It takes me several seconds to realize Vanessa is referring to Alex and me. It's such an odd question—as if Alex and I are here together, as if how I know Alex matters at all.

I laugh nervously.

"Natalie is friends with Zach. You would have seen her at my house," Alex says.

"Oh yeah, I thought you looked familiar."

I don't know what to say to that—I want to point out that we also went to school together—but I stick with my trademark move and say nothing.

"Well, I've got to go say hi to Jacqui. I'll talk to you later," Vanessa says, and she touches his arm and then walks off.

Alex sighs after she's out of earshot.

I hitch myself up onto the kitchen bench beside him. "Are you two still friends?" I ask.

"Not really. Or, yes, we are but in a weird way," he says.

"I'm sorry," I say.

"About what?"

"Seeing her makes you sad."

"No, it doesn't. I'm not sad. I'm . . ." But he doesn't finish the sentence. I raise my eyebrows.

He folds his arms as if he's not going to say anything, then says, "Fine, seeing her makes me feel a teeny, tiny bit sad."

"That sucks."

"But it's not like I still want to be with her. I don't. I just . . . I don't know. It's weird."

Alex is jiggling his leg and I reach out and put my hand on his knee to stop him. Only after I remove my hand from his leg does it occur to me that I've never touched him before. I'm suddenly self-conscious about the intimate gesture.

He looks at me, as if he's thinking the same thing about us never having touched before.

"Zach does that leg-jiggling too. It drives me nuts," I say, suddenly filled with the need to explain.

"Must be genetic," Alex says, smiling now.

"Or he learned it from you."

"That's scary. To think of all the things he might have learned from me."

"What's the best thing about having three brothers?" I ask, partly because it seems like an engaging question, but also because I am paranoid about the things I might have missed out on, not having siblings. Like, could there have been a whole other Natalie, a better Natalie, who would have existed if she'd had a cool older sibling to show her the way in life, or a younger sibling who looked up to her?

Alex makes a face at my question.

"Humor me. I'm an only child," I say.

"Never feeling alone."

"And what's the worst thing?" I'm getting good at these questions now.

"Never feeling alone."

"Ha."

"It's like . . . sometimes they take up so much space in my life I'm afraid I'll never have room for all the other people I want to fit in. And I worry about them. Zach's okay, he's so smart, and he's got you and Lucy, but I think Anthony gets bullied a bit, and Glenn thinks he's invincible, and he's going to grow up and be a bit too wild." He stops, and seems surprised at himself for saying so much.

I've never heard him talk like this. And I've never looked at him this close up before. His eyes go all crinkly when he smiles. He has messy eyebrows, like Zach used to have before Lucy started plucking them.

"My parents broke up," I say.

I have no idea why I just blurted this out.

"I know. I heard Zach and Lucy talking about it. I'm sorry. I always thought your parents seemed like a nice couple."

"You've met my parents?"

"No. But Mum talks about you, and them, so much that I feel like I have."

"It's not like a bad breakup, with yelling and fighting over money or anything like that. It's all very relaxed," I say.

"That's good."

"I mean, I'm eighteen, so there's not a child anyone needs to have a custody battle over or anything."

"That makes things easier, I guess."

"And I feel completely and totally fine about it all."

"Sounds ideal."

"Yes. It is ideal. They'll have a perfect divorce." I plan to laugh in a mature and ironic way, but what comes out is a kind of hiccupped sob. I put my hand to my mouth, more out of shock than anything, and tears start burning my eyes. The thing is, I'm not a crier. *Never* a public crier. Not even when a guy on a train said, "You've got something on your face," very loudly to me, and everyone around us looked at me and when I touched my face, thinking it was a smear of peanut butter, he said, "Oh, it's a pimple, it looked like something else for a minute," and I had spent thirty-seven minutes and missed my usual train that morning getting my foundation to a point where I thought my skin looked pretty good for a change.

I'm not about to start public crying now, at this party.

"Hey." Alex puts his hand on my arm. He looks a bit scared. Probably he's worried he's going to be stuck looking after his little brother's pathetic, blubbering friend all night.

Now I truly am crying. I put my hands over my face to catch the tears that are slipping out of my eyes.

"I'm fine," I say, trying desperately to sound it.

What is happening? I didn't even cry when they told me. It must be the word *divorce*. I haven't said that word out loud until this moment, even though I've been thinking it since they told me. I know it's coming.

I keep my head in my hands. I should go to the bathroom and hide but I can't face the idea of being caught in there again.

Alex keeps his hand on my arm and leans in. He whispers, "You probably don't know this yet, but you're not supposed to cry at parties."

I give a small laugh.

"I'm not crying." I wipe my cheeks and take deep breaths. *Get it together.* My nose gets red and swollen when I cry, and it runs like a tap. My eyes go bloodshot. I get an instant headache. Crying is not therapeutic for me.

"Oh, I know you're not crying. I was telling you just in case."

His hand is still on my arm. I don't want him to take it away. Focusing on that thought helps me to stop crying, because it's a brand-new, of-this-very-moment feeling.

I've known Alex for years and never felt a flicker of attraction. Or at least I don't think I have. He has chest hair. (I've seen him in a towel walking from the bathroom to his bedroom.) He is obsessed with soccer. He has a heavy five-o'clock shadow and sometimes a scruffy beard. He's a year older than me. He's not tall. He likes partying. I've never seen him read or hold a book. He is nothing like Zach. These are things I would have previously said were problematic for me.

I look at the wall until I've pulled myself together and I've not only stopped crying but the urge to cry has completely disappeared, and then I lift my face. Alex takes his hand off my arm, and it almost seems worth crying again to see if he'll put it back.

"Do I have mascara running down my face?" I ask him. As much as I hate to tell anyone to look directly at my face, I urgently need to know how bad things are.

"No."

"You didn't even look properly."

He leans close to my face. "No mascara running."

We hold eye contact for a long time (okay, a second or two, which is ages for me) and I feel embarrassed and ridiculously vulnerable because of my probably red post-crying nose and my bumpy skin, but I don't want to look away.

"So what other party wisdom do you have?" I ask.

"Well, every party has a guy that gets really drunk before everyone else and embarrasses himself. And a couple who get into an awkward, public argument. And an opinionated know-it-all who never shuts up and gets on everyone's nerves."

"So who are all those people tonight?"

"The drunk guy who embarrasses himself is"—Alex pauses and looks outside the kitchen window for a minute—"Benny . . . In the red T-shirt."

The guy he's pointing to is balancing a plastic bucket on his head, yelling, "Now fill it with water," with a look of total delight on his face. So that's Benny. Benny and I are almost definitely not going to fall in love.

"Yes, that seems right," I say.

"And the couple who argue?" Alex scans the backyard and shakes his head. "They must be in the lounge room. You'll know them when you see them. Annika has red hair, and Jes is wearing skinny black jeans, and they're both very loud."

"Oh yeah, I think I saw them before, arguing about returning a Christmas present one of them bought the other."

"That's where the argument will start, but it will spiral into the fact they both cheated on each other earlier this year, on the same night."

"Oh wow."

"With the same person," Alex says.

"That sounds complicated."

"And the opinionated guy—that one is easy."

"Let me guess." I look out the kitchen window into the backyard.

"Him," I say, pointing to a guy with a beer in one hand who is wildly gesturing with the other. He's wearing a T-shirt that says "Anarchy."

"Bingo. He loves conspiracy theories, arguing about politics, and telling people why the music they like is crap."

"He sounds charming," I say. I turn away from the window

and we smile at each other, and Alex looks like he's going to say something, when Owen yells at us from outside.

"Hey, Alex and Natalie!"

We look away from each other, and I jump down from the bench. My legs feel a little shaky.

"Come outside," Owen says. And just like that, I'm part of the party.

We go outside and sit on crappy folding camping chairs. A bunch of people are arguing about the existence of aliens and the best way to eat a croissant. After a while, I feel myself un-clenching. It seems almost strange that I was hiding in the bath-room at the beginning of the night. I feel nostalgically sad for my pathetic self of an hour ago—what a loser. Now I am a god-dess on a rickety camping chair pretending to drink a beer.

5

NEVER HAVE I EVER

I've been outside for about twenty minutes, occasionally chiming in on the conversations around me, and watching Owen get louder and drunker. At one point, he turns to me and winks. I pretend not to notice, because there is nothing on earth that makes me more uncomfortable than someone winking at me.

Alex checks in on me, asking if I want another drink, and then if I'm cold, and both times I smile and shake my head.

At some stage, I'm not sure how, it is decided that everyone will play a drinking game. I've never actually seen a drinking game played before, so I'm quite fascinated. I cross my legs on the chair and settle in. It feels anthropological.

The chosen game is Never Have I Ever. One person says something they've never done and everyone who has done it must drink. (There's a good five minutes of arguing and googling on how to play the game—do you drink if you *have* done it, or do you drink if you *haven't*? Everyone is very, very sure their way is correct.)

"Never have I ever . . . vomited on my parents' front lawn."

"Never have I ever . . . kissed more than five people in one night."

"Never have I ever . . . watched porn with my friends."

"Never have I ever . . . passed out naked on someone else's couch."

Predictably, most questions are sex- or alcohol-focused, and there is a fuss after each one, yelling and laughing at the people who do and don't drink. I sit my bottle on the ground so it's clear I am here to watch and not participate. In fact, I'm getting bored and not even paying attention (the game is much less fascinating than I thought it would be), wishing my phone battery wasn't so low, when Owen taps my arm.

"Your turn."

"My turn what?"

"To say, 'Never have I ever . . .' "

"Oh, crap."

Everyone is looking at me. Vanessa arches an eyebrow (a perfect eyebrow; she has the kind of eyebrows that should be studied for how perfect they are). Alex gives me a small, commiserating smile that seems to say, *I know you're going to stuff this up, but that's okay.*

I have no idea what to say. *Think, think, think. Okay, stop thinking, just say anything.*

"I've never . . . played Spin the Bottle." I don't know why, of all possible words in the English language, these are the ones that come out of my mouth. There's a pause, and I contemplate standing up and leaving, just running into the night. Does anyone play Spin the Bottle anymore? Did anyone ever play it? Does it exist as a thing outside of nineties TV shows? Does it exist outside of my own head?

No one drinks.

"What, has no one here ever played Spin the Bottle?" Owen yells. He's drunk enough that he says everything at volume.

Everyone looks at each other and they're all shaking their heads.

"Let's play," says a girl. I think her name is Lana. Or maybe Petra.

And just like that, Never Have I Ever is abandoned and an empty bottle is placed on the ground in the middle of us all.

"Wait, do you have to kiss in front of everyone or do you go off into the dark?" asks a guy called Raj.

"You're confusing it with Seven Minutes in Heaven, where you are locked in the cupboard for seven minutes together," Vanessa says.

"Has anyone played that one, either?" Owen yells.

"Nope," says Raj.

"Let's combine them. Spin the Bottle, and then the two people go around there for a one-minute countdown," Lana/Petra says, pointing to a narrow, dark walkway down the side of the house.

"How much can you do in one minute?" Benny asks.

There is a lot of laughter and teasing about what can happen in a minute. I am practically dizzy with how quickly the situation has gone from one terrifying thing (my complete failure at a drinking game) to another (my soon-to-be complete failure at a kissing game).

I edge my chair nearer to Owen's, so it will be harder to tell if the bottle is pointing to me or him, and everyone will want it to be pointing to him, so I can politely back out.

I don't want to play this game.

I don't want to play this game so badly that I take my phone out of my pocket, scroll through my contacts, and hold my finger over the word *Mum,* but then I picture myself in the future saying to my inquisitive child, *I left the party before the game started, so no, honey, I've never played Spin the Bottle,* and my child looking at me with deep disappointment. So I will stay to avoid having my future imaginary child be disappointed in my life experience, which is as good a reason as any to stay anywhere.

It's a single minute, for god's sake. No one is going to force me to do anything. In fact, I bet no one is going to do anything at all.

I can see everyone sizing up everyone else, deciding who they want, who they could deal with, and who they definitely don't want. The flip side of not wanting to do anything is, of course, the fear that no one will want to do anything with me even if I did want to.

A girl I don't know spins the bottle first. It lands on Owen. Everyone cheers. I watch him walk off with her, and an iPhone stopwatch countdown begins. We sit in silence, and after about twenty seconds, it's surprisingly boring. Seven Minutes in Heaven must really drag on. Everyone counts down the last ten seconds and they cheer again when the two of them emerge, grinning.

They rejoin the circle—Owen is looking pleased with himself in a hugely unappealing way—and the bottle is spun again. I'm so nervous I take a swill of the beer in my hand, even though beer is the foulest-tasting thing in the world and I can barely swallow it without gagging, and now I'm paranoid about having beer breath.

The game goes through several more rounds. On reflection, it seems a stupid, discriminatory game, made mostly for the enjoyment of heterosexual guys. I have no idea who is straight, gay, bi, or asexual here. One guy spins the bottle and it lands on another guy, and he gets to spin again, which is okay, I guess, because he's straight, but still. If you're queer, and not out, then you either have to out yourself or endure possibly kissing someone of the opposite sex.

I'm still thinking about how terrible the game is and working myself into a state of hating the world and feeling ashamed I even mentioned it, when the bottle one of the girls has just spun lands on Alex. They walk off together, laughing. Alex looks completely relaxed and my stomach lurches. *I don't want him to kiss her.* The thought is in my head before I can stop it.

We count down the final ten seconds, everyone looking bored now, and they walk back, all smiles.

"All right, I'm over this," Raj says as Alex picks up the bottle and spins it. It turns lazily, around and around, and we all watch it slow down and stop between me and Owen.

"It's between them. Go again," says Lana/Petra.

"Nah, it's on her." A guy points to me.

There's a pause, and everyone looks at me, and I open my mouth to say we shouldn't play anymore, but then I swallow without saying anything, and I stand up and follow Alex, who is already walking back toward the side of the house.

I'm shaking, and my legs are jelly.

There's about a meter of space between the house and a wooden fence. It's shadowy. There are spiderwebs farther down and what looks like a broken rake, an old broom, and a pile of bricks. The whole thing is decidedly unromantic. Alex leans against the fence and I stand in front of him, leaning back against the house. His feet almost touch mine. I'm worried about spiders and bugs getting in my hair.

"I didn't kiss Sarah."

"Who's Sarah?"

"The girl I just came back here with before."

"Oh cool. I mean, I don't care. We don't need to kiss either. Obviously." My face feels hot.

"I know."

"This is an awful game."

"It was your idea."

"I mentioned it. I didn't suggest we *play* it."

Thirty seconds have passed. Forty. We're not going to kiss. Of course we're not. They start the ten-second countdown. He shifts his weight and moves his foot slightly and his shoe touches mine. I can't tell if it's accidental or on purpose.

"Three—two—one!"

We both hesitate. Then I push off the side of the house at the same time he pushes off the fence, and we're face-to-face, our bodies close to touching.

It seems like he's going to say something, so I move slightly closer. He smells unbelievably good.

Alex doesn't say anything. Instead, he leans over and gently kisses my cheek. His lips are soft, and his stubble is scratchy.

My heart is hammering in my chest.

"Hey, you two! Minute's up!"

Alex turns and walks around the corner, and I follow him back out to the party.

Vanessa is staring at us both as I sit back down in the camping chair. I'm trembling a little but trying my very hardest to look normal.

The bottle has been kicked away by this point and everyone has moved on to something else. Alex doesn't look at me for the next thirty minutes—I know because I sneak a look at him roughly every minute. Vanessa looks at me, though. I catch her quickly turning away a few times.

At ten-thirty, I decide to go home. I've hardly spoken to anyone since Spin the Bottle, so I don't know if I'm supposed to tell anyone I'm leaving.

I hover near Owen for a moment, but he's deep in conversation. He looks up and I wave, and he waves back. I can't be certain, but I'm pretty sure that's the last time Owen Sinclair and I will ever communicate. I feel a surge of excitement at the fact that I don't care. *I don't care what this hot guy thinks of me.* It feels like maybe the most emotionally stable moment of my life so far.

I book a car and it tells me the driver is two minutes away. I walk through the lounge room and Alex is there, talking to a group of people, including Vanessa. He looks up at me.

"Hey," he says, smiling.

"'Bye," I say.

"You're going?"

Does he sound disappointed? Surprised? Relieved? I wish Lucy was here so she could help me figure it out.

"Yup," I say.

He gets off the couch and walks over to me. "How are you getting home?"

"Uber." I don't know why I am giving him one-word answers to every question.

"Is that safe?" He frowns a little.

"You've never got an Uber before?"

"Well, yeah, but I mean . . ."

"Safe for girls on their own?"

"Yes."

"That's a sexist question."

"Is it?"

"Yes." I actually have no idea. I am a feminist, but I don't really know the rules yet. I like the idea that he's worried about me, but I hate the idea he thinks I'm a little kid who can't get herself home.

"Take my number and text me to let me know you got home," Alex says.

"What? No." I don't know why I say this, because the thought of swapping numbers with him makes my heart speed up and my cheeks get warm, and also this is a system Lucy and I have had in place for years. But something about it feels brotherly. I don't want Alex to treat me like a female version of Zach. I want him to think of me like he thinks of Vanessa, minus the baggage.

"Come on. If Mum found out I let you get an Uber alone without checking you got home safe, she'll be so mad at me." This is true. Mariella regularly talks to her sons about how to be good men in the world, and one of her favorite topics is teaching them to think and care about the safety of women.

"Fine."

I hand Alex my phone and he adds himself as a contact. He passes it back, and we say goodbye. Is there something lingering in his eyes as we do? They seem . . . soft. Warm. Or maybe I am overthinking things, or maybe I am seeing the reflected glow of his interaction with Vanessa, or of the lamp in the corner.

I would dismiss everything between us as a figment of my imagination, but that kiss on the cheek *happened*.

Outside, I wait for my Uber, and check behind me, in case Alex is going to come running after me (in the movie version of my life, someone would always come dramatically running after me), but he doesn't, and then my car arrives, and I get in.

I text Mum to say I'm on my way home.

Then Dad texts me: *Are you still at the party?* Dad is still living in the same house as Mum. Why wouldn't they be talking to each other about this? This is a preview, I understand suddenly. Life with divorced, overly invested parents means having to tell them both where you are at all times. It means having to come up with lies that will work on them both if I need to lie about stuff. It means making sure they are treated equally in everything, down to a damn text message.

I get out of the car at my house and before I walk inside, I text Alex, *Home safe.* I was going to be cute with a gif or an emoji, but I decide not to be, because I can't think of anything that hits the right tone of I'm funny and adorable but also I don't care at all, and many men and women are in love with me and I'm probably messaging them right at this very minute too. He writes back, *Good. See you soon.* I don't write anything back to that, but later that night I lie in bed and look at the messages, and run over a million scenarios of things I might have written, and what he might have written back, and what might have happened then.

I can't stop thinking about the Kiss. On. The. Cheek. (Aka The Greatest Thing to Romantically Happen to Me, If in Fact It Is Romantic.)

Thinking of the cheek kiss is like pressing on a bruise, but instead of pain, I feel a burst of happiness. Right now is the best time—before I can be disappointed, before I find out Alex isn't interested in me at all, before I can ruin things. Tonight, everything is still possible.

6

A HOUSE FULL OF GRYFFINDORS

"What happened?" Zach says.

"Every detail," Lucy says.

The three of us are lying on the deck at Zach's house the next day. Lucy has her head on Zach's chest, hair fanned out in all directions. It still hurts my selfish heart, seeing her lying on him so casually. I love them both so much, so it doesn't make sense that I am still ever so slightly unhappy that they're so happy. But I guess it does, because they don't need my love like I need theirs anymore, and that hurts.

Today I am on edge anyway because I am nervous about running into Alex. I don't want to talk to him, but I need to see him in the light of day to formally assess my feelings. Everyone knows you can't really trust any feeling you have at night—and the later the hour, the less trustworthy it is. Anything you feel after ten p.m. is suspect, anything after midnight should be discounted altogether.

I washed my hair this morning and I'm wearing my best jeans and a top that Lucy and I call the Boob Top, for pretty self-explanatory reasons: it makes my cleavage look great. Normally little thought would go into my outfit, and I wouldn't call it an outfit, it would be just clothes I picked from the cupboard (or maybe the floor), and my unwashed hair would be in a messy bun, and I would avoid looking in the mirror because sometimes I can get stuck in a cycle of self-loathing if I make no effort in my appearance and then see myself making no effort, and start hating what I look like when I make no effort, then hating myself for making no effort, and on it goes in a really boring, looping way where I expend a lot of energy in making no effort. But this morning, I made an effort, and I wore something that makes me feel good.

Lucy said, "Why are you wearing the Boob Top?" when I arrived, and I shrugged and said, "It was the only clean thing I had," all innocent, and I could see from her face that she didn't believe me.

The thing is, I quite like my breasts. When I stand naked in front of a mirror, I like the way they look. Full, reasonably perky, and only slightly uneven in size, which is normal according to the billion times I've checked on the internet. If I were ever to become famous and be the subject of a series of tasteful black-and-white nude photographs taken by a renowned photographer, my breasts would be without a doubt the artistic highlight. Or, in an only marginally more likely scenario, if I ever have the inclination to send someone a sext, my breasts will be the pornographic highlight.

I'm pretty sure my boobs are responsible for the only time in my life I properly kissed someone. It was at the year-eleven school social, which Lucy had bullied me into going to—when I say bullied, what I actually mean is lots of positive reinforcement, emotional cheerleading, and general enthusiasm—and she pretty much babysat me all night to stop me from sneaking off and leaving. It got to the very end of the night, the time when everyone who is panicking about having kissed no one starts desperately looking around and grabbing each other, and I'm sure my cleavage was one of the major things attracting the boy to me in the three seconds he spent looking at me before he mashed his face against mine. I was a very willing participant in the mashing, as the fact I hadn't kissed anyone in my life was weighing on me—forget being a virgin, being unkissable is a worse fate, especially for anyone who has had bad skin.

"Well?" Lucy picks up a bag of chips, looks at it, and puts it down again. She's had no appetite for a few weeks now, which is worrying me. Lucy doesn't eat much when she's anxious about something. (I tend to operate at the other end of the spectrum.) Zach and I used to bring her food in the lead-up to final exams, because we knew she'd just nibble at an apple otherwise. But the thing is, exams are over. She got the marks she wanted. She'll likely get into the university she wants, studying the degree she wants, and yet I can tell she's still lugging all that stress around like an overstuffed backpack she can't take off.

"Well, what?" I answer.

"What happened at the party, obviously."

"Honestly, there's nothing to say. I went. I hung out. I came home." I shrug, as though I am the kind of person who goes to parties all the time and then shrugs about it. *No big deal.*

"Don't be ridiculous. There's so much to say. Let's start with the big stuff and work backward: Did you kiss Owen?" Lucy asks.

"No. God. I would have mentioned that."

"Did you come close?"

"No."

"Did you touch at any point?"

"No."

"Was there eye contact?"

"Not really."

"Did you talk to each other?"

Lucy is good at grilling people because this is how her mother operates—a million rapid-fire questions about your day, your homework, your train ride home, the walk from the train station to your house, the last thought you had before you opened the front door. I think the two of them see it as some weird way to practice for when Lucy becomes a lawyer.

"Not really."

"Interact in any way?"

"Sort of. He said hi and asked if I was having fun. I said yes. Oh, and he peed in front of me."

"He *peed* on you?" Zach says, his voice almost a yelp.

"Not *on* me. Near me. In front of me. For barely a second. He peed into the toilet and I was momentarily standing near him."

"Why were you in the bathroom with Owen?" Lucy asks. Her tone is gentle now, like the voice our school counselor Ms. Bennett used when she wanted you to confess to being the person who hung a used tampon off the balcony railing. (The Tampon Incident, as it came to be known, remained unsolved but everyone was pretty sure it was a girl called Marley who loved gross and shocking things and always had at least three disgusting videos primed and ready to show you on her phone.)

"I was leaving as he was coming in . . . Oh, forget I even mentioned it."

"I can never forget," Lucy says.

"Did you want to kiss him?" Zach asks.

"In the bathroom?"

"At any time."

"No."

I suspect they don't believe me.

"You are the worst storyteller today," Lucy says, and she sighs dramatically.

The thing is, her interest in my life is genuine. From the moment we met, Lucy has cared about what happens to me, and I usually put a little bit of effort into making it worthwhile for her. I always tell a story. My life has had so few things happen in it that when I go to a party *on my freaking own,* you better believe I will draw it out into a weeklong discussion, dissecting every interaction and moment. No doubt they're still annoyed I wasn't live-texting and sending them videos of every moment. My lackluster answers today are bordering on unforgivable.

So I go back to the beginning and give them a proper run-through, emphasizing the hiding-in-the-bathroom part, which they enjoy, and explaining the Owen-peeing moment, which Lucy makes me retell more than once ("What did you see *exactly*?"), but I skip over the spin-the-bottle ending, because I know Lucy will become laser-focused on that part and Zach will act weird about the fact that Alex and I got each other, but mostly because I'm not ready to say it out loud, because to speak the words of what happened might reduce it to the very small thing it really is.

If it's not already clear, Lucy and Zach are my everything. I met them both at a writing camp when I was fifteen. Several schools in my area were asked to choose two students each from year ten to attend a special writing retreat set over three days in the wilderness. There would be workshops, sessions on creativity, book discussions, and time to write. Everything about it sounded amazing to me, even the wilderness part, even though I would undoubtedly perish within thirty minutes if I ever got lost in the bush on my own.

I was one of the students chosen from my school, and I made myself sick about it. I had never wanted and not wanted something so much in my life. I had started my serious acne medication four months prior to going, and it was working, which was so miraculous I was still getting used to the idea, but it made my lips so cracked and dry they would sometimes bleed just from opening my mouth to eat something and so I had to put on lip balm every ten minutes (that's not an exaggeration, I truly had to apply lip balm up to six times an hour in order to function), and I had rough, scaly hands and elbows and a weird shiny red patch had appeared on my left cheek—all side effects that I was very self-conscious about.

Also, because of my self-imposed postpuberty social isolation, I wasn't very good at meeting new people, or staying at a house other than my own, or sleeping in a bed that's not my own, or making small talk with new people. I wasn't good at existing outside a set of very narrow confines (the walls of my house, basically). I had spent three years turning myself into a socially incapable shut-in, and I didn't know how to undo that.

On the other hand, I had wanted to go so badly it made my chest ache. I had actual heartburn from wanting it so much and knowing I would probably let myself down. I wanted to go to this camp more than I had wanted to go anywhere in my life. I was chosen because I was an A+ English student and I won the school's short story competition the year before (for an admittedly very melodramatic but honestly amazing story, if I do say so myself, called "Remember Me," about a girl whose boyfriend is dying of a mysterious disease that causes him to forget his past a week at a time and he is cured just before he is about to die, but he's lost his last memory of her), and possibly because I spent so much time in the library reading at lunchtime. But, looking back, a little part of me thinks I was chosen because of fate. I was destined to go to this camp and find the two people who would help me survive the rest of my teenage years—and the rest of my life, I hope.

Mum and Dad were overjoyed by the news that I had been

chosen. It was as though I'd been picked for the Olympics. I know they fretted about having an unbearably self-conscious hermit for a daughter, but if they broached the subject with me, it would usually end in a meltdown of tears and self-pity (mine, obviously, although Mum has a flair for the dramatic, which is where I get my best material), so my lack of social life and friends became the Topic Not to Be Discussed.

The camp invitation had opened the door to that topic again, and Mum wouldn't let it be. We went around in circles: Mum telling me I *had* to go, and me telling her I would *probably* go, I would *almost certainly* go, I would *try my best* to go, but never quite agreeing that I would definitely go. It calmed me to know that there was still the option to not go. Because what if I woke up on the first day of camp with a huge, disfiguring pimple between my eyes? This was not a theoretical concern, but rather something that had happened to me already several times in my life. I have had a pimple so big that it looked like a third eye. I have had pimples so big they should be featured on those awful, voyeuristic, disgusting pimple-popping videos.

It's hard to explain how bad skin makes me simply give up on things, but it does. I can go from being excited to feeling numb, empty, and resigned in one minute flat. I don't ever want anything badly enough that I'd still go with a giant disfiguring pimple on my face.

The heavy-duty acne medication should have given me confidence, but I didn't trust it. My body could always, always betray me. That's what I knew. And even if it was okay now, it would betray me in the future. Even my dermatologist said that—if the acne was caused by my unbalanced hormones and problematic ovaries (official name: polycystic ovary syndrome), as we suspected it was, then it would probably come back. Maybe a year after I stop the medication, maybe sooner, maybe later.

My skin was a ticking time bomb, poised to explode in the most public way whenever I let down my guard. My GP said if I go off the Pill in the future, then, as well as a return of acne, I should watch for symptoms like a disappearing period, thinning head hair, increased facial hair, weight gain, and general depression. That's a fun checklist. Also, by the way, this was a condition that would continue for a lifetime.

It wasn't just my skin and hormonal stuff, though. Meeting new people was hard and I hated it.

But Mum didn't let up. She was so scared of me missing this opportunity, the fear became palpable in our house. The signed parental consent forms were stuck to the front of our refrigerator for days, and I kept catching Dad looking at them with a worried expression. Mum surrounded them with Post-it notes, on which she drew arrows and wrote, "Don't forget!!" and "The deadline is Friday!!" and "Do it!!"

They were going to be so disappointed in me if I didn't go.

Finally, I couldn't stand it any longer. I took the forms to school and handed them in. *I was going.* Definitely, definitely going. Mum danced me around the kitchen in delight.

I made several trips to the dermatologist to beg him to fix the shiny red patch on my face, to no avail. ("Unfortunately, Natalie, this is just something you'll have to endure while you're on the medication," he had said, with a tone that implied he thought I had a limited capacity for enduring things.) I packed and repacked my bags. I chewed my fingernails. I had nightmares. I thought about changing my name. (Surely if I introduced myself as Roxy then I would magically have the confidence of a girl called Roxy.)

And I went to the camp.

Mum and Dad drove me there. It was a three-hour trip and Mum kept up a relentlessly cheerful commentary for practically every minute, as if a moment of silence would allow me to change my mind. She kept telling me I was going to have a great time, which made me want to have a terrible time just to spite her.

At the camp sign-in, I stood in line behind a boy. Mum nudged me, and I refused to look at her, because I knew she would do something unsubtle like wiggling her eyebrows suggestively. She'd done that once before when a bunch of boys were standing near us at the cinema, and I had to go into the bathroom and deep breathe in the cubicle to recover from my embarrassment.

The boy in the camp line (spoiler—it was Zach) turned around and smiled kind of goofily at me as he walked past. He was tall and skinny with messy dark curls and the friendliest face I have maybe ever seen on another human being. I quickly glanced away and didn't smile back, which is my standard response whenever anyone looks at me, but in my mind I was smiling back, and it felt like a good sign.

I was desperate for Mum and Dad to leave, but the minute I saw their car pulling away, I was hit with a wave of nausea and had to stop myself from running after them screaming, *Come back, come back, come back*. I was alone, and I had to cope without them for three days. I had to sleep in a single bed with itchy-looking blankets. I had to share a bathroom. I had to eat meals prepared by people who had no idea that chicken sometimes grossed me out and I didn't like the texture of cooked mushrooms.

Lucy walked into the cabin then. She was assigned to the other bed in my room.

Lucy was the other student from my school picked for camp. We had been in several classes together, but we'd never spoken more than a few sentences to each other before this moment.

I knew about Lucy, though. I spent a lot of time at school

watching and observing, and I generally knew a lot more about my classmates than they knew about me. I knew Lucy liked poetry and YA fantasy novels, and that she always enthusiastically volunteered for things, from reading aloud a section of a book in class to creating posters for our school's campaign for combating climate change. She was on the debating team, she was in the school musical, she was vice president of the social justice club. She was a joiner and she was aggressively *nice,* two things I have a natural suspicion of, but with Lucy they weren't fake or annoying. She acted like a good person because she really was a good person.

Lucy had one strike against her, though—she had perfect skin. Ever since the first pimple appeared on my face, skin is always the first thing I notice about someone else, the first judgment I make, even when I try to stop myself. *Do they have good skin?* Lucy was small (she was fifteen at the time, but she looked twelve), with unmarked skin and the kind of big blue eyes that could get you off a murder charge with a couple of well-timed blinks.

It was hard for me to imagine a skinny blonde with flawless skin could have any real problems. Skin, hair, teeth: the holy trinity, as I once read in an article by a Hollywood talent agent. If you had those to begin with, you were miles ahead of the competition. Lucy had them. Well, almost. Back then, she had braces on her teeth, but that meant they would be perfect soon.

Lucy's face didn't even have a mole or a slight discoloration. Almost three years later, and it still doesn't. The closest thing she has to a flaw is a scattering of freckles that appear in summer. Skin like this fascinates me. I google it sometimes. "Girls with perfect skin." "Flawless skin." "Beautiful skin." "Celebrities with amazing skin." It gives me that bad-good feeling to look at people who have what I want so much.

I went to an all-girls school, which can be a harrowing experience, but I am happy I didn't have to face boys in the classroom every day, because when my skin was at its worst, girls might have said nasty stuff behind my back, but boys straight-up yelled at me at the train station with the least imaginative insults possible: "pizza face," "fugly," and once, "GROSS BITCH." I couldn't have dealt with that all day. My classmates wrapped their insults in the packaging of unsolicited advice, such as: "If you wash your face properly every morning and every night, it will draw out all the bad toxins causing the pimples," or "Your makeup is the real problem, maybe if you went without concealer for a few days, it would get better," or "Have you tried only using organic products and washing your pillowcase in vinegar and hot water every day?" or "If you want clear skin, it's simple: don't eat sugar or carbs or fat or grains or red meat or anything processed or anything white or anything packaged or nightshade vegetables and *especially* not citrus fruit. And *drink water.*"

As if I hadn't tried everything that every random person on the internet ever happened to recommend. Honey, toothpaste, olive oil, avocado, hot water, cold water, apple cider vinegar, fish-oil tablets, spearmint tea, the juice from a sweet potato, the official ten-step Korean skin care routine, the keto diet. My skin usually got worse. It always, eventually, got worse.

I needed professionals, prescriptions, medication strong enough to deform an unborn baby. (That's what the consent form I had to sign to take the medication said: I cannot, under any circumstances, get pregnant while taking it. It gave me hope—my dermatologist thinks I'll have sex with someone one day!) After my skin got better, I needed steroid injections and laser therapy to help fix the scars on my back. And still—after all the drugs and laser beams and appointments and diets and exercise and creams and gels and injections and money and tears and worry and thousands of hours on the internet—still, my skin doesn't look half as nice as most people's. Especially on my back, which is pitted, red, and lumpy, like a constellation of the ugliest stars imaginable.

My parents tried their best to be understanding, but whenever Mum said, "It's just a pimple, Natalie, it's not a disease, there are a lot of more serious things going on in the world right now," it made me feel more alone and more awful than anything any boy at the train station said. Because half of me would agree with her—*Oh god, I'm a pathetic, weak, spineless, selfish, vain, privileged loser*—and the other half would be furious—*You don't understand a single thing about the pain I am in.*

I dreamed of waking up and not having to think about my skin. Imagine the freedom of someone who had never thought about their skin, ever. Whose first thought wasn't to rush to a mirror and check what had happened overnight—which pimples got worse, and which might be slightly better.

Lucy was that person. Of course, it didn't occur to me that Lucy might have other things to worry about when she woke up—to me, it truly seemed like if you didn't have to worry about dragging a problematic face into the world, then you didn't have to worry about anything.

Later, Lucy would tell me about how she lay awake at night worrying she wasn't doing enough: enough studying, enough preparation, enough exercise, enough reading, enough homework. That she herself wasn't *enough*. For who, for what, it wasn't clear to me, but she was tormented by a voice in her head telling her, *Not good enough, never good enough.*

Lucy's life, I would discover, was exhausting in ways I hadn't imagined.

But on this day, our first day, Lucy was just a perfect-skinned almost-stranger who was sharing my room. We smiled hesitantly at each other. Lucy made some small talk about school, and then we lapsed into silence, and I feared we had reached the end of all possible conversations we might have and the silence would stretch on forever, or at least for the next three days. But then Lucy pulled a bunch of books out of her bag, and it turned out we were reading the same novel, the final one in a long-running series, and we spent the next half hour passionately discussing the love lives of various fictional characters.

Later, when we were called down to the main hall, Lucy hooked her arm through mine and she told me she was nervous about meeting everyone. No one had ever hooked their arm through mine before. The way she did it so casually I still remember vividly, because it was the first time in years I'd felt properly *okay* around someone my age.

We sat down together in the hall, and everyone was looking around at everyone else. Most people hadn't even introduced themselves to anyone and I was already three-quarters of the way toward making a friend. It felt miraculous. I wasn't even worried that Lucy might abandon me for someone cooler. I already trusted her.

We had to play getting-to-know-you games, which is the kind of thing that normally sends me into a panic spiral but, for once, it didn't.

The first thing everyone had to say was which Hogwarts house they were in. Zach said he was Ravenclaw, Lucy said Hufflepuff, and I said Slytherin, and later we were instructed to pair up with someone who wasn't in the same house as ourselves, and Zach slid toward me saying he lived in a house full of Gryffindors and needed more Slytherins in his life. We got into a discussion about time travel, which segued into a discussion about board games and then books. Lucy joined us, and that night I went to bed with my heart full. I'd done it. I'd survived. *I'd made friends*.

The next three days were, without exaggeration, the best of my life. The teachers told me I had potential as a writer, and I should develop "Remember Me" into a full-length novel one day. Lucy, Zach, and I were inseparable, and I wasn't even mad that my mother had predicted it all.

I left the camp on a high. I had truly never been happier.

Lucy and I hung out at school after that, but it wasn't easy at first, because no one in the group she sat with was particularly warm to me. Lucy had a lot of friends—or, at least, girls who were friend-adjacent—and she was involved in seemingly endless clubs and committees. I was the opposite. My camp confidence disappeared pretty quickly once I was back.

Zach went to a school near ours, and the three of us began to hang out on weekends and message each other daily. We had game nights and movie nights. We lent each other books. We started our own little three-person TV club. We shared the creative stuff we were doing: fan fiction, short stories, poems, plays. We planned a screenplay we wanted to write together. We contemplated starting our own YouTube channel. We had running jokes. It was what I'd always dreamed having friends would be. My parents were overjoyed.

But I still didn't go to parties or join any groups. I didn't magically become cool or popular or less self-conscious. Some days I still hid in the library when I didn't have the energy to negotiate lunchtime with Lucy's friends. She would come and find me in the library, though, and our status as best friends soon became a known thing among other people in our year level. Natalie and Lucy. Lucy and Natalie. Having a best friend was like having a protective armor, something I'd never experienced before, and something I desperately needed. Lucy navigated social situations for me, and in return I made her laugh and helped her deal with her mother. In Lucy and Zach, I'd found my group, and it was small, but it was enough, more than enough, to keep my head above water. They saved me.

So yes, I probably do owe them some good gossip from my first solo party experience.

"Maybe you should text Owen," Lucy says to me now.

"Why would she do that?" Zach says.

"To say thanks for the party invite."

"That's terrible advice. Don't do that. Nobody does that," Zach says.

"It's good manners, Zach," Lucy says. Her family is big on good manners.

"Look, the thing is, Owen is really just not that interesting. I don't want to text him," I say, before they can get any further into the discussion.

Lucy and Zach solemnly nod as if I have spoken the greatest truth they've ever heard.

"And also, he winked at me," I add.

"Yuck. Okay, don't text him," Lucy says.

"You are way too good for him," Zach says. I hate it when Zach gives me compliments like this. If I was so amazing, Zach would have chosen me over Lucy. Which is a terrible, awful, self-pitying, pathetic, desperate, bad-friend thing to think, but that doesn't make it any less true. Zach and Lucy chose each other, so they have to say things like, "You are too good for him," to me to hide the fact that no one chose me. Also, "You are too good for him" usually means, "You are the less-attractive person in this equation."

At that moment, Alex appears on the deck.

"Hi," he says.

I gulp and sit up a bit straighter because there's no point in wearing the Boob Top if you're going to slouch.

"Hi. Hello," I say. I try to sound very casual but somehow instead sound very formal.

"How are you?" he says. Does he sound casual or like someone who is *trying* to sound casual? I can't tell.

"Good. How are you?"

"Good."

Zach is looking back and forth between us. Alex and I don't usually exchange pleasantries.

"So, did you have fun at the party?" Zach asks Alex.

"Yeah, it was all right," Alex says.

Oh god. There are so many bad ways I can interpret that answer, and no good ones.

"Anything interesting happen?" Lucy asks.

Why is she asking that? Would she normally ask Alex such a question? It sounds like I've set her up to ask that. I am sweating.

"We played Spin the Bottle," Alex says, grinning as he sits down in one of the deck chairs and props his feet on another.

"What?" Lucy and Zach both pretty much yell in unison.

Fuck.

Alex's eyes flick to me very quickly and then away again. I hope, in that nanosecond, I have communicated the millions of pieces of information I wish to convey to him, including: *Why the hell did you bring that up; don't tell them we got each other; don't tell them we sort-of kissed; don't tell them we didn't* actually *kiss; don't say anything about me at all; is this all a huge joke to you; are you trying to ruin my life; I hate you; your hair looks good today.*

"You didn't tell us you played Spin the Bottle!" Lucy shouts at me, her voice high-pitched in outrage and excitement.

"I didn't play. Not really."

Alex is watching me. His face is unreadable.

"Do you and your friends usually play Spin the Bottle?" Zach says to Alex.

"No. It was Natalie's idea," Alex says. He smiles at me. He's enjoying this. I am not.

"You made a party full of uni students you didn't know play Spin the Bottle?" Zach turns to me. His eyes are huge. He looks half impressed, half scared, like an alien might have taken over my body and will come bursting out of my skin at any moment.

"Hang on. That is not how it happened," I say.

"How did it happen?" Lucy asks.

"Well, everyone was playing a drinking game—"

"You played a drinking game!" Zach is being very dramatic today.

"Calm down, *Dad,* and let her finish," Alex says.

"Everyone else was playing the Never Have I Ever drinking game and I said I had never played Spin the Bottle and that's how the game started," I say.

"Why did you leave this out of your story?" Zach says.

"Who did you kiss?" Lucy asks, almost breathless.

Now there is silence. Everyone looks at me.

"No one," I say. My face feels very hot.

"Who did you see kiss?" Lucy asks.

"It wasn't like that. They went around the side of the house to kiss or whatever."

"Or whatever?" Zach says, raising his eyebrows.

"I don't think anything actually happened."

"How do you know?" Zach says.

"Well, I don't know. But they only had one minute."

"A lot of things can happen in a minute," Lucy says in a serious tone, which makes Zach blush and Alex laugh.

"Shut up and don't say a word," Zach says to Alex.

Alex rolls his eyes, lifts his feet off the chair, and wanders back inside.

"Was he an asshole to you last night?" Zach asks me.

"No."

"Did he look after you? I told him to look after you."

"You told him to look after me?" My stomach drops.

"Yes, of course I did," Zach says.

Suddenly everything makes sense. Everything that Alex said and did was out of obligation. Of course it was.

I feel a jolt of rage toward Lucy and Zach. "Why would you do that?"

"We were worried about you there on your own," Lucy said.

"I'm not *that* socially incapable." I am, but they shouldn't think that.

"I didn't mean it like that."

"Well, you don't need to organize secret chaperones for me at parties."

"That's not what we did," Zach says.

"It seems like it."

I get to my feet, and the two of them stare at me like I'm acting crazy. Which, yes, I am. But all my jittery energy finally has a focus. How dare they tell Alex to look after me? I feel stupid. Alex just sees me as his little brother's clueless friend. None of what happened means anything anymore.

"I've got to go."

"Natalie, don't go. I'm sorry," says Lucy. Nothing stresses her out more than someone being angry at her, especially me (and her mother).

But I flounce out in a huff, riding high on the knowledge that I am in the right, and they are wrong, and the world is unfair and awful and out to get me, and I can blame it all on two people. Well, four, actually, because my parents have a lot to answer for too.

7

TEN MINUTES OF FUN

I hesitate on the front porch when I realize it has started to pour with rain and I don't have an umbrella and the nearest tram stop is a seven-minute walk. I have to leave, though. You cannot return after a dramatic storm-out. I hover in the doorway, considering what to do.

Alex walks past me, shoving his feet into thongs.

"I'll give you a lift," he says.

"A lift where?"

"Wherever you're going."

"I could live on the other side of the city, for all you know."

"I know it's not far. You're here way too often for it to be miles away."

I frown at him and cross my arms. "I'm not here that much."

"The offer disappears in ten seconds."

He runs out into the rain, shouting over his shoulder, "Ten, nine, eight, seven, six, five, four, three—"

"Okay, I'm coming!" I yell, as I run out into the rain behind him.

I open the passenger door, throw myself into the car, and

tell him my address. He pulls out into the street and we fall into silence. Normally I'm good with silence, but this feels like very pointed we-are-two-people-with-nothing-to-say-to-each-other silence, which is the most stressful silence after I-am-mad-at-you silence.

After a few blocks, I lean forward and try to turn on the radio, and Alex looks at me.

"It's broken."

I clutch my hands together in my lap as if I am in prayer. I kind of am in prayer, if prayer involves chanting, *Please, please, please, please, please, please, please think of something to say,* in your mind while a trickle of sweat rolls into your bra.

"You're going to have to start directing me soon," Alex says.

"Keep going straight. I'll tell you when to turn."

I wish I could pull out my phone and pretend to text someone right now, but that would be unbearably rude. I need *something* for my hands to do. I slip them under my thighs. *Think back to that top ten tips article, Natalie. Ask him engaging questions about himself.*

"So where do you work?" I ask. (I know where he works, but he doesn't know I know this.)

"Hide Out. It's a sort of fancy pub."

"Do you love it?" I picture him in a kind of movie montage, showing off by flipping bottles and catching them, chopping carrots really fast, chatting and joking with the waitstaff, looking at a perfectly arranged plate of food with deep satisfaction. (I know nothing about pubs or cooking.)

"No. I kind of hate it, actually."

"Oh. Why?"

"My boss is the worst, the hours are long, there's lots of yelling, and my feet hurt." He turns and smiles at me as he says all this, but the smile looks a little bit pained.

"But everyone thinks you're cool for working there, right?"

"My friends do, until I tell them I can't get them free drinks."

"Oh."

"Nah, it's not that bad. But I thought I would love working in a pub, and I don't."

"You seem like the kind of person who would love working in a pub."

"What kind of person is that?"

"A person who likes to be out, doing things, talking to people."

"I do like to be out doing things and talking to people."

"I like to be home, not doing things, talking to no one."

He laughs. "I thought you had fun at the party last night."

"I did. I had at least ten minutes of fun."

"Which ten minutes?"

"When Owen peed in front of me."

"Of course."

I decide to be brave. "I also liked the part when we talked," I say, and then feel excruciatingly embarrassed the second the words have left my mouth.

"Me too," he says, which surprises me. And makes my heart speed up.

We look at each other, then away again, quickly.

"Turn left here," I say.

"What? Here? Right here?"

"Yes."

"A little warning next time."

"That was plenty of warning."

"I almost missed it."

"Because you were slow to react."

"My reaction times are faster than average. It's proven."

"By who?"

"My soccer coach."

"When did he tell you that?"

"Right before our under-elevens grand final."

"Did you win?"

"Well, no, but we came close. It was a very proud moment in my sporting history."

"It's this one here."

"With the white fence?"

"No. A bit farther. With the wooden fence. I was giving you extra warning."

He makes a face at me and pulls up in front of my house.

I could ask him to come in. I *should* ask him to come in. I am an adult now (sort of, kind of, not really). Deep breath. I could do this. But if I ask him in, then he would see *inside my house*. I need days to prepare for the idea of a guy coming into my house. Weeks, if we're talking about my bedroom. Months, if the guy in question is Alex.

"Thanks for the lift," I say.

"No problem," he says. There's a beat of silence, and I very slowly undo my seat belt, trying to give him time to say something else.

"All right, then. Goodbye, Natalie." He makes eye contact as he says my name and it makes me flustered. I turn and open the car door with a little too much force, and it swings wide, slipping out of my hand and banging into a light pole right next to us.

"Oh my god," I say.

"It's okay."

"I've scratched your car," I say, leaping out to look at the door.

"It's Mum's car."

"That's worse."

"I know."

I squat down and look at the door. It doesn't look scratched.

"Don't worry about it," Alex says.

"I feel so bad."

"If it's scratched, I'll tell Mum I did it," Alex says.

"No, tell her it was me."

"Yeah, that's a better plan, she's less likely to yell at you."

"No, I've changed my mind, don't tell her it was me." I must maintain my status as Mariella's favorite.

"I backed into the garbage bins the other day. It's fine. She has three more sons who will be driving this car. It has many scratches in its future. Especially with Zach behind the wheel."

Zach is an especially terrible driver, even worse than me. He got pulled over by the police when he was on his L-plates for going too slow, which is now one of his family's favorite stories.

"I think it's okay," I say, standing up.

"Good."

"Okay, I'm going now."

"'Bye."

"'Bye."

I walk to my gate and then turn back. He's sitting in the car. He hasn't pulled away yet. He winds down his window and waves me back to him.

"You can text me next time you need a ride, if you want."

I have no idea what he means. "Are you an Uber driver on the side?"

"No! I mean I can maybe pick you up if you're coming to my house and you need a lift and you have no other way of getting there. Like, as a favor. Or whatever. Don't even worry about it." Now he looks flustered.

"Okay," I say.

What is happening?

Later, I sit on my bed and look at my phone and will a text message from him to appear on my screen, but it doesn't.

I text Zach and Lucy and apologize for being dramatic and awful. Lucy texts me back rows of hearts, and Zach sends me the thumbs-up. I then hide my phone in my cupboard for an hour, to stop myself from checking whether Alex has texted me (even though he has *no reason at all* to text me), and then after the hour is up, I rush to look at it.

Nothing, of course.

I hate that desperate clutch of hope before you turn your phone over and then the feeling of sick disappointment when nothing is there.

8

SUN AND SAND AND GIRLS IN BIKINIS

"This is going to be so much fun," Lucy says, for maybe the tenth time.

"I know."

It's New Year's Eve, and we're at Zach's family's beach house. It's a ramshackle two-story weatherboard in Queenscliff, inherited from a great-aunt, and Zach's family shares it with a bunch of other family members. They've spent a week here every summer for the last ten years.

I've never been to the beach house before. Last summer I was invited, but I made an excuse not to go, in part because I was working most days washing dishes in the kitchen of a local café, and in part because I hate the beach. Of course I hate the beach. It's the next logical step after hating summer, and I hate summer. It's not a blanket hatred. I like sunshine. I like looking at and walking alongside the ocean. I can appreciate that *some* people like sand. I understand that it's nice to be warm. I sometimes even like being *in* the ocean (not over my head, and not if there is any seaweed or waves). But hot weather and the beach means wearing bathers, which means revealing my body, with all its scars and stretch marks and other flaws.

I hate the beach because I hate being the only person wearing a T-shirt in the water.

Winter is my season. Long coats, boots, big jumpers, puffer vests, beanies, giant scarfs, jackets with hoods. These are the safety blankets for anyone who is uncomfortable in their skin. On a really cold, wet day, you can hide everything but a sliver of your face. It is a joy. A freedom that people who aren't anxious about their bodies cannot understand. Only people with nothing to hide love summer. Plus, when it's cold and raining, no one questions why you want to stay inside and read.

But this summer I don't have a job. The café I worked in closed down and, despite me dropping my résumé into every shop and café within walking or public-transport distance, no one wants to hire an awkward eighteen-year-old with dishwashing experience and not much else. I have no money, no commitments, and no excuses (and, as our university placements aren't announced for another two and a half weeks, no direction in life).

So, here I am. If nothing else, I'm away from my parents, and that's becoming a major plus. I can't stand the way they talk to each other now. All faux-politeness, careful discussions, phrases straight from therapy, and looking at me with concerned eyes after every conversation to gauge how much they might be damaging me, even while they congratulate each other on having such a drama-free breakup. The nicer they are to each other, the less I'm allowed to feel sad and angry about what's happening, and that makes me feel even more sad and angry. Honestly, it's infuriating. Some days I can feel a hot, tight resentment building in my chest when I look at them, which can't be good for my long-term health.

Lucy and I are sharing a double bed in an upstairs room. Anthony and Glenn are sharing another room upstairs, and Zach has a room to himself downstairs, with Mariella and Sal in the main bedroom downstairs. Alex isn't here because he has to work tonight, and probably every other night too, I'm guessing. I haven't dared to ask if he's coming down, because I'm hyperaware that every question I ask could sound suspicious.

Tonight, Zach, Lucy, and I are going to walk down to the beach, where there will be a big bonfire and fireworks, and Lucy has insisted on doing my makeup in the bathroom before we leave, because she lives in an alternative universe where a cute guy might pop into my life at any time and fall in love with my smoky eyes.

"Look down."

I look down, and she gently presses the eyeliner pencil against my lid.

"Now look up."

The thing is, I hate fuss but I like being fussed over.

"I have a favor to ask," Lucy says.

"Yeah?"

"Will you swap beds with Zach tonight? Not for the whole night. Just a couple of hours."

"Do we need to switch? Why don't you just go into his bed?"

"Well, his parents are downstairs. We'd feel better in the upstairs bed."

"So you're okay with Zach's brothers hearing you have sex but not Zach's parents?"

"Gross, no. No one is going to hear anything. But you know what Mariella is like. She's a very light sleeper and the farther away from her we are, the better."

"I'm happy to switch."

"Thank you. I love you."

Lucy doesn't turn eighteen until February, and Zach not until March, and because they're both only seventeen and also for a multitude of other reasons, they're not allowed to sleep in the same bed. Lucy's mother only agreed that Lucy could come to the beach house if she and Zach weren't sharing a room, and Mariella was brought up as a strict Catholic and is squeamish at the thought of any of her sons in a bed with any girl. Her worst nightmare is one of her sons getting a girl pregnant, and Lucy's mother's worst nightmare is Lucy's life not going according to plan, so they're in sync when it comes to thwarting opportunities for Zach and Lucy's sex life.

It doesn't seem to have occurred to Mariella or Lucy's mother that Zach and Lucy have spent countless afternoons locked together in his bedroom after school or in the den on a Saturday afternoon, doing whatever they like to each other. I know Lucy often lies to her mother and says I'm there too when I'm not. I don't mind. I'm happy to facilitate Zach and Lucy's plan to be together. It's probably sad (scratch that, it's definitely sad), but it makes me feel more involved. It means I'm still needed in our group.

I saw Zach falling in love with Lucy before anything happened, so I knew it was coming. But before it started happening, there was a moment of something almost happening between Zach and me. It is one of those things I have always felt certain of, but I have never discussed it with anyone, and I have no real evidence, other than my own feelings.

It was the school holidays, Lucy was away for two weeks, and Zach and I were watching *The 100* together. We had five seasons to get through at the time, and so we were spending all day together, lying on the couch, saying, "Let's watch one more," and sharing packets of licorice. The couch was long enough that we could both lie stretched out, with our heads in the middle on a pile of cushions.

One afternoon, I was lying with my hands tucked under the pillows, and Zach must have put his hands under the pillows too, because our fingers touched momentarily. Only the slightest touch, for a moment. But after a few seconds, Zach's fingers bumped against mine again. The first time was probably an accident, but the second time felt like it couldn't be an accident. His hand had touched mine, moved away, and then moved back. Our fingers were now resting against each other.

I couldn't concentrate on the show because all I could think about was the fact that our hands were touching. What did this mean? I was never sure of what my feelings for Zach were, exactly. Whenever my parents questioned me, I would become defensive and point out how ridiculous it was that I couldn't just be friends with a guy without everyone assuming there was something going on. It was predictable and, frankly, offensive, and it was bad enough that TV shows and movies never let guys and girls just be friends, but worse, that everyone had to make the assumptions in real life too. And, even worse, no one made any assumptions about Lucy and me, which is so backward and heteronormative.

Outside of my standard rant, though, I wasn't exactly sure whether I believed what I was saying. I mean, I believed in principle, but whether it actually applied to me was another question. Zach was *the* guy in my life, so I was never sure whether I was projecting feelings onto him, or really feeling them. He was cute, in a gawky way. Sometimes I found him attractive and sometimes I absolutely didn't. I had occasionally had a sexual dream about him, but I had also had sexual dreams about a middle-aged, not-especially-attractive teacher before, so I couldn't trust whatever my subconscious thought it was doing there.

Zach was funny, and kind, and he made me feel safe. I still

wasn't comfortable around him when my skin broke out, and I had never let him see or even know about the terrible acne scars on my back, or how bad my skin was before I met him, but, otherwise, I was always relaxed with him. The best way to describe my feelings for Zach was a deep, familial love accompanied by a fluctuating semi-romantic crush that could come and go in an instant. I couldn't picture myself *actually* kissing him, but I had such limited kissing experience, I couldn't trust that instinct either.

There were people who I was very clearly, definitely, instantly attracted to: the boy who caught my train and had cheekbones I couldn't look away from; the fill-in PE teacher we'd had once who had the most breathtakingly athletic body I had ever seen up close; the lead guitar player in a Battle of the Bands night I was forced to attend, who held himself in the sexiest way I've ever seen; the guy who worked in my local library who had gloriously long eyelashes. And there were many people I was definitely not attracted to. And then there's this whole section of people who fall somewhere in the middle. People who you don't even notice until they say something unexpected and then you realize they are smart and funny, or people who look bad in a school uniform but then you see them in a coat and scarf and everything changes. That's where Zach exists, in this in-between place.

Zach also felt achievable for me. I knew he liked me as a person. I knew I could make him laugh, that we had similar interests, that we could pass an entire day together and not be bored or sick of one another. That we never ran out of things to say, and that he challenged me to do better at things, more than anyone else did. If anyone was going to fall in love with me . . . well, Zach was the only possibility, really. It came down to basic math. I don't spend enough time with any other boy for love to be possible. The chances of me meeting and falling in love with someone else were minuscule. I simply didn't have a social existence that allowed for that, and I didn't want one, let alone know how to get one.

I mostly imagined Zach and me getting together later in life. In our twenties. Maybe our thirties. I wasn't in love with Zach now, but I was confident I could be one day. He was the potential future love of my life.

If my life were a TV show, then my character and Zach's character would eventually get together in season three or four, after many episodes of banter, pining, and meaningful looks, and the audience would love it. Everyone would ship us.

So we lay there with our fingers touching, and my heart pounding, and we watched the rest of the episode and half of the next one before either of us moved. My arm was aching and uncomfortable, but I wasn't going to move it because the next move either needed to be something more (actively holding hands) or something less (moving my hand away entirely). I didn't want to be the instigator of either of these actions. I wanted to leave my hand right there and see what happened. I was holding the door open for Zach to walk through it.

Zach didn't walk through it.

He got up to get a glass of water, and when he came back, he didn't put his hands under the pillow again, and I didn't either.

That was it. For thirty-seven minutes our hands had touched, and we lay in silence thinking about what to do next, and we chose nothing.

Lucy came back from her trip changed. She had met someone. A friend of the family whom she hadn't seen in years. She was staying next door to him in Perth. Her parents were busy and distracted, and Lucy and this boy—Travis—spent all their time together. Travis taught Lucy how to surf, and he had three dogs, called Alvin, Simon, and Theodore, and he rode everywhere on his bike. And his skin tasted salty, and he was a good kisser, and Travis and Lucy had sex.

Travis and Lucy had sex.

I have never felt as panicked as I did when Lucy told me this. Here I was, grappling with the hand-touching incident, and she had met a whole new person and his three cute dogs, and had kissed this person, and learned to surf, and then had sex with this person. *She had sex.* She didn't even think to call me and discuss it before she did it. She'd just done it.

We were almost equals when she left, and now she was so far ahead of me.

"Oh my god."

"I know."

"I can't believe it."

"I know."

"Was it . . . ? What was it like?"

"Some parts were a bit boring, other parts were quite good."
She made it sound like the latest Marvel movie or something.

Which parts were good? I wanted to scream. *Tell me which parts, tell me what to do. Stop, stop, stop, and wait for me to catch up.*

"I can't believe it."

"I know."

I was ashamed of how unhappy I felt (a recurring theme, as it turns out, when it comes to Lucy's love life). But I could feel Lucy slipping away from me. First it was sex with a surfer, then it would be wild parties, and dating terrible boys with cool haircuts, and then we would drift apart and finish high school and she'd become a high-powered lawyer, and I would do who knows what (even in imaginary scenarios I have no direction) and we'd never talk again. Lucy was my safe place, my favorite person, and she was smashing that safety to bits. I wanted to physically grip her arm.

"You look weird," Lucy had said to me.

"I feel weird." I had become used to letting Lucy see me and know me, so it was hard to hide myself from her.

"Why?"

"Well, I feel like . . ." I wasn't sure how to put it. "I feel like you are so far ahead of me in life."

"Well, one of us had to have sex first."

"And there was never any doubt it would be you," I said, probably with a touch too much self-pity.

"Are you kidding? Have you met my parents?"

"How come they trusted Travis?"

"They didn't, by the end, but it was too late then."

We lay together on my bed and I calmed down a little. Lucy chattered on, and things started to feel more normal again. She wasn't a different person. She just had a great story to tell. Everything would be okay.

Everything would stay the same.

It didn't, though.

Zach took the news about Lucy and Travis better than I did. He seemed unaffected and cheerful about it at first. I thought that was nice. It was refreshing, because I was worried Zach would be jealous if Lucy or I got a boyfriend. (And I am sure we would have been jealous if he got a girlfriend.) Hell, I was jealous of Lucy and Travis. But it was also somewhere around this time that I noticed the vibe between Lucy and Zach change. Maybe the Travis story was a jolt to Zach, and he was scared of losing his chance with Lucy. Maybe it made him look at her in a different way. Maybe he was thinking about the almost-something that might have happened between him and me, and he realized Lucy was who he wanted. Or maybe they just fell in love, as simple as that. Or maybe I have no idea what happened, and I never will, because they have their own secrets.

The first thing I noticed was in the early weeks of year twelve. Lucy and I were stressed. To be fair, *everyone* was freaking out. Our school was pretty intense. But Lucy was especially stressed. Her parents wanted her to do well. They wanted her to set the example for her younger sister. They wanted her to be top of her class in at least two subjects. They wanted her to be better than as many people as possible.

"I *have* to do well," she said one afternoon when we were all studying together.

"I know. Me too," I said, chewing my pen and not really paying much attention.

"Your parents don't care," she said.

Now I looked up. This wasn't true and she knew it. "My parents do care, actually. They show it in different ways. And anyway, *I* care."

"I know, I know. I know it's bad for everyone." She bent over, pretending to look for something in her schoolbag but, really, she seemed to be just trying to breathe.

"I keep thinking about everything I need to do this year, and I feel sick," she said, still bent over.

I looked over her head at Zach.

"Luce?" he said, and put a hand on her arm, and bent over to try to see her face.

"What?"

"You'll be okay. We'll make sure it's okay."

The tenderness in his voice, the tenderness in his hand on her arm. I noticed it. I'm not sure what I thought, exactly, but I remember noticing how he was with her that day.

A week or so later, we were all on the train together, and a bunch of guys from Fullers College got on, in their distinctive green and yellow uniforms. They were the guys who used to scream at me about my acne. I hated them, but, even more, I hated that I was scared of them. I looked away.

The train was busy, but not packed. We were near the doors, and they got on yelling and laughing, and they walked past us, deliberately ramming into Lucy's bag and almost knocking her over.

"What the hell?" she said, stumbling backward and grabbing the pole.

The boys laughed.

"Hey," Zach said.

"What?" One of the boys turned to him.

"Watch what you're doing. You almost knocked her over."

The guy rolled his eyes. He was summing Zach up—taking in how much more muscular he was than Zach, and how many more friends he had around him, how much the situation was to his advantage. And yet Zach's eyes were flat and unafraid. He looked calm and serious. He wasn't trying to start a fight, but there was something forceful in his voice.

"All right, mate. Whatever. Tell your girlfriend I'm sorry."

The guy turned away, said something to his friends, and they all laughed.

"I'm standing right here," Lucy said, looking cross, putting her hand on her hip.

"What do you mean?" I said.

"He said, tell your girlfriend I'm sorry, as if I wasn't standing right here listening to him." This outraged Lucy a lot more than the original bump did.

But I had seen the way Zach's face changed when the guy called Lucy his girlfriend, and then again when Lucy repeated it. There was something flickering there.

I became sure that he was falling in love with her. I wasn't sure how I felt about it; a little bit sick, a little bit fascinated. I thought it was an unrequited love, at first. Lucy didn't give much away.

Then one afternoon, I felt a shift. They were laughing, and I saw Lucy gently pushing Zach's arm and he was staring at her with soft eyes, and I knew it was coming—something was going to happen between them. And the minute something did happen, things would change between the three of us forever, and I wasn't in a hurry for that to happen. Still, I imagined Zach would come to me and tell me about his feelings for Lucy and ask for my advice. I imagined Lucy would confess to me first too, and I would guide them both toward each other.

I imagined I would be part of things.

Instead, everything happened when I wasn't looking. I was busy with assignments one weekend, and I didn't see Lucy or Zach, and then the next weekend I went with Mum to see my grandmother who lived a two hours' drive away. On the way home, I asked Mum to drop me at Zach's house so I could pick up a book.

I didn't message him to say I was coming by, and I let myself in the back door. I knew I was doing this to see if Lucy was there, to see how she and Zach were interacting without me. I was imagining flirting, maybe catching them snuggled together watching a movie.

"Hello?" I called out, knowing that if they were in the den, then they probably wouldn't be able to hear me.

I walked to the den and gave the door a small push. At first I thought it was empty, but then I saw Lucy and Zach on the couch, kissing passionately, completely entwined in each other.

"Oh," I said, and jumped back. They didn't hear me. I shut the door, turned too quickly in my hurry to get out of there, and tripped over a pair of shoes in the hallway. My knees hit the floorboards really hard, and I sat on the floor for a minute, looking down, deep-breathing, feeling shocked, feeling stupid for coming there with the intention of catching them, because I wasn't prepared to see that.

I limped home slowly and, to my shame, I started to cry about halfway there. I pretended to myself I was crying because my knees hurt and I was cold and tired. But I knew I was crying because Zach and Lucy hadn't needed me at all to get together, and even though I had known they were going to get together, I hadn't expected them to be *that* together. I was picturing lingering looks, and they were well on their way to who knows what. Well, I did know what. Lucy had had sex before, so why wait now? I could hear a nasty tone in my own mind. I was slut-shaming my best friend in the privacy of my thoughts. I was a gross, horrible person. A sad, single, unlovable, horrible, repulsive person.

I limped and cried the rest of the way home, and then I had to sneak into my own house and hide in the shower until my face looked less red and tearful.

My left knee had a gigantic bruise on it.

"Oh my god. How did that happen?" Lucy asked me at school the next day.

"I fell over."

"Ouch."

"Yeah. It hurt."

9

AULD LANG SYNE

Zach, Lucy, and I are sitting on a sand dune and sharing a bottle of pink champagne. I take a small sip and hand it to Lucy, who swigs a couple of times before handing it to Zach, who drinks and then makes a face. He doesn't like pink champagne. Neither do I. We got it for Lucy, because drinking pink champagne all together on the beach on New Year's Eve is something she wanted to do, and we like to make her happy, especially at the moment. She still occasionally gets that faraway look in her eye, the look that says she isn't as happy as she seems to be.

"We did it," Zach says, holding the bottle of champagne up to the starry sky.

"To finishing school," I say.

"To our future," Zach says.

"To staying friends forever," Lucy says.

"To all going to the same uni," I say. We all want to go to Melbourne, mostly because we were told that was the university to aim for. I will do arts, then maybe honors and a Ph.D. (I am the kind of person who will just keep automatically doing the next study option until there are none left.) Lucy will do commerce, then postgrad law, and Zach will do science, then medicine, and we'll be together as a codependent unit for six years or longer and I won't even have to try to make a single new friend until I'm at least twenty-five.

"To getting everything we want," Zach says, which feels like a bit much, but he's never had any reason to think that's not possible, to be honest.

I lie back in the sand, close my eyes, and listen to the sound of the waves.

"What is Alex doing tonight?" Lucy says, startling me, because I was just wondering the same thing.

"Working, remember?" Zach says.

"And then what?" I ask.

"Then he'll probably go out and sleep with a bunch of girls."

"A bunch of girls?" My voice almost squeaks.

"Okay, maybe just one girl. Or no girls. I have no idea."

My mind is still stuck back on the sleep-with-a-bunch-of-girls part. I feel ridiculous for thinking a kiss on the cheek meant anything. It's like the hands-touching moment with Zach. I fixate on tiny nothings while everyone else is off having mind-blowing sex. I'll be on my deathbed still thinking about the one time a guy was kind of nice to me.

"I'm going for a walk," I say, mostly because I feel obliged to make a show of leaving them alone so they can kiss at midnight.

"The fireworks are about to start," Lucy says.

"I'll be back."

"Don't be a martyr. We are counting down together. All three of us. No arguments," Zach says.

"Fine."

I stand up, and we all look at the sky together. I'm torn between feeling like a charity case and feeling like I have the best two friends in the world. The crowd counts down from ten, everyone cheers at zero, and the fireworks begin.

"*Wooooooo*," Zach yells, running to the water, leaping goofily until he's waist-deep and then diving under fully clothed.

"Come in," he yells.

Swimming in the dark seems like a surefire way to get eaten by sharks, but this might be my one opportunity to go swimming in clothes without feeling ridiculous. I figure there are enough people out there that if a shark came past, the odds are reasonably good I wouldn't be the one chomped.

Lucy runs into the water, and I follow her. It's colder than I am ready for, and I edge my way in, until I reach Zach and Lucy.

"Let's all say three things we like about each other to start the new year," Lucy says, as we stand shoulder-deep in the water. She suggests stuff like this all the time. She says a group therapist her family once went to made them play "feel-good games," as he called them, and now Lucy is kind of addicted. Sometimes Zach and I play along, and sometimes we don't.

"Lucy is kind, generous, and caring. Natalie is funny, smart, and interesting," Zach says quickly, swimming in slow strokes with his head out of the water.

"Interesting," I scoff.

"What's wrong with interesting?" Zach says.

"It's a placeholder word," I say, flicking a bit of water at him when he swims by me.

"A placeholder for what?" he says, scrunching his face when my flicks of water hit him.

"Weird. Unpopular."

"It is not. Interesting is the highest compliment I can give," Zach says, standing up and pushing his hair out of his eyes.

"I think you can do better."

"Well, you say yours and let's see if you can do better."

"Why do you guys always ruin my game?" Lucy says.

"We can't help it," Zach says.

"It's in our nature to ruin things. Hey, that can be one for you, Zach—excellent at ruining things."

"That's a very undervalued quality," he says, grinning.

I dive under the water, trying not to think about sharks, rise to the surface, and dive under again. Last year, I spent New Year's Eve with my parents, doing what had become our tradition over the years: eating fancy cheese and watching old movies. As much as I love Zach and Lucy, and as happy as I am to be with them right now, a part of me can't help thinking about how I'll never, ever have another New Year's Eve like that with my parents again.

I float on my back for a while and watch the last of the fireworks burst across the sky. My ears are under the water, so it's a silent, colorful explosion surrounded by stars. I could stay like this forever.

10

HUMILIATING THINGS

It's two a.m., and I jolt awake at the sound of the front door creaking open. Everyone is back at the house and in bed, and I've been asleep for about half an hour. After coming home, showering, dumping our wet clothes in the washing machine, and saying good night to everyone, Zach and I secretly switched rooms.

I'm currently alone in the downstairs bedroom that's closest to the front door, and I'm scared. Why didn't I think of the risks of bed-swapping? I'll be the first person murdered because of Zach and Lucy's horniness. The front door creaks closed, and I pull the blankets over my head. *Dear God or Whoever Might Be Listening, don't let me die before I learn how to drive. Don't let me die before I launch my podcast series about current teens watching old teen shows from the nineties. Don't let me die before I get to travel somewhere, anywhere, outside of Australia. Don't let me die before I have an orgasm with someone other than myself. Don't let me, don't let me die, don't let me die—*

There are footsteps headed toward the bedroom door. When is the appropriate time for me to scream—when the murderer starts opening the door, when they actually enter the room, or do I wait until they pull the sheet off my head? I want my phone, but it's charging on the other side of the room.

The murderer is definitely hovering on the other side of my door. Except now there is another set of footsteps, and whispers. Two people whispering. I pull the sheet down off my head.

"Alex?" It's Mariella's voice.

"Mum?"

"You almost gave me a heart attack! What are you doing here?" she says.

"I drove down after I finished work. What are you holding? Is that a cricket bat?"

"I thought you were someone breaking in."

"So you left Dad asleep and came out to confront an intruder on your own with a child's plastic cricket bat?"

"Your father doesn't have a killer instinct. He'd hesitate at the crucial moment. You know that."

"True."

"What are you doing driving on New Year's Eve? That's dangerous, honey."

"I wasn't drinking. Trust me. I was pulled over and tested by a booze bus twice on the way down."

"Driving for an hour and a half in the middle of the night after a long shift is how you fall asleep at the wheel and die."

"You're right. I shouldn't have done it. I just had a bad night and wanted to get out of the city."

"What happened?"

"Nothing, I just—let's talk in the morning."

"Well, Zach's in there asleep, and the trundle bed is still in the cupboard in Glenn and Anthony's room. I don't want to wake them up."

"I'll share with Zach, then. You know how he sleeps. He won't even notice I'm in the bed until morning."

"Sweetie, come here."

"Mum—"

"I just want a quick hug."

"Mum, come on."

"You can't hug your mother now?" The universal mum-guilt tone.

"Fine. Careful with that bat."

There's a beat of silence.

"Your T-shirt smells like beer. And chips."

"Yeah, I work in a pub."

"Good night, honey. I love you."

"'Night, Mum. Love you too."

I'm so busy eavesdropping that what is about to happen occurs to me in a rush. I pull the sheet back over my head.

The bedroom door opens and then closes. I am waiting to make sure Mariella has gone back to her room before I speak, but I hear the sound of Alex taking off his jeans, and my mind turns into a white-noise buzz, it's so panicked.

"Wait," I say. My voice comes out in a huffy breath. The sheet is still covering my head.

"Shit! Who is that?" Alex must have one leg half in, half out of his jeans, because I hear a hop as he jolts in surprise, and then a soft thud as he falls onto the floor.

"Are you okay?" I ask.

"Natalie?"

"Yes."

"Sorry. Shit. Mum said Zach was in here."

"He was. We swapped, don't tell her, so he and Lucy could share."

"Oh."

I pull back the sheet and squint into the dark. He's standing up, yanking his jeans back on.

"Bloody Zach," he says.

"It's New Year's Eve. They wanted a night together."

"So what do we do? I guess I'll sleep on the floor," he says, but sits down on the bed. Then he flops onto his back, putting his hands over his face, like we're facing the greatest predicament two people could ever endure.

"I'm so fucking tired and I've had the worst fucking night ever and I can't stop fucking swearing, sorry. I don't even like swearing," Alex says. There's a brokenness in his voice that makes my heart hurt.

"Get in," I say, because it seems like the kindest thing to say right now, and I want to offer him some small kindness. About a millisecond after I have uttered the words, I want to die. I just told Alex to *get in bed with me*. I resist the urge to pull the sheet back over my head. Maybe I will self-combust and disappear into thin air before he answers. I can only hope.

He lies still for a second, and then he sits up and crawls up the bed until his head is on the pillow next to mine.

"Thank you," he says, his voice a little shaky.

It's ridiculous he's thanking me, because this is his family's house, not mine. I want to say, *And take your jeans off*, because the thought of him sleeping in jeans on a warm night makes my skin itch, but telling him that sounds even more suggestive than telling him to get in the bed, and also I'm not sure I want him to take his jeans off.

I can't sleep in a bed with a pantless Alex. I might legitimately have a heart attack.

Thinking about his jeans makes me realize I'm wearing my distorted-face Prince Harry T-shirt and oversized pajama shorts with hot dogs on them that I bought from the men's section at Kmart. So, my pajamas are not sexy. They are the opposite of sexy.

Alex shuffles around, and then leans over to the side of the bed and grabs two pillows off the floor (Mariella loves pillows, every bed has at least three more than are needed) and puts them under the sheet between us.

"What are you doing?" I say.

"Creating a pillow barrier. I can't sleep in jeans."

Oh god, oh god, oh god. He is going to be pantless. He will be Without Pants.

I'm in a fan fiction of my own life. Except I want to be safely reading it on the screen, not lying here in hot-dog-patterned shorts, sweating and self-consciously braless.

"Are you going naked?" I ask, my voice a weird squeaky version of what it normally sounds like.

"No! I'm wearing my jocks. Is that okay? If it's not okay, I can keep the jeans on."

"No, no, it's fine, take them off," I say, dropping my voice a little to try and sound like a worldly woman who is unconcerned about the amount of clothes being worn in the bed beside her. (I always imagine worldly women as having sexy, raspy, it-might-be-a-cold-or-it-might-be-too-many-cigarettes kinds of voices.)

I listen to Alex wriggle out of his jeans and drop them to the floor. That's it. The jeans are officially off. *Deep breaths, Natalie. This is really happening.*

"When are you and Zach switching back?" he asks through a yawn. How can he be so relaxed? This is the most high-stakes moment of my life, and I say that as someone who considered her final English exam a matter of life and death.

"At six-thirty. I've set my alarm," I say.

"Are you really okay to share until then?" he asks.

"Yes. Alex, it's your house."

The only thing more terrifying than sharing the bed with pantless Alex is losing the chance to share the bed with pantless Alex.

"Exactly. It's my house. Which means you're the guest who has to sleep with a random guy who bursts into your room in the middle of the night."

"You're hardly a random guy." If he knew how much space he had occupied in my brain in the past four days, I would die of shame.

"I know. But it feels weird. Anyway, the pillow barrier is here to create the illusion that we're in separate beds."

He has a lot of faith in this pillow barrier.

"I feel very reassured. In fact, it feels like we're in separate rooms. Separate houses even," I say.

"That's the power of a good pillow barrier," he says, and his voice has a smile in it.

We are both lying on our sides, facing each other. It's dark enough that I can only see an outline of his features, more a sense of his face than his actual face.

"So why was your night so horrible?" I say, feeling braver than usual because it's two a.m. on New Year's Eve and I've had a small amount of pink champagne.

He's quiet for a long time. "I got fired," he says finally.

"Oh my god." I was not expecting that answer. "Why?"

"Because my boss is an asshole."

"Wow." I don't know what to say. I feel terrible, because I know how much that job meant to him. Zach told me what a big deal it was when Alex chose to do an apprenticeship instead of going to university and how much their parents disapproved.

"Yeah," Alex says.

"I'm so sorry," I say.

"It's not your fault."

"I'm sorry it happened."

"Me too. I've never been fired before."

"What does it feel like?" I say, without thinking. What a terrible question. I honestly shouldn't be allowed to talk to people.

"Pretty bad," he says.

"What happened, exactly?" It feels a little nosy to ask, but I sense he might want to talk.

Alex rolls over and lies on his back.

"Long story short, my boss, Garry, likes to scream and yell at people. Like, I know that's a thing all chefs do, or something, but this guy is really bad. I think there's something seriously *wrong* with him. Anyway, tonight he was picking on me and this other guy, Felix. Mostly I just ignore him, but Felix lost it. He and Garry got into a huge argument and I sided with Felix. I told Garry he was being unreasonable, and that he can't treat people like this, and at the end of my shift Garry told me not to bother coming back."

"That's awful."

"Yeah. The thing is, he didn't fire Felix, who said a lot worse than me. I think he just wanted to get rid of me. I'm not the greatest cook yet, but I'm getting a lot better."

"You didn't do anything wrong, though."

"Maybe I did. Maybe I should have kept out of it. Anyway, Mum and Dad are going to be furious." He lets out a long breath.

"They'll understand," I say.

"They'll say they knew this was going to happen," he says.

"You can get another job," I say, with more confidence than I should, since I know nothing about the industry.

"I just feel like . . ." He pauses, and then he rolls over and looks at me. "You know what? Let's talk about something else. What did you do tonight?"

I ignore his question. "You just feel like what?" I say.

He's silent for a few seconds, and I can feel him wavering, hedging his bets on how much he wants to say.

"I just feel like, no matter how hard I try, I'm screwing everything up right now. My whole life feels like a huge mistake," he says quietly.

I know that feeling. The one that says my life isn't how it's supposed to be, that I've made all the wrong decisions.

"It's a new year. You've got a clean slate," I say. I'm naturally a pessimist, but tonight I'll play the role of optimist for Alex.

"Technically, I was fired this year. About ten minutes into this year, to be precise," he says.

"Anything bad that happens in the first hour of a new year still belongs to the previous year. It's a rule," I say.

"That's a good rule."

We've shuffled a little closer to one another during this conversation.

"Now forget everything I just said," he says.

"Why?" I say.

"Because I just told you a very humiliating thing about myself and . . . it's embarrassing." He gives a little uncomfortable half laugh.

"See, I don't think you realize who you are talking to. I'm the queen of humiliating things. My life has been one big humiliation," I say. I regret the words as soon as they are out of my mouth, because I know what his next question will be.

"Like what?"

I try to think of something I would actually want to tell him, something funny and easy, a humble brag that sounds embarrassing on the surface but is actually designed to make me sound cool, something that doesn't involve me being ashamed of the state of my body or the state of my personality. Nothing comes to mind.

But it's dark, and he's waiting, and I have to speak.

"Like, all of my high school years, I guess," I say.

"Give me an example."

I reach for the safest option I can think of in the moment, something he already knows. "Well, the other night at that party. You saw me hiding in the bathroom. You saw me *cry*."

"You went to a party where you didn't know anyone. That's brave."

"You have a low bar for brave," I say.

"No, I don't."

"What's the bravest thing you've ever done?"

He thinks for a while.

"I'm not sure I've ever done anything truly brave."

"What about tonight? Standing up to your boss?"

"Maybe." He sounds unconvinced.

"It sounded brave to me."

"Well then, maybe *you* have a low bar for brave," he says, reaching across the pillow barrier to gently poke my arm.

His very brief touch gives me goose bumps. "Or maybe we're both incredibly courageous people," I say.

"We're heroes, really," he says.

"They'll write books about us."

"And make movies."

"Little kids will dress up as us on Halloween."

"That means we need superhero costumes."

"Mine has a silver dagger with a poisoned tip, and a black hooded cape," I say. I've always wanted a cape, so I can sweep out of a room with purpose or pull the hood back to dramatically reveal my identity.

"Are you a superhero or an assassin?" he says.

"A bit of both," I say.

"Well, my superhero costume will have a jetpack, and a sword."

"I'm not sure a jetpack and a sword really fit together, thematically."

"You think that now, but when you see a sword fight in the air, you'll change your mind." He sounds very sure of this.

"But how are you fighting with the sword and steering the jetpack at the same time? It's logistically very dangerous."

We argue about swords and jetpacks for a little while, and I can hear in his voice that he's relaxing.

"Thank you," he says suddenly.

"What for?"

"I came in here feeling terrible. And now I feel a bit less terrible."

"Less terrible, but still not good?"

"Well, let's not get ahead of ourselves."

I laugh, and then close my eyes. I listen to him breathe, and I can tell the moment he falls asleep because his breathing changes.

I lie there listening to him sleep for a long time, which is a thrillingly intimate and kind of creepy thing to do. I can't help it, though, because I feel wide awake. I've never spent the night in a bed with a guy before. I want to document every moment, although after a while it becomes clear that with Alex asleep, there is very little to document.

It feels like I've just closed my eyes when my alarm starts quietly buzzing.

11

AN INCOMPLETE LIST

Here is an incomplete list of my actual greatest humiliations from high school that I would never say out loud to Alex, or anyone:

- A woman in the supermarket asking me what happened to my face, because my acne was so bad it didn't even look like acne anymore.
- Crying in my doctor's office when she showed me the smallest kindness by saying, "Oh, honey, you poor thing."
- Crying in my dermatologist's office when he said, "You should have come to me sooner," and it became clear that everything was my fault.
- Crying in my naturopath's office when she was listing the foods I needed to stop eating and she had been listing them for a while and I realized she probably was only halfway through and I would never enjoy a meal again.
- Having a public fight with my mother in the Myer

fitting rooms while bra-shopping, because I didn't want the bra fitter to come in and see the acne and scars on my back.

- Not looking anyone in the eye for days at a time, and then being called rude, and having a terrible flood of realization of what other people must think of me.

- Feeling okay about my skin for the first time in a long time, and then a little girl asking if I'd fallen over and skidded my chin along the road, and realizing my skin only looked okay relative to how bad it was before.

- Giving up sugar for six months and not having a birthday cake or dessert at Christmas or a bowl of ice cream on a Friday night (my favorite), and my skin breaking out anyway, making all that sacrifice pointless.

- My parents going away for a weekend and calling me and asking in a hopeful tone if I had invited people over, and realizing later they were wishing I would throw a party in their absence (even just a small party, even if I'd just invite one friend over), and instead I read fan fiction and watched YouTube tutorials on cross-stitching and wrote a list of names I would call my dog if I had one, and felt happy I didn't have to see anyone.

- Crying when I'd see myself in the mirror on a Monday morning and realizing I had to endure a whole week of being out in the world.

- Deleting and then reinstating my social media accounts every two weeks for a year, and agonizing for hours every time, even though I never posted pictures of myself anyway.

- Spending literally hours on other people's social

media—people from school, friends of people from school, celebrities, complete strangers—and dreaming of having their lives.

- Turning eighteen and knowing I had never been liked, romantically, by anyone, at all, ever, in my entire life.

A FAVOR TO ASK

Lucy nudges open the door to our shared bedroom with her foot and walks in carrying aloe vera gel, an ice pack, a wet washcloth, a bottle of water, and a candle. I am lying prone on our bed with the blinds down because I am sunburned. (Of course I am. This is why I hate summer. No other season physically *burns* you for doing what everyone tells you to do—going outside and enjoying the nice weather.)

It's my own fault. The super-strong acne medication I used to take has left me with a semipermanent sensitivity to the sun. I went for a walk on the beach today, while Zach and Lucy were surfing and Alex was off somewhere, and even though I lathered myself in sunscreen, I couldn't find my hat and, in an act of vanity, didn't wear the very old, slightly dirty spare baseball cap hanging by the front door.

Even though I was just going for a casual walk on the beach, the truth was I was hoping to run into Alex.

I had pictured myself walking along the beach, the breeze in my hair, my sunglasses giving me an air of mystery, my short denim shorts giving me a hint of sexiness. Alex would be swimming, and he'd look up and see me on the shoreline. I wouldn't know he was watching, I would be simply walking along, lost in my own deep thoughts, beautiful but oblivious to my beauty. Like footage from *The Bachelorette*, when they're reflecting on the lead's journey as an emotionally troubled but extremely desirable woman looking for True Love. Except I would be thinking about important things, like housing affordability and climate change and health care.

In reality, I was hot and sweaty within seconds of being outside, the denim shorts chafed my thighs quite badly, and I stepped on a nonpoisonous (I hope) jellyfish and it squished between my toes, which made me shriek loud enough that an older woman rushed over and asked if I was okay. And I got sunburned in splotches on my legs, my arms, my chest, my nose, my forehead, and my neck. Plus, I didn't see Alex all day.

So now I'm lying on the bed upstairs, being pathetic. Lucy is very good at sympathy, much better than my mother, so I like to play things up to her. We both slot easily into carer/being-cared-for roles.

"Did you wear a hat?" Lucy asks, popping the cap off the aloe vera gel.

"No. But I wore sunscreen."

"You need both."

"I know."

"How do you feel?"

"Hot. And cold."

"You might have sunstroke."

"Is that serious?"

"I'm not entirely sure. You'd better drink some water."

"What's the candle for?"

"It's scented. Sea mist. It smells like the beach. Mariella said it will relax you."

"We're at the beach. The air here already smells like the beach."

"Yes, but the scented candle version of the beach is supposed to be more relaxing."

Lucy lights the candle, sits down on the bed, and frowns at me. "There's sand on the bed," she says.

"I know."

"How did you manage to get so much sand on the bed?"

"It sticks to me, even when I try to rinse it off." I look up at her with my most pitiful face.

I rub aloe vera gel all over myself until I am shiny, and then Lucy drapes the wet washcloth over my face.

"Do I really need this covering my whole face?" I ask, muffled.

"Yes," Lucy says with authority.

Then Zach walks in.

"Hello, O Burned One."

"No teasing. I'm in a fragile state," I say.

"Did you wear a hat?"

"I don't care for that line of questioning." I can see everyone is going to keep harping on this no-hat fact.

Zach sits down on the bed and frowns. "Why is there so much sand everywhere?" he says.

"God, you and Lucy spend too much time together. Your brains are melding together."

There are footsteps walking down the hall and into the room, and then the one voice I am both dreading and dying to hear.

"Hey, guys . . . what's wrong with Natalie?" Alex says.

"Sunburn," I say.

"Oh no," he says, but he has laughter in his voice.

"She might have sunstroke," Lucy says in her most serious carer's voice.

"Why are you so shiny?" Alex says, and his voice is closer.

"Aloe vera gel."

"I'm not even going to ask about the washcloth over your face."

"Please don't. I'd prefer it if everyone just looked away from me, actually." Motto of my life.

Later, after dinner, I'm in the bathroom brushing my teeth and examining my sunburn (red and getting redder) when Zach walks in.

"I've got a favor to ask."

"Okay," I say, through a mouthful of toothpaste. I know what he's going to say.

"It's a big one." He's got his serious face on.

"I'm listening." I spit into the sink.

"Can we switch rooms again tonight?"

"And where will Alex be sleeping?" I ask.

"On the trundle bed."

"I don't know." I can't look too eager, because then Zach will be suspicious. Also, Zach doesn't know I like Alex, and if I didn't like Alex, then sharing a room with him would be scary, in a different way than the way it is scary now, and Zach should feel bad about asking me to do it. Zach is a good person, but he's also a teenage guy with priorities: Lucy, having sex with Lucy, then a lot of air, then me and his family, then the rest of the world.

"You won't have to talk to him or interact in any way, I promise," Zach says.

"Does he know about this plan?"

"Yes."

"And what did he say about it?"

"He said it was fine."

Fine. What a small, ungenerous word. Fine is not excitement, or hidden desire, or even pretending not to be excited. Fine is indifference. Fine is *fine*. I want Alex to feel anything but fine.

"Hmmmm."

"You guys are sort of friends now, aren't you?"

"Sort of." I busy myself packing up my toiletries bag, which is large enough to almost be an overnight bag: I have an inordinate, embarrassing amount of skin-care products that I lug with me everywhere. While I am at the beach house, I am sleeping in a very small amount of tinted moisturizer, just to cover the redness of my old scars, so there is never any chance of anyone seeing my face completely bare.

"And sharing with him last night was okay?" Zach asks.

"It was a bit weird."

My stomach hurts, thinking of it. I have another chance to be alone in a room with Alex. I want it, I want it so much, but I also want to put nice, safe obstacles in the way of me being able to have it, because that way I can't ruin it.

"Okay, let's not do it, then," Zach says.

"Are you disappointed?" I ask, testing the strength of this obstacle.

"No."

"You have a terrible poker face. I can tell you are."

"It's okay. I don't really expect you to be comfortable sharing a room with my brother. Lucy said I shouldn't even ask. And I feel bad that's what happened last night."

We look at each other in the mirror.

"I'm happy to swap beds," I say.

"I don't want you to," Zach says.

"It's fine."

"No. Now I feel bad."

"I want to do it."

"No, you don't."

"I kind of do." He can't know how much I kind of do.

"No, you don't."

"Shut up and stop telling me how I feel. I'm doing it. That's it. No more arguing."

"Okay. All right. Good. Thank you," he says.

"You owe me."

"I know."

"Big-time. You owe me big-time."

"I know."

A NIGHT IN FEELINGS TOWN

I tiptoe into the room and shut the door quietly behind me. I hope Alex is on the trundle bed, fast asleep and snoring. That way I can fantasize about us kissing without it being a possibility. Nothing can happen, and I can be safe in the knowledge that it wasn't my fault, the opportunity simply never presented itself.

I shuffle forward tentatively, worried I'll walk into the trundle bed.

"I'm in the bed," Alex says.

"Zach said you were going to sleep on the trundle."

"It's got a broken spring—it's like someone is poking you in the back."

"I'll sleep on the trundle," I say, delighted I have the opportunity to show how little I care about sharing a bed. *I'm just a girl here to sleep. I most certainly do not have a desperate, all-consuming, so-intense-it-hurts crush, and I will unequivocally prove this by sleeping on the trundle.*

"Don't do that."

"I'm doing it," I say.

I stub my toe on the edge of the trundle bed as I'm trying to find it, and give out a sort of muffled yelp of pain.

"What happened?"

"I banged my toe."

"That fucking trundle."

I crawl onto the trundle bed and lie there for a few seconds. It is extremely uncomfortable. "Okay, the spring is really poking into my back," I say.

"I told you." Alex sounds amused.

"I'll sleep on the floor," I say, determined not to give up.

"Don't be ridiculous."

"I'll make a little nest with blankets and pillows—it'll be cozy." It seems very important I put on a show of not wanting to be in a bed with him. Denying the thing I want the most is very soothing.

"Natalie. Don't."

I like it when he says my name. I don't want to like it as much as I do.

"It's fine," I say, and start dragging pillows and blankets onto the wooden floor. Then I lower myself onto the pile.

"It's actually not that bad. I think it's going to be good for my back."

I swear my back already hurts, down here for two seconds.

I try to find a comfortable way to lie, but the floor is too hard. I am not an animal, I cannot sleep like this. I don't even know why I'm doing it. I *want* to share a bed with Alex. What is wrong with me?

I'm scared of him—of anyone—knowing what I want. I'm scared that we'll share the bed again and nothing will happen again, and I'm not sure I can handle having all these chances that pan out to nothing. On the flip side, the thought of something happening between us is so scary-good stressful, I can't handle that either. Why are good things so terrible?

"I'll make a pillow barrier again," Alex says.

I want him to want to kiss me. I want him to want to kiss me so badly that he would never think of a pillow barrier.

Jesus, calm down, Natalie.

"Okay," I say, and get into the bed.

"I'll sleep on the floor, if you want. In your nest," he says.

"No, stay in the bed. The nest is not comfortable."

"I'll build a big pillow barrier."

"It's fine. We don't need a pillow barrier," I say. I am now regretting that I have pushed us in this direction.

"I'll sleep on the couch, until you and Zach switch."

"Alex. Stop. I want us to share the bed."

There's a beat of silence. I can't believe I said that. It feels starkly revealing. *I want us to share the bed.* It is worse than last night's "Get in." I can already imagine how many times I am going to regretfully replay this sentence in my head in the future. I need to backtrack, fast.

"I mean, I don't *want* to, but I'm perfectly fine sharing," I say, my voice veering close to embarrassed babble.

"Good. Because I was beginning to feel like a creep," Alex says.

"You're not a creep."

We lie in awkward silence. Any chance of something happening has definitely disappeared.

I close my eyes and count to fifty. I should be grateful. I get to share a bed with the guy I have a crush on, for the second night in a row. That's not *nothing*. It's almost nothing, but it's not completely 100 percent nothing.

"Are you asleep?" he says.

"No. Are you?" I mean, obviously he's not.

"No."

I turn onto my back. I'm wide awake, even though I barely slept last night.

"Let's play a game," he says.

"Uno?" I ask hopefully. I love Uno. I would definitely beat him too, and nothing relaxes me like winning a card game.

"Not that kind of game," he says.

"I'm not drinking," I say, suddenly wary. Jesus, maybe he has a flask tucked under the pillow.

"No, not that kind of game either."

"What, then?" For a second I think he's going to say Spin the Bottle and my heart races, even though of course he won't and we're lying in bed and we don't have a bottle and it's not a two-person game and there's absolutely no reason he would say it, but—

"Truth. We ask each other questions, and you have to answer each one truthfully, but you get three passes."

"That sounds like a very intense game."

"It's easier when you're drunk," he says.

I wonder who he has played it with drunk and who he has played it with sober.

"You start," I say. I need time to formulate some questions. I have no idea how deep we're going.

"Okay. Do you have feelings for Zach?" he says, without hesitation.

Shit, okay, so it's going to be like that. "No, I don't have feelings for Zach," I reply. "And that's actually an insulting question. Zach and Lucy are my best friends. Do you think I'm plotting to break them up or something?" I'm suddenly so annoyed that I've forgotten I even have a crush on Alex, and I turn toward him in the dark, ready to continue whisper-yelling. I hate that he, or anyone, might think that of me. Even if I was in love with Zach, absolutely head over heels crazy-in-love, I would *never* do that to Lucy. Never. I don't know all my limits, but I know that one. Lucy comes first for me.

Alex turns to me, clearly startled by my response. "I phrased that wrong. I meant before. Before they got together. Like, have you ever had feelings for Zach?" he says.

"Where has this question even come from?" I say, buying time, because I don't know whether to be truthful or not, and also I'm not sure what the truthful answer really is.

"Mum used to tease Zach and say he was going to marry one of you. I guess she put the idea in my mind," Alex says.

"Really?" Oh god, I hope Mariella doesn't think I'm in love with Zach and sadly trailing him and Lucy around like some kind of stalker/sad puppy.

"I'm sorry. I should have picked an easier question to start with. Don't forget, you can pass," Alex says. I have the urge to push him out of the bed.

"No, it is an easy question. I don't have, and I have never had, feelings for Zach." The truth is a slightly more complicated version of that statement. But this is not the time to be revealing my true self to Alex, even if whispering in the dark makes me want to start telling secrets.

"Great. Your turn," he says.

"Are you still in love with Vanessa?" I say. I don't really want to know the answer to this, but I need to ask him something equal to what he asked me.

"Nope."

"You didn't even pause to think."

"Didn't need to."

"You don't have any feelings about your ex you still need to process?"

"That wasn't the question."

"Okay. Your turn."

Now he hesitates. My stomach clenches a little.

"Have you ever been in love?"

He's good at this, I'll give him that. My automatic response is, *Fuck, fuck, fuck, I can't answer that.*

"That's a big question," I say, stalling for time.

"We don't have to keep playing."

"I'm having fun," I lie, because even though it's killing me, it would be much worse to stop playing this game and spend days and weeks (and, depending on how my future social life goes, potentially months and years) wondering what would have happened if I'd kept playing.

"No, you're not," he says.

"Yes, I am. And no, I haven't ever been in love. My turn. When are you going to tell your family that you got fired?" I throw back something as fast as I can, so he won't have time to dwell on my answer.

"Tomorrow." He pauses and then laughs. "Maybe tomorrow. By the end of the week."

"Your mum will understand," I say.

"It's more complicated than that."

"Tell me."

"I will if you ask the right question."

"It's your turn."

"Hmmm. Okay. Did you want to kiss Owen in the Spin the Bottle game at the party?"

"No. How many people have you slept with?"

He makes a small choked noise that makes me laugh. I knew that one would throw him.

"Pass," he says finally.

"Is that a point for me?"

"You don't really score this game."

"Well, new rule. We're scoring, and I'm winning."

"If I'd known that, I would have answered," he says, shifting a little closer to me.

"No, you wouldn't have."

"I might have."

"Your turn."

"I've got to think of a tough one, now it's about winning points."

"I have nothing to hide."

"Sure you do."

I pretend to scratch my arm but really use it as an excuse to shuffle a little nearer to him. We're now lying close enough that if I moved my foot a tiny bit, it might brush against his.

"Okay. That night at the party, when we got each other in Spin the Bottle, did you want to kiss me?" he asks.

There's a long pause, and I'm so glad that it's dark because my face is so hot it might be on fire, and that's only half due to the sunburn. "Pass," I say.

"I knew you had something to hide."

"Well, now it's my turn," I say quickly. "And I'm asking the same question back at you." I can't actually bring myself to say the words, *Did you want to kiss me?*

"Yes."

"What?"

"Yes, I wanted to kiss you."

My heart, my heart.

"Oh." I have no idea what else to say. My mind is completely blank. I can't even think of another question for the game.

"I mean, I did kiss you. On the cheek," he says.

"I know."

"So my answer should have been obvious."

"A kiss on the cheek is a different thing."

I can't believe we're having this conversation. I especially can't believe we're having this conversation without me having a heart attack.

"If you wanted to kiss me that night, why didn't you?" I ask, ignoring that it's actually his turn. We've been talking quietly, but I'm whispering now. These are scary words.

"Pass," he says finally.

I don't know what to do with that.

"Do you want to kiss me now?" he asks, so quiet I can hardly hear him.

"Pass," I say, because even in this moment, even with every opportunity in the world, I'm still too scared to say it.

That's two passes each. The next person to pass loses, but, for once, I don't care about winning. I can't bring myself to ask him the same question in return. My hands are trembling. But I don't want to change the topic. *Please, dear God, never let us move on from this very important topic of kissing and wanting to kiss.*

"Have you ever had the urge to kiss me before the night of the party?" I say.

He's quiet, and I listen to his breathing.

"Yes. Once."

"When?" I'm holding my breath.

"That's another question. You don't get another question. It's my turn," he says, and pauses to think. "Do you want me to kiss you right now?" he says.

"You already asked that," I say.

"No, I asked if *you* wanted to kiss *me*. Now I'm asking if you want *me* to kiss *you*."

"They seem like very similar questions."

"Similar but different." He's smiling, I can hear it in his voice. We're facing each other, but I have my eyes closed.

"Yes, I want you to kiss me," I say, my voice rushed and shaky. It feels like the single bravest thing I've ever said.

Before I have time to go into a full neurotic meltdown, he leans over and kisses me. His kiss is so quick and soft, a gentle touching of lips, that I could almost convince myself I imagined the whole thing. I open my eyes, and our faces are only inches apart on the pillow.

"Your turn," he says. And I know he's probably saying it's my turn to ask a question, but instead I decide that he's saying it's my turn to kiss him, and before I can rethink my decision, I take all my courage and I move forward and put my hand on his stubbly cheek and kiss him.

FIFTY-TWO MINUTES

I'm kissing Alex.

I'm kissing Alex.

He kisses my neck and my collarbone, and it feels more reckless and thrilling than anything I've ever done or anything I may ever do again. I feel like I am bursting, like I can't hold the particles of myself together anymore, like I could power a city with the electricity coming off my skin.

We kiss for fifty-two minutes, until the red numbers on the digital alarm clock on the bedside table say 12:42 a.m. For a lot of that time, Alex's hands are in my hair, on my face, on my shoulders, wrapped around me. After a while, though, they venture farther, sliding under my top. I'm not wearing a bra, it's not hard for him to find the bits of me he wants to find. I put my hands under his T-shirt and feel the bare skin on his stomach and chest, and it makes me breathless.

I can feel things getting more intense, and I pull back a little. I stop kissing him, mostly because I feel like I'll lose control of myself. He kisses my forehead, then shuffles back, creating space between us, but then reaching his hand out to touch mine. We don't say anything, we just lie facing each other, holding hands, until we fall asleep.

15

A DAY AT THE BEACH

The next day, while we're having breakfast, I am nervous. I'm keeping my head down and hoping no one notices the faint rash I have near my mouth from Alex's stubble rubbing against me, and if they do, that they think it's just part of my sunburn or my acne scarring.

Alex is not currently at the table. I think he's still asleep. He barely stirred when I snuck out of the bed early this morning. I artfully arranged the blankets on the trundle on my way out the door so it looked like someone had been sleeping there.

I nibble on a scone and try to stop myself from thinking about last night's kissing, even though my mind keeps looping endlessly back to it.

The kissing was glorious. The kissing was terrifying.

At about the seven-minute mark, a little voice wormed its way into my head, reminding me that Alex's hands were touching my body and my body is a minefield of potential humiliations. When his hands went near my hips and stomach, I kept thinking about how flabby they might feel, and when he put his hands on my back, under my T-shirt, I flinched away, because if he went any higher on my shoulders, he would feel the scars.

I want, so badly, to be the person who loves and is proud of her body, who says, *I am not giving in to the bullshit that is pressed on every girl from birth that what she looks like matters more than anything else.* But the truth is, what I've looked like *has* shaped my life, or at least my recent life. So I am not the enlightened person I want to be. I wish I didn't care what Alex thinks of my body, but I do. I've never let anyone as close to me as I let Alex last night. I don't even like people kissing me hello or goodbye, and last night I let someone press his face against my face for fifty-two minutes.

I didn't let him into my underwear. (He didn't try, in truth.) That's an area of my body that represents anxiety I've never needed to fully contemplate before. For a start, I am not completely hair-free. I'm trimmed down and waxed enough to wear bathers, but there is still lots of hair there and I'm not sure if I am supposed to have hair there. I mean, obviously I know I am biologically supposed to have it, and that women can do whatever they like with their body hair, but I still have a bubble of fear that maybe every single other girl my age keeps everything completely waxed or shaved off, all the time. I know Lucy gets waxed regularly, and I'm pretty sure she's getting everything removed.

I once read online that guys my age watch so much porn they don't even realize that women naturally grow pubic hair. Surely that can't be true. *Can it?*

Not to mention, what if I am . . . weird down there? Maybe I'm lopsided, or my insides are on a weird angle or curve the wrong way or are too long or too short or too big or too small or just don't feel right or look right or taste right. I wish there were some way of verifying for sure if I have a regular, standard, run-of-the-mill vagina and vulva before anything more happens with Alex. I could see a doctor, but I would be too embarrassed to actually ask the question. ("Hello, Doctor, do you think a nineteen-year-old guy with an unspecified amount of sexual experience would think it all looks generally okay down there?") The internet says genitalia come in all shapes and sizes, that there is no right or wrong, and I know, intellectually, that's true, but it gives me no real reassurance because I've never had to face the real prospect of someone interacting with mine before.

I thought I had cataloged and processed all my bodily anxieties years ago, but being with Alex has made me realize there are so many more possibilities.

I am also worried about Alex's expectations. He's nineteen and he's had a girlfriend. Who knows what he's already done. We were in a bed. At night. Kissing. *Enjoying* the kissing. Any other person in my situation would probably have had sex, no problems. Well, maybe not, but they would have at least considered it. But we didn't even get to the halfway point of having sex. (I don't know what the official halfway point is, but I doubt we reached it. We might not have gotten to a quarter of the way.) I don't regret not having sex, but I regret not being the person who would have had sex.

I just feel like I am so bad at this.

I keep secretly worrying about my vagina and eating breakfast while Zach chats with his father about politics, Mariella listens to Glenn talk about dinosaurs, Anthony plays a game on his phone, and Lucy stares into space, sipping at her tea every now and then.

Alex walks in the door, panting. He's not still asleep after all. He's in exercise gear and he's covered in sweat. I can hear the music blasting out of his headphones from across the room.

"Where've you been?" Zach says.

"For a run."

"That's not like you, sweetheart," Mariella says.

Alex frowns. "What does that mean?"

"You don't run," Mariella says, lifting a jar of Nutella out of Anthony's reach so he can't spread a third layer on his already-Nutella-covered toast.

"I run all the time," Alex says.

"When?" Glenn scoffs.

"At the gym. On the treadmill."

"Yes, but you're not a *runner.* You're not someone who gets up early specifically to go for a run outside, in the morning, before breakfast," Anthony says.

"You should all be out there running, making the most of this glorious day," Sal says, in his most dad-like voice.

"Dad, when's the last time you did any serious cardio?" Zach says.

"Your mother and I are going for a bike ride this afternoon."

"We are?" Mariella asks, looking up in surprise.

"Dad, you haven't been on a bike in over ten years," Zach says.

I stop listening, because I'm a little bit mesmerized by a sweating Alex. Sweat is ostensibly gross, but somehow it's not gross on Alex. His thick hair is pushed back, and when he rubs a towel over his face, little droplets reappear almost immediately. It should be disgusting, but it's not. It's appealing.

Maybe this is what falling in love is: you're not grossed out by someone else's sweat.

"Do you guys want to come to the beach with me today?" Alex says, looking at Zach and Lucy but flicking his eyes quickly in my direction and then away again.

"With you?" Zach looks confused.

"Yeah. I'm meeting some friends at the back beach. I thought you three might want to come too."

"I'll come," Anthony says, but no one responds to him.

There's a pause. Alex doesn't invite Zach places. Zach doesn't invite Alex places. Their brotherly relationship is complex, and part of that complexity is maintaining very different social circles and activities at all times.

"That's very nice of you, darling," Mariella says.

"Sure, we'll come," Zach says, glancing at Lucy and then at me. I try to make a very, very subtle I-don't-want-to face at Zach, but I think Zach reads it as an I'm-hungry face because he pushes the last scone on the table toward me.

"What time?" he asks Alex.

"About two."

"Cool."

Alex goes off to shower, and then leaves before lunchtime, saying he'll meet us there.

By the time the afternoon rolls around, I've decided I really, truly, absolutely don't want to go to the beach and hang out with Alex and his friends. I *cannot* go. But I dutifully change into my bathers anyway, because Zach and Lucy ignore my protests.

I am wearing a one-piece swimsuit that I am quite proud of myself for finding. It, amazingly, has a full back, and tiny little cap sleeves. I never thought such a thing existed until I saw it online. It zips up the front, and it's sleek, and it doesn't look too weird—in fact, it's designed as a fashion choice, a kind of slinky cat-suit type of bathers. So the scars on my back are hidden. The only parts of me that are very visible in a stressful way are my thighs. But if I unzip the top enough to show a bit of cleavage, I figure I can draw people's eyes up to my boobs.

I put on a loose dress over the bathers, and Lucy gives me her big floppy straw hat—a hat that looks adorable on the shelf, and adorable on Lucy, and adorable in Lucy's hands as she reaches up to put it on my head—but the moment it actually touches my head, it ceases being adorable and becomes ridiculous, as all hats do when they're on my head.

But with the hat and my sunglasses, I feel somewhat safe and hidden.

It takes about ten minutes to walk to the back beach. I trail behind Zach and Lucy, half listening to them chat but mostly fretting about seeing Alex with his friends.

"What happened between you two last night, that Alex is suddenly inviting us to the beach?" Zach says, turning around and walking backward, looking at me.

"Nothing," I say, a little too quickly and forcefully. At some point, I'm not exactly sure when, I decided that I wouldn't tell them about Alex. Not yet. Lucy would be too excited, too over-eager to analyze every detail and turn it into something bigger than it is. She would get my hopes up. She'd convince me of things that might not actually be true. She'd make me believe in love, and I need to be tougher and more sensible than that. I need to protect myself.

Zach, on the other hand . . . I'm not telling Zach mostly be-cause I'm scared of how he will react. I don't have siblings, but I know kissing the brother of one of your best friends is a big deal. And Alex and Zach already have a messy relationship. I don't want to squeeze myself into the middle of that.

So now it's a real secret.

We see Alex and his friends up ahead of us. They are playing Frisbee in the water, shouting and laughing and diving to catch it. I see Alex, and Owen, and a couple of other familiar faces from the party, a few entirely new faces, and . . . Vanessa.

Vanessa is here.

I stop walking, and Lucy turns back.

"What's wrong?"

"Nothing."

"You look pale," she says, peering under the brim of my giant hat.

"Her face is sunburned. How can she look pale?" Zach says.

"Are you okay?" Lucy asks me, ignoring Zach.

"Yes, I'm fine," I say, but my mouth is suddenly very dry. What the hell was I even thinking, coming to the beach and kissing Alex and acting like I had any business being a part of any of this?

"Let's just sit here," I say, not wanting to get any closer.

We lay out our towels. It's very hot, but I'm not going to go into the water or call any attention to myself. I get out my book and start reading.

At some point, Alex sees us. Zach waves at him, and he waves back, motioning for us to come closer, to come into the water, but he doesn't walk over to us, and my stomach twists.

I've been reading the same page of my book for fifteen minutes, because I'm not really reading as much as holding it as a prop while I watch Alex and his friends.

Alex seems happy. He runs around, diving into the sea for the Frisbee, tackling and wrestling with his friends. At one point, he and Vanessa both run after the Frisbee, and she bumps into him, pushing him out of her way, and he laughs. She's wearing a simple navy-blue bikini, and her dark hair is up in a messy topknot, and she runs and leaps and swims and dives with the confidence and joyful abandon of someone completely at ease in her body.

"Let's go for a swim," Zach says.

"I'll stay here," I say.

"No, you won't," Lucy says, pulling me to my feet. The three of us walk down the beach a little, getting closer to Alex and his friends. I'm still wearing my dress and hat and sunglasses. Lucy is in her red-and-white-striped bikini, as bright and cheerful as a lolly, with red sunglasses and bouncing blond curls. She looks like she should be playing beach volleyball in an ice-cream ad.

Alex and his friends are all in the water, and Lucy and Zach walk into the waves and wade out toward them.

"Coming?" Lucy calls over the sound of the waves.

"In a minute," I say, pretending that I just love wading in the shallows by myself.

Lucy and Zach swim out, and I sit down in the wet sand, where the last of the small waves reach, and let the cold water run over my feet and legs, recede, and run over them again. They are having shoulder fights now, one person sitting on another's shoulders and trying to knock another person off someone else's shoulders. Lucy is on Zach's shoulders and she squeals as she falls into the water. Alex is on Owen's shoulders. He gets flipped backward into the water and surfaces laughing. He looks at me, and yells something out, I think, but I can't hear him, and then he's pulled back into the game.

They seem to be rotating through all the options, so I know what's coming. Vanessa gets on Alex's shoulders, and my heart races. He grips her thighs (her lovely, lovely thighs) and they laugh as she fights against a girl on Owen's shoulders. She yells at Alex, and he yells back at her, and they are both grinning, and Vanessa knocks the other girl off Owen's shoulders. Alex lowers Vanessa back into the water and she slips off and dives under in one smooth motion. I've never felt more repellent or more pathetic in my life.

I should swim out and join in. I should strip off my dress and not care about what I look like. I should joke, laugh, and flirt, and show Alex the best parts of me. I should be the Natalie from last night, the Natalie who kissed him. But I'm stuck here in the shallows, watching, too scared to go out there.

I can't do this. I'll never be able to do this.

What the hell was I thinking? Outside of the bubble of sharing a bed at night, Alex and I don't work. I can't frolic with his bikini-clad friends on the beach, I can't go to bars and do whatever people do at bars (drink, I assume, but what else, there must be more to it). I just can't handle any of it.

This realization builds up inside me like an uncontrollable storm, and suddenly I can't stand it anymore. I get up and walk back to our towels, pick up my things, and keep walking, all the way back to the beach house. Somewhere along the way I start crying, which makes me feel even more pathetic, and I feel even more sorry for myself, which makes me cry even harder.

I would give anything to be someone other than me, just for one afternoon, just for a goddamn *minute*.

16

TWO STRIKES

That night, Lucy and Zach assume we'll keep doing the same thing as always and swap beds. It's our last night in Queenscliff. I agree, because what else can I do, but I am feeling sick about it.

Alex doesn't come back to the house until late. I hear him come in when I'm standing in the bathroom brushing my teeth. He chats with Mariella and Sal for a few minutes, laughs about something, and walks into his room. He sounds happy. I don't know if that's a good sign or bad one.

Lucy and I lie in bed and talk until we're sure Zach's parents are safely asleep. Then I tiptoe down the stairs, passing Zach on his way up.

"You okay?" he says, pausing and looking at my face.

"Yup." I force a smile.

A whole new idea has occurred to me. Alex wasn't interested in hanging out with me today. I've overthought this whole thing. Maybe he was bored and just wanted to hook up. Maybe? Definitely. God, I'm so naive. I am a distraction, a way to fill in time, a stand-in, an it's-dark-and-I'm-horny-so-she'll-do hookup. He probably thinks we're going to *have sex* tonight.

By the time I've reached the bedroom door, I've worked my-self into a state and I'm furious. It feels so much better to be angry than sad.

"Hello, stranger," he says, as I slip into the room. He's trying to be cute.

Oh no. Not tonight, buddy. I will not be tricked by cuteness. "I'm not having sex with you," I say. The words burst out of my mouth, a little louder than I'd intended. I don't often say the word *sex* out loud, I realize in this moment. Other than discussing it with Lucy, I haven't had many occasions to say it to another person. Certainly not in the context of me having, or not having, the sex in question.

"Keep your voice down," he hisses in a panic.

"Well, I'm not." I put my hands on my hips. This part of relationships, being mad about something and in control, feels like the part I can probably do quite well.

"What are you even *saying*?"

"I. Will. Not. Have. Sex. With. You." It's easier to say the second time. I'm getting good at this.

"There was no part of my mind that thought we were having sex tonight," he says, sounding a little horrified at the thought.

"Oh," I say. That's a little offensive. I mean, I would have at least liked him to *think* about it.

"So you can calm down."

"I am *calm*." There is nothing more unattractive than a guy telling a girl to calm down. That's two strikes against Alex to-night and I've been in the room for less than a minute.

"Okay," he says. He sounds a little scared.

I lie on the bed, but don't get under the sheet.

"Are you mad at me?" he asks eventually.

"No," I say, because admitting I'm mad at him seems like I'm admitting I care more than he does, and everyone knows the person who cares the least is the person who wins. (*Wins what?* I can hear my mother asking, in the way she does when she thinks I'm being ridiculous but she wants me to reach that conclusion myself. *Wins at life, wins at self-protection, wins at surviving the utter hell that is liking someone,* I yell back at her in my mind.)

But then I change my mind. This is our last night together in this bed, potentially our last night together forever, and I'm so mad at him that it's making me crazy.

"Actually, yes, I am mad at you. I'm mad at you because you're ashamed to be seen with me," I say, as loud as I dare. I can hear how dramatic I sound, but I don't care.

"No, I'm not," he says, sounding indignant.

"You ignored me today!" I whisper-shout.

"What? You ignored me!" he whisper-shouts back.

"I came to the beach, and you didn't come anywhere near me."

"I waved at you, twice, no, three times, and then the next thing I knew, you were gone."

"That's not what happened."

"That's exactly what happened."

It's actually quite thrilling to be in a middle-of-the-night argument with a cute guy, but I wish we were disagreeing over something more exciting than waving at each other on the beach.

"So, what? You thought you would wait for me to swim out to you and your friends and introduce myself and start playing Frisbee?" I ask.

"Yes." He sounds bewildered. He hasn't the faintest clue.

"That's not how this works."

"How *what* works?"

"You want me to make all the effort when I'm . . ." I can't find the words. Surely he understands this part: that the less attractive, less popular, less experienced, less *everything* person should not have to be the one to put themselves out there.

"Never mind," I say.

"I want to know," he says, and his voice is soft now.

"Why did you kiss me last night?"

"Because I wanted to. And if I remember correctly, you kissed me too."

"Right. But were you just bored and filling in time?"

"Filling in time?" He sounds incredulous. "If I wanted to fill time, I would have just gone to sleep," he says, laughing.

It's all a joke to him. It's all easy to him. He kisses so many girls in so many beds, he doesn't *need* to overanalyze the situation.

I roll onto my side, and I hear him sigh and roll onto his side, so we have our backs to each other. I play mindlessly on my phone for a while, and then a message pops onto my screen.

It's from Alex.

—Turn over

I turn over, and he's looking at me.

"I don't like that you're mad at me," he says.

"Okay," I say.

"That's a new feeling," he says.

"You've never had someone mad at you before?" If he truly believes that, he's in for a shock.

"No, it's a new feeling that I care that *you* are mad at me. You specifically."

"Oh."

"I should have walked over to you at the beach today."

"So why didn't you?"

"I'm not very good at this kind of thing," he says.

I nod as if I know what he means, but really I'm thinking, what kind of thing, exactly, are we talking about here? Are we talking about dating, or romantic feelings, or liking someone, or talking to someone the day after you kiss them, or dealing with someone else's insecurities, or just social interactions in general?

"Me neither," I say, which, no matter which thing we're talking about, is bound to be true and probably an understatement.

"I'm sorry about today," he says.

He reaches over and takes my hand, interlaces our fingers, and cradles our joined hands against his chest. Then with his other hand he traces his fingers up and down my arm. It feels so nice that I make an involuntary murmuring noise.

It had never occurred to me before tonight, before this very moment, that there could be tenderness like this when you are with someone. I'd always thought about kissing, and everything that comes after kissing. I thought about passion, and ripping off clothes, and sweeping everything off a desk or a table so you could go for it on a horizontal surface. Or negotiation, of testing boundaries and seeing how far the other person was comfortable in going.

But I never thought about how nice it would be to just have someone touch you softly and gently. I guess I never thought a boy would *want* to. I thought it was sexy stuff or nothing.

Alex spends a long time gently tracing his fingertips up and down my arm, and it feels as nice as anything I've ever felt before.

17

WHAT HAVE YOU DONE?

"Get up, boys," Mariella shouts, and bangs on the door.

Boys, I think, groggy, not comprehending. *Why is she calling Lucy and me boys?* The times we have both stayed over together in the past, she never wakes us up like this. She gently taps the door. She says things like, "Don't want to waste the day, darlings," and "I'm making pancakes especially for you both," and "The shower is free and there's still some hot water left."

The door bangs again. Alex groans.

I sit bolt upright and kick him.

"Shit," I hiss.

"What?" He speaks at normal volume, and I kick him again.

"I forgot to change beds last night."

He opens his eyes, blinks a few times, looks at me.

"It's fine," he says. "You can go now. She's gone upstairs, I think."

"Which means I'll run straight into her when I go upstairs."

"Pretend you are coming out of the bathroom."

"What if she just passed the bathroom and saw it was empty?"

"You're overthinking this."

"I'm not—"

I stop talking, because there are footsteps coming back down the hallway. I flop back onto the bed and pull the blanket over my head. I try to make myself as flat as possible.

The door swings open.

"I said, get up, boys. You're on breakfast duty this morning." Mariella likes to appoint tasks to her sons in a very military way. She has a chore wheel at their house, and she spins it each week to assign tasks for each son. Zach complained after he got the bathroom four weeks in a row and the integrity of the chore wheel was called into question.

In my house, there is no chore wheel. Dad does most of the cleaning during the week, and Mum and I usually clean together on Saturday mornings while listening to a podcast or our official Saturday Morning Cleaning playlist on Spotify. (Both of us have to approve a song before it can be added to the list, and we have to both agree to skip a song before it can be skipped.) In my worst, most friendless, most acne-prone years, cleaning the house with Mum was actually something I looked forward to every week.

I wish I were cleaning with Mum right now. I wish I were basically anywhere but in this bed.

"What's Zach doing?" Mariella says.

I hold my breath.

"What do you mean?" Alex says, sounding disinterested and croaky and like it was any other morning. He's a better actor than I realized. Lying to his mother might be a regular occurrence for him, though. I don't know if this is something I should be worried about or not. Either way, now is not the time to think about it.

"Why isn't he on the trundle?" she says.

"His back got sore," Alex says.

"That bloody spring. I don't know why you boys didn't just share from the beginning."

"Well, we are sharing now, so . . ."

There's a beat of silence, and it seems like we did it, we got away with it, and everything will be fine.

"Zach, get up, please."

"Let him sleep, Mum. I'll do breakfast."

Another beat, another moment when I think we've got away with it, but Mariella knows her sons too well. She knows Alex would never be so considerate to his brother.

"Zach, up."

I keep lying there, my face scrunched, praying to every god or goddess I've ever heard of to be teleported out of here.

"He can't get up," Alex says. He still sounds calm. He hasn't resorted to praying. He thinks we can wriggle out of this.

"Why not?" Her voice is closer. She's right beside me. I try to breathe in the way I imagine a sleeping teenage boy would.

"He's sick," Alex says.

"Sick? In what way?"

"Feeling sick. Ill. Under the weather."

I contemplate faking a cough, maybe a slight groan. No. Too much.

"Alex, what is going on? Is Zach drunk?" Mariella's voice goes up an octave.

"No, he's not drunk. It's a rash, I think. And a sore throat. Looks contagious—"

Mariella pulls back the blanket and I open my eyes to her face peering into mine.

"Natalie!" she says, and nothing else. I think it's the first time she's ever been speechless.

CONFESSIONS

"Mum, it's not what you think." Even now, in the most embarrassing moment of my life, Alex is calm and relaxed. Though he is talking a little faster than normal. The hole he needs to get us out of is getting deeper.

Thank god I'm still sunburned, because I am blushing harder than I have ever blushed in my life.

"What do you think I think it is?" Mariella says, hands on her hips.

"You think there's something going on between us."

"There's not," I say, sitting up, finding my voice. It doesn't occur to me to tell even a hint of the truth. Lying seems the only option.

"Did Zach ask you to swap beds, Natalie?" she asks.

"Yes," Alex says, betraying his brother in less than half a second.

"No," I say, at the same time. We glance at each other.

"It was my idea," I say.

Alex raises his eyebrows.

"I thought Zach and Lucy would prefer to share a bed, and I don't care where I sleep, so I suggested we swap," I say.

Mariella is squinting, watching me. Then she turns on her heel.

"Let's see what Zach has to say," she says, and she leaves the room in a flurry of outrage. I know Mariella well enough to know she quite enjoys a flurry of outrage, but usually I get to listen to her story about the person or persons who have inspired the outrage, rather than be one of them myself.

"I messaged him," Alex says, pulling his hands out from under the blanket.

"Saying what?"

"Mum run."

"That's helpful."

"Actually, it says 'num rum' because I typed it without looking."

"Oh god." I hope Lucy is dressed when Mariella walks in. I pull the blanket back over my head.

"Is she really mad?" I ask, making a little hole between blanket and pillow to speak out of.

"She'll be mad at me and Zach. For breaking her no-sleepovers-in-the-same-bed rule. She's paranoid about her home being turned into a den of underage sex." Alex yawns. He sounds like he's been down this path before.

"We're not underage."

"Underage in her mind is anyone under thirty. Also, she hates lying."

"Well, we are telling the truth."

"No, we're not. You said there's nothing going on between us."

"I panicked," I say and, I want to add, *We haven't clarified what is happening between us, is it something, and if it is something, is it the kind of something you mention to mothers?*

"You're eighteen. I'm nineteen. It's none of Mum's business what happens in this bedroom."

"Right," I say, but I'm not as confident as he is in this assertion. This is Mariella's house and I obey all kinds of other rules she has. Also, I don't feel like an adult. Or at least, not the adult Alex is describing, one who has a sex life and is confident in her life decisions.

I get out of bed and I catch sight of myself in the mirror.

"My sunburn looks worse today, somehow."

"You look cute."

"No, I don't."

"Like a tomato."

"Tomatoes aren't cute."

"A cherry tomato."

I sit back down on the bed. I want to go upstairs and change out of my pajamas, but I'm too scared of seeing Mariella again. Alex is still lying in bed, watching me.

"I can't believe I fell asleep and forgot to swap back," I say.

"Well, so did Zach."

"I hope Mariella isn't too mad."

"You know Mum. Overreaction is her favorite kind of reaction."

"Lucy's mum will be furious," I say.

"Lucy's mother is not here," Alex says.

"Your mum might tell her. And it's the principle of the matter. The lying."

"Well, I haven't lied about anything."

"You told your mum that it was Zach under the blanket."

"Oh yeah. Well, aside from that."

"I'm so embarrassed. I can't ever look your mum in the eye again."

"Now you are overreacting. It's not like she caught us in the middle of something."

"But she thinks she did, which is the same."

"She doesn't know what to think yet."

I poke my head out the door, hoping that Mariella is not around and I can safely scurry upstairs.

"Natalie?"

Mariella has seen me.

"Can you and Alex come out here, please?"

"Okay."

We walk out into the lounge room, where Lucy and Zach are sitting at the table. Zach looks grumpy, but he always looks grumpy in the morning, and Lucy is staring down at the table, with her hands folded like a nun. She looks up, meets my eye, smiles, and suddenly I am overcome with the urge to giggle.

I bite down on my lower lip, hard enough to feel pain, to stop myself from laughing.

"Okay, everyone." Mariella claps her hands. She looks Very Disappointed, in that universal parent way.

Lucy reaches over and holds my hand in hers. I want to laugh again, because the situation feels both serious and absurd. I squeeze her hand and she squeezes back.

"Firstly, I want to say I feel really let down by you all," says Mariella.

We all nod.

"Especially Alex and Zach."

They nod solemnly.

"Mum, can I say something?" Zach says.

"Not until I'm finished."

"Fine."

"Well, now I've lost my train of thought."

"You were talking about your deep disappointment in everyone, but most especially your sons," Alex says, leaning his chin on his hand.

"That's right. And do you know what I'm disappointed about?" She pauses. Lucy and I look at each other. Are we supposed to guess?

No one says anything. Alex yawns. I frown at him.

"I'm disappointed in the fact that I trusted all of you, and now you've broken that trust."

"Mum, can I just say one thing?" Zach says again.

"I have always been very happy for you to have people over," Mariella continues, ignoring him, "on the proviso that you'll abide by the rules. And now that you have broken the rules, I'm going to have to be much stricter."

Lucy raises her hand like we're in a classroom.

"Yes, Lucy?"

"I just want to say I'm really sorry, and I appreciate how welcoming you've always been to me, and I promise not to be deceitful again."

"Me too," I chime in.

"Girls, I love you like daughters, and I want to feel comfortable having you in my home. But I can't feel comfortable if you're sneaking around behind my back." She dramatically puts a hand over her eyes.

"Mum, there's a really easy solution here," Zach says.

"What's that?" Mariella says, removing the hand.

"Let Lucy and me share a bed."

"Absolutely not." Mariella's hand goes back over her eyes and she sits down at the table.

"We're both adults."

"You are not! You are still only seventeen years old, Zachary. And so is Lucy! I promised Lucy's mother that whenever she was in this house, you would be under my supervision. Now you've made me look like a fool."

"Well, only if Lucy's mother finds out," Alex points out.

"Yes, this is your choice, Mum. You can make a drama out of it or not," Zach says, which I think is putting Mariella in an unfair position.

"What if Lucy got pregnant and it happened under my roof, on my watch?" Mariella says, her voice getting higher and higher pitched, and Lucy goes bright red.

"Mum, it's fine," Zach says. "There is no way that's going to happen. You've been talking to us about using condoms since I was eleven. You texted me a link to an article about gonorrhea two days ago."

I want to die a little, because there's no scenario in which I want to be present when Zach and his mother discuss details of his and Lucy's sex life, and also the word *gonorrhea* is so unpleasant said out loud.

"Well, I hope you're using condoms. Two of them at a time, even," Mariella says.

"Jesus," Alex says under his breath. I look around, wondering if there is a way to escape. Lucy has my hand in a death grip.

"Mum, I don't think—" Zach begins.

"And I hope you're using another contraceptive method as well, just to be sure. You can never be too careful at your age," Mariella says, talking over Zach.

We all sit in silence. I don't want to be part of the discussion on how many kinds of contraception are being used, even though I already know Lucy secretly went on the Pill a few months ago, and they also use condoms, because Lucy might be even more paranoid than Mariella.

"I mean, I can't believe I let things get this far without having this conversation. Lucy could already be pregnant right now,"

Mariella says. She is working herself into a state. She's known about Zach and Lucy from the very beginning, of course, but I think seeing them physically in bed together makes it all too much for her. It's because Lucy is so fairy-like, all big-eyed innocence. And Zach has those who-me? dimples and reads eighty books a year. They look like they'd spend all their time playing chess and talking about their feelings. In actuality, they've been having sex multiple times a week after school for the past six months.

"I'm not pregnant," Lucy says, her face bright red.

"She's not pregnant," Zach says. He looks two-thirds irritated, one-third terrified.

"We all need to be one hundred percent sure." Mariella waves her hand around the room, as if the "we all" encompasses Alex and me. I'm scared she's going to make Lucy take a pregnancy test.

"Mum, this conversation is deeply uncomfortable for everyone sitting at the table," Alex says.

"And we haven't even got to you and Natalie," Mariella says.

Everyone looks at us.

"What do you mean?" Zach says.

"Well, what's going on there?" Mariella asks us.

At this moment, the front door swings open and Sal bursts in, carrying bags and a tray of coffee cups, bellowing, "It's another gorgeous day out there, everyone!" and kicking off his shoes.

"Sal, come here. We've got a bit of a situation," Mariella says.

Sal puts the coffee down on the table and pulls out a tray of croissants. "Tuck in, everybody! They're still warm!" Sal is the kind of man who puts an exclamation mark on the end of as many sentences as possible.

"I said, we have a situation, sweetie," Mariella says. The

way she forcefully says "sweetie," it doesn't sound much like a term of endearment.

"Well, now, what kind of situation?" Sal says, looking faintly concerned but still mostly focused on the croissants.

"The kids swapped beds last night," Mariella says, in the same tone you might say, *The kids took heroin last night*.

But Sal doesn't seem to get it.

Mariella sighs. "Zach and Lucy spent the night in one bed, and Natalie and Alex in the other," she says.

"Natalie and Alex!" Sal says, clapping his hands together. He sounds like the MC at a wedding, announcing us as a couple.

"Dad, there's nothing going on with Natalie and Alex," Zach says.

"No, I didn't think so," Sal says, chuckling a little.

"Well, hang on. Why is that idea funny?" Alex says.

My stomach twists a little. On the one hand, I have the same question. On the other hand, this is dangerous territory to dig into.

"It's not funny, per se, so much as unlikely," Sal says.

"And why is it unlikely?" Alex asks.

"Because you're you and Natalie is Natalie," Zach says, biting into a croissant.

"What does *that* mean?" I say, suddenly not caring about the dangerous territory.

"It means you're very different people," Zach says.

"Haven't you heard the saying, opposites attract?" Alex says.

"I don't believe in that," Zach says, still eating his croissant, as if we're simply having a friendly philosophical discussion rather than making sweeping pronouncements about my dateability.

"With your wealth of life experience?" Alex asks. He's annoyed now.

"Alex is a Leo and Natalie is a Scorpio," Mariella says, as if that explains everything.

"You would be the last two people I can ever imagine together," Zach says. He seems very firm on this.

"Natalie's an intellectual," Sal says. (Sal holds this delusion because I once knew the answer to a crossword clue he couldn't figure out.)

"And I'm stupid?" Alex says, looking more and more irritated.

"No, honey. He means Natalie is book-smart and you're street-smart," Mariella says, using her fingers to make air quotes around the words *street-smart*.

Zach hoots with laughter, and Alex shakes his head. I used to think it was fine that Alex was often the butt of his family's jokes because he was the older and cooler brother, but now I want to tell everyone to shut up.

"You work in a bar and Natalie doesn't even drink," Zach adds.

I wait for Alex to mention that, technically, he doesn't work in a bar anymore, and that it's not a bar, it's a pub-restaurant, and I like eating food and Alex likes making food, so we're actually very compatible in that way, but instead he just looks furious.

"This is a ridiculous discussion," I say before anyone can open their mouths and make a comparison between Vanessa and me, which is where I fear the conversation is headed next.

"Exactly. Natalie and Alex are not together," Zach says.

"Actually, you're wrong," Alex says, standing up dramatically.

I feel a stabbing pain in my heart. I'm going to have a heart attack and die before I can hear Alex clarify that statement.

"We are together," Alex says.

Mariella actually gasps and puts a hand to her chest.

"What?" Lucy and Zach say in unison. Zach looks disbelieving, Lucy scandalized. She has let go of my hand, and I wish she hadn't, because I need her now.

"Well, then," Sal says. He opens his mouth like he's going to say something else, but then closes it again.

If my life were a movie, this moment would be underscored with heart-swelling music. Alex has just publicly declared we're together! Except it doesn't feel romantic at all. It feels like all the air has been sucked out of the room. And I'm not sure if what he's saying is *real*.

I make fleeting eye contact with Alex. My face says, *What the hell are you doing?* and his says, *I will say anything to prove my family wrong.*

Everyone turns to look at me.

"Is this true?" Zach says. I can tell he's hoping I will deny everything.

"Um, sort of," I say. My left eye has developed a twitch. I've moved into a state beyond emotion. I am numb, calm, serenely detached. This must be what people mean when they say they're having an out-of-body experience. Or else I have actually died.

"The two of you are a couple?" Lucy says, speaking more slowly than usual.

"Well, I wouldn't say that," I say, pressing a fingertip to my twitching eyelid. Is an eye twitch the sign of something more serious? Should I be seeking medical attention? That could be my way out of here.

"What would you say?" Zach asks.

"I would say it's complicated," I say. The calm feeling is quickly disappearing and panic is flooding in. I give Alex a help-me look. He has the expression of someone who thought they were in control of a situation and has just realized that maybe they aren't.

"When did this happen?" Zach says, standing up next to Alex in an aggressive way. Are they going to *fight*?

"And *what* happened?" Lucy adds, as if I'm going to go into the nitty-gritty in front of Mariella and Sal.

"I swear to god, Alex, if you are just using Natalie because she happened to be in your bed . . ." Zach says, and even though I accused Alex of the very same thing the night before, I am utterly outraged by this, especially the fact he would say that in front of everyone.

"Zach!" I say.

"It's nice that you think so highly of me," Alex says, glowering at his brother. They really are standing quite close to each other. Before this moment, I would have said the idea of two guys physically fighting over an issue relating to me was quite interesting, but now that it's closer to happening in reality, the very thought is making my other eye twitch as well. I close both my eyes, briefly, and take a deep breath.

"Why are we being interrogated like criminals anyway? We are two consenting adults," Alex says.

Good, okay, he's deflecting. Except for using the word *consenting*. I wish he hadn't said that. It implies we had sex. I can tell that's Lucy's interpretation, because her eyes have widened.

"Honey, we're all rather shocked by this. Give us a moment to digest it," Mariella says. She looks like she can't decide how to feel. On the one hand, it's gossip and she loves gossip, especially about her sons, especially about her sons' love lives. On the other hand, we're not a couple she has anticipated, and we're possibly a couple she doesn't want.

Sal has gone to the kitchen and returned with butter and various condiments. He sits down, cuts open a croissant, and spreads it thickly with strawberry jam. Sal takes great pride in the fact that he makes the jam himself. He labels every jar "Sal's

Super Splendid Strawberry Jam," and he spent a whole weekend working on the design of the labels and made everyone in the family vote for their favorite of three options.

He takes a big bite of his croissant, and then speaks, mouth full. "What exactly are we talking about here? How serious is this thing? Alex, what are your intentions?"

What are your intentions? Now we're in a Jane Austen period piece, apparently. I choke a little while trying to swallow a sip of my latte. Sal looks like he's settling in for a long discussion.

"That's it. I'm leaving," Alex says, turning and walking out of the room.

"We're still discussing this," Mariella says.

"You can discuss it all you want. I'm getting dressed," he says over his shoulder. Then he pauses and looks at me.

"Natalie?" he says, as if I've missed something obvious.

"What?" I say. I hope he's not about to make any further declarations.

"Do you want to, um, come into my bedroom for a second?" Mariella's face looks stricken.

"To *talk*, Mum. So I can apologize to Natalie for having to endure the horror show that is this family," Alex says.

"Natalie has been aware of the horror show that is this family for years!" Zach yells.

I stand up and follow Alex into his bedroom with the stilted gait of someone who has forgotten how to walk. I have forgotten how to do anything.

19

EVERYTHING I EVER WANTED

I close the door to Alex's bedroom behind me, and we stand in silence for a few seconds, before we both start whisper-yelling at each other.

"What the hell did you do?" I say. I'm suddenly really mad at Alex, and it's a relief to give all my pent-up anxiety a target.

"I'm sorry. It kind of slipped out. I was angry about how they were talking about us."

"Me too. But that doesn't mean you just start saying things!"

Especially *meaningful* things. In front of *everyone*. In an ambiguous way where it's not clear if you actually *mean* them or not.

"I know, I know."

I lie on the bed and look at the ceiling. "This is a disaster," I say.

"*Disaster* is a strong word." Alex sits down next to me.

"Everyone *knows*."

"So what?"

"So what? Now it's this big thing. Everyone will want to know what is happening, and Zach is angry about it, and your parents will watch us every second, and I'll have to tell my parents, and they'll have a million questions and want to use it as a distraction from their breakup, and it's all this fuss over something that might be . . ."

"That might be what?" Alex prompts me.

"That might be nothing," I say in a rush.

"Do you want it to be nothing?"

"I don't know. Maybe they're right. We're not very compatible."

I walked home in tears after attempting to hang out with him and his friends at the beach. That's not a *great* start.

"Fuck them. I want this to be something."

"You're just saying that because you want to prove your family wrong."

"Ah, but see, I can want to prove my family wrong and I can also want to be with you. It's win-win."

"But which option is your driving motivator?"

He leans over me and looks down at my face. "Being with you. And I really like proving my family wrong, so that should tell you how much I like being with you."

He kisses me, and my eye finally stops twitching. But then he stops kissing me and leans up on one elbow, and my eye twitch is back.

"But *you* haven't said what you want," he says.

"That's true."

Is it possible to know exactly what you want, and also have no idea what you want, at the same time? I do know that I don't want to tell him what I want, because that would be exposing too much of myself.

"So, what do you want?" he asks.

"I like kissing you," I say, trying to avoid looking in his eyes, because eye contact when making any kind of confession increases the stress tenfold.

He laughs. "Good. What else?"

"I like you. You know, in general, as a person," I say, which feels big and momentous enough that I am proud of myself, even though I know adding "as a person" is a total cop-out. He kisses my forehead, and I am surprised again at his tenderness.

"Well, what are we telling everyone out there?" I say.

"We're telling them to mind their own business."

"It's too late for that."

"We say we're seeing where this is going."

"Okay, good, that sounds good," I say.

That's something. That's a relationship status of sorts. In the world of *The Bachelor* and *The Bachelorette*, that means you're getting a rose, you'll be around for another week. (It's fucked up that I'm automatically assigning Alex the role of Bachelor in my mind, and me the role of underdog—the unconventional contestant that the audience is cheering for but the one they know will never win.)

I leave Alex's room, and I go straight to the bathroom, because I can't face anyone yet and I need a moment to run cold water over my wrists and take deep breaths.

This is what you want, I tell myself.

My throat feels dry. It's a little sore. I think I'm getting sick. I've caught something off him. Glandular fever, maybe. Or scarlet fever, which I thought was an old-fashioned disease that didn't exist anymore until a girl at my school caught it after kissing too many people at a music festival. Alex probably kisses so many girls that he's a walking bacteria incubator. He's probably built up an immunity to all the germs he's carrying, and I have zero immunity because I've been kissing no one, and I will collapse under the exposure.

I need to get a grip. A boy might like me. This information should not send me into total emotional collapse.

I can do this. I can do this.

20

A GREAT LOVE STORY

Sal is driving us home to Melbourne. Mariella has been careful to divide us into non-couple groups: Lucy and Glenn in her car, and Zach, Anthony, and me with Sal. Alex is left to drive home on his own. A part of me wanted to drive off with Alex, windows down, music blaring, sunglasses on (a pair much cooler than the ones I actually own), everyone openmouthed in the rearview mirror as we roar away, but I don't think Mariella could take it, and she's been kind enough to host me.

Zach and I sit in the backseat, turned away from each other, looking out our respective windows. We've settled into a silent fight. We don't need to say a single word to know how mad we are at each other. Sal and Anthony talk as we drive, but their conversation doesn't penetrate the cold, hard tension in the backseat. Zach and I are sealed off in our own little cube of hurt feelings and angry thoughts.

I am arguing with him in my mind ("You're selfish and immature and trying to block my only chance at love." "Natalie, I'm sorry—" "NO, I'M NOT DONE, LET ME FINISH!") when we pull into a petrol station. Sal gets out to fill the tank, and

Anthony leaps out and runs inside to buy food. Zach and I are alone in the car. We glance at each other and then away again.

"Can we talk for a second?" I say.

"Sure," Zach says, turning toward me a little.

I expected him to say no, and then I could be smug in the knowledge I tried to be the bigger person, and I could text Lucy and say, *I wanted to talk but he didn't*, and she would yell at Zach for me, and everything would be resolved in a day or so. Now I need something to say.

"Well?" Zach says.

"Well, I don't know what I'm going to say yet," I say defensively.

"Okay, let me go first. When did this thing with Alex start?"

"Two days ago."

"So you just started kissing out of the blue?" he says.

"Pretty much," I say. I mean, if you skip past all my agonizing feelings, that sums it up.

"Because you were in a bed together and why not," Zach says flatly.

He's trying to make it sound as bad as possible, but really, "we were in a bed together and why not" sounds kind of hot to me.

"Sort of. I mean, we talked first," I say. How much detail does he want?

"Do you actually like him?"

"Why are you using that tone?"

"What tone?"

"You know what tone. *That* tone. I hate that tone."

"Because I'm mad at you. You're hooking up with my *brother* behind my back, and you weren't going to tell me. I'm allowed to be mad."

"Says who?"

"Says the rules of the universe. When have you ever heard of someone being happy with their sibling and best friend getting together?"

"All the time. The normal response is joy and happiness."

"Give me one example of someone being happy in this situation."

"I hate it when you do that give-me-an-example crap." It's Zach's go-to move in an argument and it's annoying.

"Well, look, I can't help how I feel, and I'm mad."

"At who?"

"Both of you."

"And how long are you going to be mad?"

He frowns and my heart lurches a little, in the way it does when you look at someone and suddenly think, *Wow, this person is so precious to me,* while simultaneously thinking, *Wow, this person is more irritating than anyone else on earth. I hate you, I love you, I want to slap you.*

"I don't know. Maybe a while. How long is this thing with you and Alex going to last?"

"I don't know. Maybe awhile."

Zach kind of half snorts, half grunts.

"What?" I say. Someone half snorting, half grunting at the idea of me being in a relationship confirms all my worst suspicions about myself.

"I don't see that happening."

"Wow. Thanks, Zach. That's a really lovely thing to say."

"Not because of you. Because of him."

"Still terrible."

"Think about it for a minute. Alex likes going out and partying. Most of his friends are awful. He gets bored easily. He's probably still in love with his ex-girlfriend. He doesn't go to uni. He works weird hours. He's on *Tinder.* You are not right for each other."

"We could be right for each other," I say, as if this is a solid rebuttal to anything on Zach's deeply unnerving list. The very word *Tinder* sends a shiver down my spine. The ex-girlfriend mention makes me want to vomit. I am way out of my depth.

"Can you hear yourself?" Zach says.

"Yes, I can hear myself. Can you hear what you're saying? You're basically saying there's no way Alex could possibly like me."

And I agree, a part of me wants to shout, but I would never give Zach the satisfaction. The more he voices my deepest fears, the harder I am going to push back.

"That's not what I'm saying at all," he says.

"Yes, it is."

"Natalie, I'm saying that I'm worried that this thing won't work out and you'll be the one to get hurt. He has a history of stuffing things up."

"Do me a favor and stop worrying about my ability to cope with things, thanks," I say, as viciously as I possibly can, even though I have admittedly spent years of our friendship establishing myself as someone who can't cope with things.

"Fine. But don't come running to me when he breaks your heart," Zach says, as Anthony opens the passenger-seat door.

"Don't worry, I won't," I say.

You are being a shitty friend to me, I want to scream at him, even while a part of me is worried I am being a shitty friend to him.

Anthony hands us icy poles, and then jumps out of the car again to show Sal where the toilets are.

"I would never be with a member of your family," Zach says, unwrapping his icy pole.

An irrelevant point when I have no siblings.

"You and Lucy got together, which is kind of the same thing," I say.

In fact, it might be worse.

I bite off a chunk of my Frosty Fruit, which I know will irritate Zach, because his teeth hurt when he sees someone biting into anything frozen.

"No, it's not," he says, visibly cringing at the sight of my teeth on the ice.

"You don't think that was hard for me?"

"That was different. For a start, we fell in love." He swallows after he says this. I know he and Lucy have said, "I love you," to each other, I know that they text each other hearts and *love you's,* but he's never said it so explicitly to me before. I can't help making a mental note to tell Lucy later, because I know it will make her happy that he said it, and that his eyes softened when he did.

But right this second, I need to be angry. "You think you are so much better than me, don't you?" I say.

"No, I don't."

"Yes, you do. You and Lucy are this great love story, and I'm just a pathetic loser who's going to get her heart broken and won't be able to handle it."

"I don't think you're a pathetic loser."

"But the rest of it, you think that's true, right?"

He stops and looks at me, letting a drip from his icy pole fall into his lap. "I don't think Alex is going to be your great love story, no," he says.

We stare at each other, and then Sal and Anthony get back into the car, and we don't say anything for the rest of the trip.

21

MOVING-DAY BLUES

The next day, Dad and I stand and survey his new lounge room. There are boxes everywhere: boxes that have detailed labels like "Books—Literary Fiction, A–G," "CDs—Jazz and Classical," "Clothes—Winter," and then boxes that just say "Fragile," "Kitchen," and, mysteriously, "Good Stuff"—they're the ones from after we got tired of labeling things.

I've never moved house before. Not that I'm moving now, but I've never experienced anything to do with moving before. I thought packing could be fun (it wasn't, at all) and that unpacking would definitely be fun, because I like putting things in their proper places. But now we are staring at the room filled with boxes and it feels like a momentous task we will never get through.

The last time Dad moved house was before I was born, so this feels all new to him too.

"Dad?"

"Yeah?"

"How long has it been since you lived on your own?"

Dad takes off his glasses and rubs his eyes. He looks tired. But even at his most tired, he is patient. He will always answer me, no matter how irritating my question, and his answer will be considered and thoughtful.

"Well, let me see. Your mother and I got married when I was twenty-eight. And we lived together for a while before that. So, twenty years, give or take?"

Honestly, I don't know how they could be *bothered* separating at this point.

"Honey, don't sit on the boxes—you'll break them."

I sigh and stand up. Dad's apartment building has a lift, but even so, I am gruesomely sweaty from helping the movers carry boxes in from the truck, up to the lift, and into the apartment. The glasses are still packed, so I walk to the sink and drink water straight from the tap.

"Natalie, no. Please don't do that."

"There are no glasses and I'm dying of thirst."

"I should have bought some paper cups and plates."

"Or we could just unpack the kitchen stuff."

But we don't. We just stand there looking at it all. Some of the kitchen stuff isn't even in moving boxes—it's in its original packaging, because Dad went out and bought a whole lot of new stuff. We had a good time discussing the merits of various blenders and toasters. ("Dad, if you don't buy this four-slice toaster you could regret it for the rest of your life.") It felt so important that he should buy the spiralizer at the time, but now it definitely feels like there's too much stuff.

"I like the nautical look," I say, patting the big blue-and-white-striped cushions he bought for his new couch.

"Oh yes, I've had my eye on those for a while." I don't know why, exactly, but hearing him say this makes a solid ball of sadness form in the pit of my stomach.

"Let's leave everything for an hour and go and get some food," I suggest. This is the kind of idea Dad would normally hate. He's a great believer in "getting things done" and "enjoying the reward after doing the hard work." But not today. Today he's living on his own for the first time in twenty years and moving sucks.

"Let's get food," he agrees.

Dad and I walk down Port Melbourne's main street and I make excited conversation about all the new things he has to discover here, even though surely he knows because he's the one who decided to move here and I actually know nothing about the suburb. He nods along, but I get the sense his mind is elsewhere. I was planning on getting sandwiches, but Dad says we should get ice cream.

Dad and I love ice cream. It's our thing. Mum will eat it, but it's never her first dessert choice—she likes cakes and baked goods—but Dad and I have always known that ice cream is the superior option.

We walk all the way along the beach to Albert Park to get Jock's famous homemade ice cream. We walk mostly in silence. Dad seems lost in his thoughts. I'm obsessively thinking about Alex, and then forcing myself not to obsessively think about Alex because I am superstitious enough to believe that if you think about a good thing too much you can turn it into a bad thing, and, also, it has been twenty-four hours since Alex and I last spoke and he hasn't texted me yet. To balance out thinking about Alex, I dwell on my fight with Zach and the still unbelievably raw fact that my parents are no longer together.

I can't quite believe that *my father has moved out.* I symbolically removed his favorite R2-D2 magnet from the fridge and hid it so he couldn't take it with him. I put it in a drawer where I cruelly hope Mum will one day find it and feel a piercing pain of regret in her heart. I have been trying to work up the courage to say, *I don't want you to leave,* but I haven't found a way to work it into the conversation. I kept hearing Mum and Dad having extremely polite whispered conversations about who owns what. ("You can have the rice cooker." "Oh no, you keep it, you like rice more than I do." "Do I?" "Yes, you went through that phase of eating brown rice with everything, remember?" "Oh, I'm over that now.") I wanted to smash everything so they'd have nothing left to talk about.

We reach Jock's and that eases my anxiety, because this is like heaven for us. We stand in line and discuss flavors.

"Hokey pokey?" I suggest.

"It's a highly recommended flavor," Dad says.

"Or peach sorbet. Or fig ripple."

"Or chocolate and vanilla. Mix the originals," Dad says. He is a big believer in traditional flavors.

"Walnut espresso?"

"I do love coffee and nuts."

"But I think something chocolate today," I say.

"It's moving day. We need chocolate," Dad agrees.

"Cone or cup?"

"You know my feelings on that topic, Natalie. Cone, always cone."

"You get more ice cream with the cup."

"But you get to eat the cone."

"But eating out of a cup is less messy than eating out of a cone."

"It separates the men from the boys."

"Mum and I hate that saying," I say.

Dad says it all the time, I think to tease us. "I know, honey," he says, and his voice isn't cheerful anymore.

We are silent then. Mentioning Mum seems to have taken all the air out of the conversation. I turn to Dad, ready to finalize our order, and his face looks strange.

"Order for me, will you?" he says.

"Okay. Where are you going?"

"Outside for a second." He pushes money into my hand and leaves the shop.

The lady behind the counter is smiling at me.

"What can I get you, dear?"

I point wildly at options, mixing together flavors that don't even complement each other like a complete amateur, and ask for both ice creams in cones. The woman takes a long time to carefully scoop the ice cream, and my heart is racing every second I'm in the shop and Dad is somewhere outside. His face was weird. Maybe he's having a heart attack. Or a stroke. I get out my phone and open the keypad, my fingers hovering, ready to call an ambulance if I do step outside and see him on the ground.

Dad could be dead because I dithered over ice-cream choices.

I pay and rush outside. I spot him sitting on a bench. His shoulders are a little bit hunched and his hands are resting carefully on his knees. If I walked past him on the street, I would think, *That man is sad*, and my heart constricts at the realization that my kind, wonderful dad is the kind of man other people might walk past and feel sorry for.

"Dad, are you okay?"

"I'm fine, honey."

I hand him his ice cream and sit down next to him.

"It was too hot in that shop," he says, not looking at me. His eyes look a little red and watery.

I'm embarrassed to admit it, but this is the first time I've thought about how awful the breakup might be for my parents.

22

THE DATING SCENE

"You're dating now?" I say, in my most victimized tone of voice.

I've come home from helping Dad move and I'm watching Mum twist and turn in front of the mirror. She's wearing a wrap dress and cute sandals with sparkles on them. Her toenails are painted in a way that I can tell she paid for. I've never known her to pay for a pedicure. This is new, and I am not on board with it.

After my time with Dad today, I made a vow to be more sensitive to my parents and what they're going through. I was going to be the mature, openhearted, caring daughter they need right now.

That vow lasted for one hour. I have since replaced it entirely with anger at Mum, which is much easier and less taxing on me.

"It's not a date. It's dinner with three other people," Mum says.

"Two of whom are Aunt Jenna and Uncle Ian."

"Right. Very boring."

"No, I mean, it's a couple, plus you, and who else? Who's the fourth person?"

"A friend of Uncle Ian's. I told you that."

"You're dating. They are setting you up on a date."

Mum turns to me and gives me a long look. I stare back at her, triumphant.

"No, it's not a date. And even if it was, Natalie, so what?"

"So what? So what? You told me you were breaking up less than two weeks ago, on *Christmas Day*, which, quite frankly, I'm not over yet, and Dad just moved out *today*, and you are already dating? I mean, that's ridiculous. And hurtful. And emotionally scarring. I'm not ready for any of this."

"We haven't handled this whole thing very well. I know that. I'm sorry. But all that's happening right now is that I'm going out for dinner. I'm socializing with my sister and her husband. That's it."

"And another man."

"Yes. A friend of theirs."

"What's the rush?" I throw myself on her bed, lying across the clothes she's already tried on and discarded. All of Mum's clothes smell faintly of the rose-and-sandalwood body cream she always wears. No matter how I'm feeling about Mum at a particular moment, this smell makes me feel safe.

"There's no rush," Mum says, but I can't trust anything she says anymore.

Mum is forty-eight. That's too old to get pregnant, surely, even with IVF, even with donor eggs? But maybe not. Forty-six is the new thirty-six, I think I read in a headline somewhere. I try to picture Mum pregnant, I try to picture myself with a sibling. A stepfather and a baby and my mother having an entire do-over, and Dad and me standing outside their lounge room window, peering in while eating ice cream and gently weeping.

"Do you want to get married again?"

"I'm not divorced yet, so getting married again is the last thing I'm thinking about."

"I doubt it's the *last* thing. After all, you are going on a date right now."

"It's not a date."

"It's date-adjacent, at the very least."

Mum holds different earrings up against her ears, turning to me.

"Which one?" she says.

"The left."

"Are you sure?"

"Yes. The other ones are too much with the shoes."

"You're right."

"See, that question about the earrings? That's a question you would only ask if you were going on a date."

"Natalie." Mum sounds tired.

"What?"

She turns around. "It's one dinner. Please let me have this."

"You have it. I can't stop you, can I?"

"If you really don't want me to go, I won't."

"Oh please." Arguing with Mum is almost comfortingly predictable. I knew she would say this, because when we fight, we throw guilt back and forth like a ball.

"I'm serious."

"You'd love that, wouldn't you? I tell you not to go, and then you get to sit home and feel sorry for yourself, and *I* have to feel bad."

"I wouldn't love it. I'm looking forward to this dinner. But I'll give it up if you want me to."

This is Mum at her passive-aggressive best, and she knows it.

"The last thing I feel like doing is spending the night with you, to be honest," I say.

"Good, then. I'll go with your blessing."

"You do not have my blessing."

She ignores me, staring into her mirror and tweezing her eyebrows. I seethe silently, and let the silence between us draw out, knowing she'll speak first.

She stops plucking and turns around. "Look, this isn't a date, okay? I am not going to bring a man back to this house. It's dinner with my sister and her husband and his friend. It's *not* a date. Please don't make me feel bad about this."

My greatest power over my mother is making her feel bad about things. Being considered an inadequate parent is one of her fears. I once saw her Google history and it included a late-night search for "signs you're a bad mother" and I went out and bought her a "World's Greatest Mother" mug that week. I gave it to her as a joke present but that was three years ago and she still uses it all the time and seems to care about it, which makes me feel a little bit worried for her, and also for myself, because, when you really think about it, she would only think she's deficient as a mother if she thought there was something wrong with her child. Sometimes last year I used that very thought to motivate myself to study more and study harder, which is probably psychologically unhealthy but it worked pretty well.

Right now, though, I am motivated in the opposite direction. "You can just add it to the list of things you should feel bad about. Which includes lying to me for a year, ruining your marriage, and destroying our family," I say. I can see from Mum's face in the mirror that I've hurt her, and I quickly get up to leave.

"How did I raise such a horrible daughter?" she says as I walk out of the room, which hurts me, so now we're even.

I lie on my bed with my door shut. After a while, Mum comes and stands outside the door but doesn't open it.

"'Bye, Natalie. I won't be home until late. Call me if you need anything."

I say nothing. There's a long pause, but I know she's still there.

"I love you," she says.

I continue to be silent.

"I'm sad too, okay? Your dad moving out is hard on me too. I'm trying to do something to cheer myself up, that's all."

Still, I say nothing. For all she knows, I might have earbuds in. For all she knows, I might be dead.

She sighs and walks away. I hope she feels bad and I hope that feeling bad ruins her night.

God, I am a horrible daughter.

After I hear the front door close and her car start and drive away, I wait to see if I'm going to cry. I feel like I want to cry but tears don't come. I scream into a pillow, which feels good the first time I do it but very over-the-top the second time.

23

UNSENT

I spend a lot of time that night drafting text messages to Alex and then not sending them.

—Hey

(Too serious.)

—Hi!

(Too eager.)

—Hey . . .

(Too suggestive.)

—Hi :)

(Completely desperate.)

—Hey what's up

(Trying so hard it takes my breath away.)

—Yo

(Utterly, utterly ridiculous.)

—Hello Alex

(A robot would sound less formal.)

Alex and I last saw each other yesterday at lunchtime when we all left the beach house. He said, "Talk soon," and I nodded. One of us should have contacted the other by now.

I need to stop thinking about him. I can't stop thinking about him.

I am considering Photoshopping my face next to Alex's, and comparing it to a photo I found deep in someone's Instagram history of Alex and Vanessa, just to see if Alex and I are a comparably cute couple, but I quickly abandon that idea when I picture a scenario where Alex somehow stumbles across this Photoshopped image. The thought is so horrifying I want to wipe my laptop completely clear of all images I have ever saved and immediately get hundreds of hours of therapy.

I spend the rest of the night trying to distract myself by reading theories about celebrities who might be in secret relationships, writing down a list of all the evidence I might have missed that my parents fell out of love, and being mad at Zach, who I have also not heard from since our fight in the car.

Mum comes home from her non-date date and I ignore her and pretend to be asleep. Then, when she is in the shower (a couple of years ago, Mum became the kind of person who showers at night and Dad remained a shower-in-the-morning person, and really, now that I think about it, there might be no stronger indicator of impending divorce than this), I take being a horrible daughter to the next level. I sneak into her room and look at her phone, feeling mostly like a psychopath but also a little bit like a really cool spy.

There is a series of text messages between her and a man called Eric. They're not sexy texts. I'm not completely sick, I would not read sexts between my mother and a stranger. They are barely even flirty. In fact, Eric seems very polite. He invited my mother to play golf and he also sent her a promo code to use to get 20 percent off when buying printer cartridges online. I don't know which is worse—the thought that this was related to an actual conversation they had, or that he sent the code unprompted. Eric has the personality of a spambot.

My father will die alone, and my mother will marry a man who uses cheap printer ink as a seduction tool.

And now I also have to consider the fact that Eric texted my mother three times within an hour of dinner finishing. Either he is a stalker or I should definitely be freaking out that I haven't heard from Alex in thirty-four hours.

Or both things could be true. Eric is a stage-five clinger, *and* Alex is ghosting me.

After her shower, Mum comes into my room in her bathrobe, combing her damp hair. I'm not fast enough putting my phone down, so she knows I'm not asleep.

"Let's talk," she says, lying down on the bed beside me. She is a big believer in never going to bed angry, which really gets in the way of my desire to hold petty grudges and stew on things at three a.m. instead of sleeping.

"What do you want to talk about?" I say.

"How was your time at Zach's?"

"Fine."

"What did you do?"

"Not much."

"Natalie."

"What?"

"Don't do this."

"Do what?"

"Give me nothing answers."

There was a period of time, when I was in my early teens, when Mum and Dad banned me from saying "Nothing much" and "Fine" in response to questions about my day. I had to think of something interesting to say. Sometimes I just made things up to appease them. Sometimes I would research random facts, because I knew if I said, "In Switzerland, it's illegal to own just one guinea pig," then Dad would be completely distracted by that information and they would both forget to ask any more questions about my day.

But I don't have any random facts on hand tonight, and Mum was never as easy to distract as Dad anyway.

"Fine. Let me see. I went to the beach, I got sunburned, we watched some movies, and I kissed Alex."

A part of me has been bursting to tell Mum this, because I want to shock her and show her how she doesn't know as much about me as she thinks she does. *I guess you've been so busy dating other men, you can't keep up with my life anymore.*

I also want to tell her because we haven't been talking as much lately and I am scared we are going to drift apart, that maybe she'll fall out of love with me in the same way she did with Dad, which is ridiculous because parents don't fall out of love with their kids, but maybe they do and no one talks about it.

"You . . . what?" Mum says. She sounds as shocked as I was hoping she would.

"I kissed Alex, Zach's brother."

Mum sits up a little and turns to me. "When?"

"We were hanging out and it just happened." I shrug, trying to look nonchalant.

"Do you like him?" Mum's eyes are lit up with excitement and also slight panic. This must be what I looked like when Lucy told me she'd had sex.

"Well, I kissed him."

"I thought you liked his friend Owen."

"No." I scrunch up my nose.

"But you said in the car—"

"That was ages ago."

"It was a week ago!"

"Well, it feels like ages ago."

"I guess I can't keep up with your love life anymore," Mum says.

"Well, I just told you the biggest thing that has ever happened to my love life, so consider yourself all caught up."

"Honey, this is . . . this is great. I'm excited for you. We're excited, right?" She's looking at my face, trying to gauge my feelings. I'm not giving her much.

"It's semi-exciting," I say. I mean, it's nice to have one person in my life excited by Alex and me, but she's excited for the wrong reasons, and her excitement is like an alarm bell. *Ding, ding, ding, sad desperate Natalie should be over the moon that anyone is paying attention to her.*

"I should meet him."

"Mum. Calm down. You definitely don't need to meet him."

"You could invite him over for dinner."

"I'm absolutely not doing that."

"Not now, obviously. Next week or the week after."

Oh god, she's going to suggest a golfing double date with Eric next. "We might not even be a thing next week," I say.

"What kind of thing are you now?"

"The smallest thing possible, too small to even classify. We're seeing where things go. Which is nowhere, since I haven't heard from him since yesterday."

"Why don't you text him?"

Very easy for her to say, a woman who's just had three texts from the man she left a couple of hours ago. Her eyes are bright, and I can see her next thought will be to help me decide what to write to him. It's all there, flashing through her mind right now, the fun we'll have being two single ladies figuring out the dating world together.

No, no, no, no, no, no. *No, we are not doing this.*

"I don't want to talk about this with you."

"Oh. Okay." Her shoulders slump. Here we go with the guilt again.

"Mum, can't you see I'm still upset with you? For lying to me for *months*."

"I know."

"And for breaking up with Dad."

"You keep saying that, honey, but the truth is, we made the decision together."

This can't be true. Someone had to be the instigator, but they clearly don't want me to know who it was.

"Well, it was a terrible decision," I say.

"This is not how I wanted my marriage to go either. Trust me. I didn't plan to be single in my late forties."

"Well, why did it go this way? I don't understand."

I think of the list I wrote a few hours ago, of evidence I had missed. There wasn't a lot of tangible proof. As a family, we're not shouters or criers, not in the traditional sense. Our fighting style is all quiet viciousness: sharp-edged comments, sarcasm, eye-rolling, and pointed silences. They sometimes argued about money, but in a way that was so detailed and intricate I was too bored to listen in. Here's my list of things I do know:

- Dad doesn't like the way Mum makes Vegemite on toast (too little butter, too much Vegemite), but she doesn't change her method when making it for him.
- Mum hates the brand of toothpaste Dad buys, but he still always buys it.
- Mum once said Dad would never survive in the zombie apocalypse (I mean, of course he wouldn't, it didn't even need to be said), and Dad was so offended he wouldn't watch the next episode of *The Walking Dead* with us.

- Dad thinks Mum interrupts him too much.
- Mum thinks Dad fails to defend her when she disagrees with other people.
- Dad thinks Mum has poor time-management skills.
- Mum hates Valentine's Day, but is also offended when Dad does nothing to celebrate it.
- Dad doesn't like Mum stealing his good work socks to wear around the house.
- Mum has always wanted a cat, but Dad is allergic to cat hair, though Mum questions the severity of this allergy.
- Mum thinks Dad is bad at apologizing.
- Dad snores.
- I once found Mum crying, alone, in the car and I got the feeling that maybe she'd gone to sit and cry in the car before.

None of these things seems enough to end a twenty-year marriage, but maybe, when you add them all together, they are. The thing is, there was lots of good stuff too. I'm sure of it. They laughed a lot. They loved talking to each other. They genuinely seemed to enjoy each other's company, and they always wanted to know what the other thought of things.

"It's complicated," Mum says.

"I am capable of understanding complex things, you know," I say. I can't seem to stop saying everything in the bitchiest tone possible.

"I know. I just . . . I don't think it's appropriate for me to share all the details with you."

"All the details" makes it sound like there was a scandalous affair.

Mum can see where my mind is going. "No, it's not what

you're thinking. Your father and I just no longer felt like we worked as a romantic couple."

"Don't all marriages go through that phase?"

"It wasn't a phase."

"But did you actually try to fix it?"

"Yes. For a long time."

"But . . ."

But, but, but. But this doesn't give me any answers. And it doesn't explain to me how to know if a relationship is good or bad or wrong or right.

"I hate that you're breaking up," I say, and, finally, the bitchy tone is gone.

"I know."

"Do you think you'll get married again?" I am so scared of the answer to this question.

"To your father?" she says.

"No. To someone else." I don't want my mother to spend the rest of her life alone if she doesn't want to be alone. I want her to be happy, but I don't want to share her with other people either—she's mine.

"I don't have any plans to."

"I'm scared of having awful stepparents."

"I will never marry someone you don't like, I promise."

"Well, that's a lot of pressure to put on me. I might be a terrible judge of character. Don't give me that much power."

"Fine. You have some power but not veto power."

"No, I've changed my mind. I want veto power."

"Sweetie, you're jumping way ahead. A lot is going to change in your life in the next few years too. We don't know where any of us will be in five years, or how we'll be feeling about things."

"Don't say that."

Growing and changing is only fun if my parents stay the same and I can show them how different and better I am without having to process their stuff too.

"Are you worried about next week?" she says.

Next week is when university places are announced, and the *rest of my life* will be decided. Of course I'm worried.

"A little."

I've decided I actually quite like the safety of this limbo period. Nothing is certain or decided yet. Next week, my choices will become concrete and I might have made the wrong ones and I'll have to live with that forever and I don't know how anyone makes these kinds of decisions and feels good about them. The whole thing makes me feel sick.

"No matter what happens, I'm so proud of you, honey."

There she goes, with the no-matter-what-happens stuff again. She has no idea that bringing up the fact that *anything can happen* is as unnerving as hell to someone like me.

I'm feeling bad now about how awful I have been to her tonight and for the phone snooping, and I'm about to apologize, when she turns to me.

"Natalie, there's something else I need to tell you."

My stomach hurts preemptively. "What's that?"

Mum clears her throat a little. "We're selling the house."

"This house? Our house?"

"Yes. I can't afford the mortgage on my own."

This probably should have occurred to me before, but I have been too busy wallowing in my own self-pity and thinking about Alex to consider logistics. *I hate this.* Without a big piece of shared real estate, the chances of Mum and Dad getting back together someday just got much, much smaller. (I didn't even know I was holding out hope for them getting back together until this moment.)

"Where will I live?"

"With me, at my new place."

"Which is where?"

"I don't know yet. There's a lot to organize before I get to that point."

I swallow, afraid I'm going to cry, and wait until I know my voice won't wobble to speak. "What if I want to live with Dad?"

"You can do that," Mum says, and she looks like she's trying to stop her voice from wobbling too.

"So I have to *choose* one of you?" I knew it would come to this. If Mum had kept the house, then staying with her wouldn't have felt as much like choosing, because I would be at the home I've always known, my real home. But if they are both renting new apartments, in new areas, then it is a direct choice between them.

"I wouldn't put it like that."

"But it is exactly like that."

"You could do one week with one of us, and then a week with the other. Or a month each. Or a year. There are lots of ways for us to share you," she says, squeezing my shoulder, and then smoothing my hair back from my face.

As long as I am shared. As long as my life is sliced up into equal pieces for them both to enjoy.

24

FIVE STAGES

The next morning, I lie prone on the couch and watch Netflix. It has been almost forty-eight hours since I last spoke to Alex. I have cycled through the five stages of rejection. (Stage one: I am too busy and carefree to even keep track of when he last contacted me. Stage two: he's probably busy, I'm busy too, we are both busy people. Stage three: it would have been nice to hear from him by now but everything is fine. Stage four: maybe he dropped his phone in the toilet or left it somewhere. Stage five: it's over and fuck him.)

Then a text from Alex appears on my screen.

—Hey, what are you up to tonight?

I clutch my phone and look at the words with relief and delight, grinning like a goof for a sad and shameful length of time before realizing I need to respond. I consider saying, *nothing*, but I actually do have plans. Lucy invited me to see a movie with her and Zach tonight, which is a transparent move on her behalf to smooth things over with me and Zach, but I figured I should go and give Zach the chance to apologize in person.

—I'm seeing a movie with Zach and Lucy

The more I look at that sentence on the screen, the colder and harsher and more closed off those words seem, so before I can second-guess myself, I send another message.

—Do you want to come?

No. I've gone too far in the other direction now. I've asked him out. I've literally *asked him out*. He ignored me for two days and this is how I respond.

I need a paper bag to breathe into or one of those stress balls to squeeze or a block of chocolate to stuff into my mouth: *Please, God, give me something to do with my hands before I recklessly send any more soul-exposing texts.*

The little "I'm typing" dots appear, then they *disappear*, and my text sits there unanswered like a humiliating stain on the fabric of humanity.

Seconds tick by. I start the stopwatch on my phone, because it feels important to know the exact details when I analyze this with Lucy later.

A whole minute passes.

At one minute and twenty-three seconds, the typing dots reappear. At one minute and twenty-nine seconds, he finally replies.

—Sure, what movie?

Does that mean, *Sure I'll definitely come, what movie are we seeing*? Or is it more, *Sure, I might be interested, depends on the movie*? And why did he need one minute and twenty-nine seconds for *that* reply?

I wait for exactly one minute and thirty seconds to pass before I respond, to maintain a shred of dignity.

—The Final Reckoning

—It's a horror movie

—We're seeing the 6:30 p.m. session

—It's had some good reviews

—Well good might be an exaggeration, it's had mixed reviews

—Here's the link to the trailer

I stop myself before I can send a seventh text message in a row. I put my phone down. It's okay if he takes a while to respond now. He might want to watch the trailer, or read some reviews, or look at the Rotten Tomatoes score, or—

A new message pops onto my screen.

—Sounds good. Should I pick you up?

Last time I was alone in the car with him I couldn't think of anything to say for most of the trip. Nope. Best to meet him there.

I send him the details of where to meet and he writes, *see you then,* and I angst over whether or not that needs a reply, and if it does, whether or not I have waited too long to reply, and then I finally send a thumbs-up emoji, throw my phone away from me, walk into my bedroom, and collapse facedown on my bed.

If every step of dating is this torturous, I won't survive.

25

ARE YOU HAVING FUN YET?

"Hi."

"Hi."

"Hi."

"Hi."

Ten seconds in, and this double date is a disaster. We make small talk about popcorn and choc-tops, and I am acutely aware of how far apart Alex and I are standing and that Zach and Lucy are holding hands, which I suspect is so Lucy can grip his hand tightly as a warning if he starts to say the wrong thing, but, still, it makes me feel extremely aware of their closeness and our separateness. A double date, I realize, means you are pitching your coupling into direct comparison with another couple, and Alex and I have no chance of measuring up to Zach and Lucy. Zach and Lucy are the Olympic champions of coupling, and Alex and I are amateurs trying out a sport for the first time, stumbling around confused about the rules.

Alex and Zach are being overly polite to each other in a way that's making me tense. They're not polite brothers. Every word between them has an undercurrent of darker meaning. Zach and I are simply avoiding eye contact or directly speaking to each other at all. An apology does not seem to be forthcoming. I am also avoiding making eye contact with Alex because looking into his eyes makes me nervous. I am attracted to him with an intensity that feels deeply embarrassing and I'm worried that might not be normal.

Because of the weird tension floating between the three of us, Lucy is left to do a lot of social heavy lifting, but, luckily, she's good at filling silence with cheerful chat that doesn't require any input from anyone else. ("I keep seeing that poster for that movie everywhere, and I have no idea what it's about at all, and I just think if you look at a poster and have no idea what the movie is about, if you can't even guess the *genre,* then the poster is a failure, but then again, I'm talking about it, so maybe it's a success.")

We walk into the theater with Lucy leading the way, which means I end up sitting between Zach and Alex.

I can see Zach glancing at us all the time out of the corner of his eye, and I keep thinking about his Alex-is-not-going-to-be-your-great-love-story comment. I am determined to disprove that theory, but it is difficult under surveillance.

I am 70 percent sweaty anxiety and 30 percent paranoia, but that might be pretty normal for a first date, I don't know.

The movie starts, and it has a creepy doll, which is my least-liked horror trope, and lots of jump scares, my second-least-liked thing about horror films. I am very sensitive to jump scares, and I practically leap out of my seat at the first one, which scares Alex.

"Jesus, you frightened me more than the movie," he whispers.

"Sorry, I'm not good with horror."

He lifts the armrest between us, thank god, because I wanted to raise it from the moment we sat down but I wasn't sure of the etiquette of when that should happen.

I push my face into Alex's shoulder every time the movie gets scary, and suddenly I'm seeing the appeal of horror movies. Alex smells very, very good. He has a very particular masculine smell that I always imagine handsome celebrities in magazine photo shoots wearing leather jackets and sitting on motorcycles have.

Alex looks at me at one point and smiles, and his eyes do that crinkly thing, and I want to die with how adorable he is.

Then the movie ends and everything goes to hell again.

"What did you think?" Lucy asks.

"It was pretty bad," Alex says.

"That's rude," Zach says.

"What is?" Alex says.

"Telling my girlfriend, who was kind enough to invite you along, that the movie she chose was crap."

"Actually, Natalie invited me. And I wasn't aware we weren't allowed to criticize the movie."

"It's fine, Alex, of course you can say it wasn't good," Lucy says, making a what-the-hell-are-you-doing? face at Zach.

We file out of the cinema in silence and I can feel the tension between Zach and Alex crackling. We reach the foyer, and I turn around, about to say something to Lucy, but Zach speaks before I can.

"Why are you even here?" he says to Alex.

"Don't worry, I won't come again," Alex says.

"You won't be invited again."

"What is going on right now?" I say. Alex and Zach might argue and tease each other a lot, but what is happening now is different—it has undertones of something sour and long-lasting.

"Zach has a problem with you and me spending time together," Alex says, and takes my hand in his, which I don't like, because I am not here to be a prop in their fight. I let go of his hand, and I see Zach notice me doing it, and I want to shout, *That wasn't for you.*

"Yeah, I do," Zach says.

"Let's get a hot chocolate!" Lucy says, with hopeful enthusiasm. She believes in the power of a nice warm drink to diffuse a situation. I think she learned it from Mariella, who routinely distracts her sons with food and drink when they are fighting or getting on her nerves—it's her signature move as a mother.

"It's weird that you are going out with Lucy and trying to control Natalie's love life at the same time," Alex says.

Lucy and I look at each other. This is awkward.

"No, it's weird that you're socializing with me now after years of ignoring the three of us," Zach says.

"Let's all just take a deep breath and relax for a second," Lucy says.

"Well, what exactly do you want? That Natalie and I never talk to each other again? Is that what would make you happy?" Alex says.

I am acutely aware that we're making a scene in the cinema foyer.

"Yes, to be honest, that would make me happy," Zach says.

"And do you care about what makes me happy?" I say, because I can't stand to listen to them fight any longer.

"Yes. Obviously, I do. That's what I'm trying to say," he says, turning to me.

Alex's jaw is clenched. "You must really think I'm a piece of shit," he says to Zach, his voice cracking as he says it.

My heart lurches.

Zach shakes his head. "I don't think that," he says quietly.

"It seems like you do," Alex says.

"You cheated on Vanessa," Zach blurts out.

Oh.

Oh.

This is not a piece of information I can process in front of other people.

"You cheated on Vanessa, and I don't want you to cheat on Natalie," Zach continues.

"You don't know what you're talking about," Alex says.

"My mum is picking us up in five minutes," Lucy says, grabbing Zach's hand and dragging him toward the escalator. Mariella, thankfully, has not told Lucy's mother about catching Lucy and Zach in bed together, so Lucy is still allowed to socialize out in the world.

"I've got to go too," Alex says.

I wait for him to offer to drive me home, but instead he hugs me goodbye, and leaves quickly, head down, hands jammed in his pockets, practically running. This is all the confirmation I need that the cheating must have happened.

"My mum can drive you home," Lucy says to me.

"No, it's okay, I'm getting picked up," I lie. I had assumed Alex would drive me home.

"All right, then, 'bye," Lucy says.

"'Bye," I say. We exchange wide-eyed looks that acknowledge we will be texting each other about this later tonight.

"Zach," I call out to their backs as they are walking away.

"What?" he says, turning around.

"Thanks for ruining my first date," I say.

He looks appropriately devastated, and I walk away quickly before he can defend himself.

26

THE TRUTH OR SOMETHING LIKE IT

Alex messages me that night. I'm at Dad's apartment, my first night staying over, and I'm trying to figure out how to work the dimmer on the light switch when I hear my phone ping.

—That went badly

There it is. The inevitable text I always knew I would receive after my first date. I can't deny getting a secret thrill out of having my low expectations met. So there, Mum. Sometimes the pimple does get worse, the jeans don't fit even after stretching them out for a day, and the date you thought was bad really was that terrible.

I write back.

—Yes it did

No point in denying it. Alex's response appears on my screen seconds later.

—So about what Zach said

Oh god. The thing I have been avoiding thinking about even though the words have been haunting me for hours. *Alex cheated on Vanessa.* Everything I have read about relationships on the internet or seen on TV has taught me that once a cheater, always a cheater. Alex is a Bad Person, and Zach is right, he'll let me down. (Of course, in one way, this has only made Alex more attractive to me, because Bad Person is very close in characterization to Bad Boy, and TV has also conditioned me to love the Bad Boy.)

I take a deep breath. I need to protect myself. I need to be tough.

—Which part?

—The cheating part

—Is it true?

—Yes. No. Kind of.

—Kind of?

Alex is a cheater, which means he's a liar, which means I shouldn't trust anything he says or does.

—It's more complicated than it sounds

—Isn't that what guys who cheat on their girlfriends always say?

The little typing bubbles appear for a long time before his next message appears. I imagine all the things he could be writing. *It wasn't me, it was a guy who looked like me. I was tricked into it. Someone took a photo of us from a weird angle and it looked like we were kissing, but we weren't. I was possessed by a demon. It was a dare. It was a scheme. We were rehearsing a scene from a play. It was one small part of a complicated jewel heist.*

If he actually writes any of these things I won't believe him, but I want him to care enough to try to lie.

His response finally appears on my screen.

—Vanessa and I were on and off for months . . . it was very messy . . . one weekend we had this really big fight and I was upset and I kissed someone else at a party . . . a kiss that lasted about two minutes . . . I'm not proud of it, it was a mistake

I don't know what to say to this, and I type a single-word response that would probably stress me the hell out if I got it.

—Okay

—But I'm not a bad person. At least, I really hope I'm not. Or if I was, I'm not now.

—Okay

—What does okay mean???

—Okay means I am thinking about that information

—What are you thinking?

—I haven't decided

I believe him, which makes me think I shouldn't believe him, because I don't know what I'm doing, and my instincts are probably all wrong. I am a naive, inexperienced know-nothing. (But all my years of reading relationship-advice columns online! Surely that counts for something! I guess it depends on who is doing the counting.) The Natalie I was before we kissed, she knew better. She knew not to trust Alex. She was strong, unwavering. She rejected secrets, and lies, and pretty much the entire male population. Now I am weak and disgusting with feelings.

Also, there's the glaring fact that I didn't notice my parents weren't together for *ten months*. This, more than anything, tells me that I can't trust my judgment anymore.

If I can see Alex's face, and look into his eyes, maybe then I can know. I once read a book on how to spot a liar. I've forgotten most of it, but I know looking someone dead in the eyes without blinking makes it much harder for them to lie, unless they're a psychopath, and then they'll stare straight back at you and lie with ease and you'll probably be caught in their web of lies forever.

—Come over

I type it without really even thinking, but once I've written it, it feels very exciting.

—Okay

—I'm at my dad's place

I send him the address, and he says he's on his way. Dad calls out to me then, asking if I'm ready to watch the next episode. We're watching a new Netflix series that is very, very slow and it takes all my strength not to look at my phone every two seconds, but I'm trying not to ruin our first night together, because that might set the tone for the rest of our lives. Dad and I have to figure out a whole new relationship, one without Mum's presence, and I have no idea how to get it right.

I walk into the lounge.

"Dad, someone is coming over."

"What, now?"

"Yeah."

"It's after ten." After ten p.m., to Dad, is a time for quietly drinking a cup of tea and eating shortbread biscuits. It is not a time for going outside, being loud, or doing things of any kind, most especially socializing.

"I know. I'm sorry. It's important."

"Who is it?"

"A friend."

"Coming here?"

"Sort of. I just need to talk to them for a second. I'll go downstairs, I won't bring them up here."

"You can bring your friend up here."

"I'd rather not."

He looks at me and frowns. "You are being very mysterious."

"Says the man who lied to me for ten months."

"Well, now . . ." He pauses.

He and Mum are still really struggling to come up with ways to get around the fact that they did a terrible thing to me. They still won't admit it was terrible—they won't say it, but we all know it was.

"For my peace of mind, tell me who it is," he says.

"A boy."

"What boy?"

"A boy called Alex."

"Is this boy called Alex nice?"

"I'm still deciding."

"Okay. Are you going to go somewhere with him?"

"No. I'm just going to sit in his car and talk."

"All right. What are you going to talk about?"

"That's private," I say, which is a mistake, because now he probably thinks it's about sex.

Dad sips his tea and puts the cup down with a rattle. "You know you can always talk to me, don't you?"

"Yes." This is true: Dad is far less judgmental than Mum.

"I'm good at giving advice."

"I know," I say.

"And I was once a teenage boy, so maybe I have insights you don't know about."

"You would have been a very different kind of teenage guy than Alex."

"So he's not a *Star Wars* superfan who collects rocks?"

Dad was very much an eighties nerd stereotype as a teenager, as far as I can gather. I saw a picture of him once as a fifteen-year-old, and I felt instantly sorry for him, even though he looked happy with his arms slung over the shoulders of two friends, all of them grinning, one of them delightedly pointing to his T-shirt, which had an image from a movie I didn't recognize on it.

Then I imagined my own child looking at pictures of me at fifteen and feeling sorry for me, except that was easier to know why, because of my skin, and the way I can never, ever relax in front of a camera, which comes through so clearly in every single photo. I'm always looking down, looking away, half turning, straining, enduring, smiling in a closed-mouth, get-this-over-with way. "Gee, you're not photogenic, are you?" a friend of Lucy's once said to me, choosing which group shot to post on Instagram, and I said, "It's good because people are never disappointed when they meet me in person," and she nodded earnestly, like it was my master plan all along.

"Not quite," I say now to Dad.

"Still, try me."

"Fine. *Hypothetically,* and I'm *not* saying this is Alex, but if someone cheated on their previous girlfriend, does that mean they'll cheat again?"

"Yes," he says, without hesitation.

"So if you do something bad when you're young, that defines who you are for the rest of your life?"

"Well, no."

"So which is it?"

He takes another sip of his tea, thinking.

"I don't know, sweetie. People aren't all good or all bad. You can learn from mistakes. Or you can keep making them. You can always become a better person."

"That's not very helpful."

"I do know I don't like the sound of this boy."

"I said it was hypothetical."

"Well, I hypothetically don't like him."

I've introduced Dad to the idea of Alex with the worst story possible, which is incredibly stupid, but I can't imagine Alex ever actually meeting my parents. That feels years away, if it ever were to happen at all. It's the problem of a different Natalie. This current Natalie just needs to know what to do tonight, here, now.

When Alex messages me to say he's outside, I hurry down

the three flights of stairs as fast as I can, and then I feel ridiculous. *Calm down. Don't be the girl who trips and dies because she's rushing to see a boy who took two days to text her and who once cheated on his ex.*

I walk out of the apartment building and over to his car, trying to look casual.

"Hi," he says, smiling when I open the door.

"Hi," I say, getting in the car.

God, he's cute. I wish I didn't think that every time I saw his face, but it's involuntary now. Alex. Cute. Alex. Cute.

He takes a deep breath. "Let's start over."

"From when?" I say.

"From before the movies."

"But after Queenscliff?"

"Yes."

So we're keeping the kissing but erasing my knowledge of the cheating? I frown, and the car falls quiet. For once, I don't feel the need to fill the silence. This is his silence to deal with, his problem.

"It wasn't *cheating* cheating," he blurts out.

"I thought we were starting over."

"I know, I know. I just feel like you've heard about one of the worst things I've ever done and we're not going to get past it."

"I think the less we talk about your ex, the better."

"It wasn't Vanessa's fault."

"Okay, that's the opposite of what I just said."

"I know, I just want you to know I'm not blaming her or anything."

On the one hand, I'm pleased he said this, because the idea of him bad-mouthing Vanessa after he cheated on her would make me furious, but on the other hand, it also doesn't make me feel any less insecure about him maybe still being in love with her. I flash back to watching her sitting on his shoulders and feel a stab of jealousy at the ease of their bodies together.

"Clearly, you two still get along, so there's no reason for me to be mad about it if she's not."

"I wasn't always a good boyfriend to her."

"Obviously, because you cheated on her."

"I feel like the word *cheated* is being overemphasized."

"In what way?"

"Look, I was seventeen, I wasn't even sure if we were together anymore, I was drunk and sad, and I kissed a stranger at a party for a minute."

"You said it was two minutes before. Now it's one minute."

"It was a very, very short amount of time."

"Did Vanessa consider it cheating?"

"Yes."

"Was she upset?"

"Yes."

"Well, there you go."

"I'm not saying I wasn't in the wrong. I'm just saying what happened. It wasn't something that I'd planned. And I told Vanessa about it straightaway."

"So it was spontaneous? The kind of thing you might do again at any moment?"

"No!"

I don't know how mad I can be with him about this. Am I just a horrible, judgmental person, hassling him about something that is largely none of my business? Or am I doing the right thing, the smart thing, finding out everything I can before I get too attached? Surely things shouldn't be this messy after one date. We're barely a week in. I should be asking him his favorite color or favorite TV series or favorite something. We should be exchanging *boring facts*. Not traumatic secrets.

"Look, I don't know how to talk about this stuff," Alex says. There's real panic on his face. This is hard for him.

"You don't owe me an explanation," I say. This is all Zach's fault. Damn him and his big mouth and his need to ruin my life.

"I would have told you about it. Probably not on our first date, but at some point," he says.

"Well, I know now." I wish I didn't.

"I just don't want you to think of me as the kind of person who would cheat on you. It's not who I really am," Alex says.

I look at his face, half lit by the nearby streetlights, and I do believe him. He doesn't want to hurt me.

In that moment, I decide to trust him and what he's telling me. Which feels reckless, like I'm giving him something I can't get back. A leap of faith. I even decide not to mention that he didn't text me for two days. (Maybe I am more emotionally mature than I thought.)

"Well, at this point, I mean, would it even be cheating?" I ask, opening a whole new can of worms. *What kind of together are we?* If I'm trusting him, I need to know the answer to this question. I'm glad it's dark, because my face feels very red. I think my hands are shaking.

"I meant cheat on you in the future. If things get, you know, more serious," Alex says, glancing at me and then away.

"Oh, right."

"But also now. It's not like I'm seeing anyone else." He looks at me again, but this time he doesn't look away.

"Me neither." I repress the urge to laugh hysterically at the very idea. God, every step in this process feels like a competition in making yourself the least vulnerable person in the equation.

"I'm not even thinking about anyone else," he says, still holding my gaze.

"Me neither," I say again, my heart hammering. I give him a little smile.

He leans over and kisses me then, and we kiss for a long time, and I forget we're on a public street until my phone buzzes and I assume that it's Dad texting me and if I take too long to respond he'll come downstairs to find me and we'll never be able to look each other in the eye again for the rest of our lives.

"Okay, I should go back upstairs now," I say, pulling away.

"I don't want you to."

"My dad is waiting. It's my first night staying at his new place."

"Okay." He rests his forehead against mine very briefly and it takes all my strength not to reconsider and stay in this car forever.

"You could come over to my mum's house tomorrow." These invitations just fly out of my mouth now.

I want to be around you all the time and that desire makes me feel sick.

"Yeah?" he says.

"Yes."

Every second of this is terrible and confusing and wonderful, and I love it and hate it in equal measures.

27

THE FIRST TIME

I've thought a lot about my first time having sex. Maybe I've overthought it, but overpreparation and overanalysis are better than none at all. I've read as much as I can online and in books, and I've come to have three expectations—one: it might hurt; two: it's very, very unlikely I'll have an orgasm (I know how to have one on my own but there seems to be a lot of logistics, multitasking, and detailed communication involved in having one with someone else); and three: I won't know what the hell I'm doing, in a general sense.

I wish I could skip the first few times—maybe even the first ten times, or twenty, or thirty (sex might be one of those things it takes ten thousand hours to become really good at, like golf and playing the piano), and get to the point where everything works perfectly and I either look good doing it or I'm enjoying it so much I don't care what I look like.

When I was younger, I thought I wouldn't have sex with anyone unless they loved me with an all-consuming movie-star love. Then I got bad skin, and I changed my stance—maybe the person didn't have to love me, they just had to like me a whole lot and have really good shoulders. Or like me a little bit. Or be willing to look at my face without making fun of me. Or just be simply willing.

Lucy and I decided one day (this was before she was with Zach, and before she had sex with Travis) that we'd figure out sex, and all the other stuff that goes with it, once we got to university. We'd magically find low-stakes, low-maintenance boyfriends (or, in Lucy's case, maybe a girlfriend, she was open to either). They'd be people who were cute and fun but who we didn't care about that much, and we'd get good at sex while sleeping with them, without worrying too much what they thought of us or the pressure of anyone having *feelings*.

But now there is Alex.

Alex and all the Alex-feelings that go along with him.

He's the person I want to have sex with. The sooner, the better, before this whole thing falls apart and I miss my chance.

I figure today is the day. Alex is coming over, like we agreed in the car last night. Mum is at work. If we do it now, in my room, on my terms, on my invitation, then I'm more in control of the situation. I'm in control of how much—or little—he'll be able to see of my body in the process.

I might not be in control of what happens with my parents, or where I will live, or what university program I get into, or what I will do with the rest of my life, but, fuck it, I will have control over *this*.

I've tidied my room and put clean sheets on my bed. I've bought a box of condoms from the supermarket. I've double-checked I haven't missed a Pill in the last month. I've had a shower and put on my expensive skin moisturizer, the one I save for special occasions. I've brushed my teeth twice. I blow-dried my hair this morning, and kept going until all my hair was dry, which is a big deal because I usually lazily leave the underlayer damp. I even stretched my hamstrings and watched a meditation video on YouTube to center my spirit, whatever that means.

I text Lucy and say, *I might have sex with Alex today,* because it doesn't feel real without telling her. She immediately calls me.

"Natalie!" she shouts.

"It might not happen," I say, putting her on speakerphone so I can examine my eyebrows at the same time.

"Are you sure about this? It seems very fast," she says.

"Yes," I say. I am sure. I think. I'm eighteen. It's time. It has to be time. It feels like my moment. I could start university ahead of schedule.

"What are you wearing?"

"The Boob Top."

"Okay, good. How are you feeling?"

"Nervous," I say, leaning as close to the mirror as I can. My eyebrows need to be sex-ready. I don't know what that is, exactly, but I know how they currently look is not that.

"Do you want . . . advice?" she says, a little hesitantly.

"What kind of advice?"

"About . . . any of it."

"Okay, tell me your top five tips," I say, suddenly realizing Alex is going to be here any minute.

"I'm not a BuzzFeed article."

"Quick, just tell me the most important things."

"Um, okay. Go slow. Have fun doing other stuff first, but don't do anything that you don't want to do. Use lubricant. And stick to the basics."

I have a million questions (*What are the basics!? How necessary is lubricant!!?*) but the doorbell rings and it's all too late.

"He's here. I have to go!" I hiss into the phone.

"Good luck!" she says.

I hang up, take three deep breaths like my YouTube video said to, and walk to the front door.

"Hey," he says, when I open it.

"Come in. No one's home," I say, already on the edge of nervous babble.

I lead him immediately toward my bedroom. I'm jittery. I suddenly just want this to be over with. I picture myself an hour from now, as a sophisticated person who has had a satisfying sexual experience. I want to jump ahead to that moment.

He's looking around, as though I'm going to give him a tour, but I shepherd him straight into my bedroom and I sit down on my bed.

"We have two hours, maybe three, before my mum gets home," I say. Mum doesn't normally get home until six, but I'm building in a buffer.

"For what?" he says, looking a little confused.

"For whatever we want to do." I keep my tone light, but I hope he gets my meaning. I don't want to resort to smiling suggestively.

"Okay." He still sounds confused as he sits down next to me. We look at each other. He didn't shave this morning and he's wearing a plain gray T-shirt. The combination of a stubbly cheek and a well-fitted top is irresistible.

I stand up, and pull down my blinds, then shut the door.

"What are you doing?" he asks, looking at me like I'm about to commit a murder.

"Just giving us privacy," I say.

"Right. Isn't the house empty, though?"

"Extra privacy."

I sit back down on the bed, leaving a space between us. It's not completely dark with the blinds down, but it's dark enough that he won't be able to see my skin properly. If I'm going to take my top off, I can't let him see my scarred back in natural light, that's for sure.

"So," I say.

"So."

I lean forward and kiss him, and he kisses me back, but he seems a little hesitant. After a few minutes, he's lying on top of me, and the hesitation is disappearing. I tug at his T-shirt, and start to pull it up, putting my hands on the bare skin of his back. Now he stops.

"What are we doing?" he says, propping himself up on one elbow.

"What do you think we're doing?" I say, feeling a little twist of nerves in my stomach but trying to play things cool.

"I feel like . . . I don't know."

"Well, we're doing whatever we want," I say. I can picture someone else—someone cooler, the kind of person with the confidence to wear black nail polish, the kind of person who could cut their hair into a pixie cut without regretting it, the kind of person who's done more than the sex basics with at least two different people—being able to say this line in a really seductive way. I sound like a child.

"You keep saying that," Alex says.

"I'm hoping you're going to catch on," I say.

"You want to have sex?" he says.

Okay, finally.

"Yes," I say, feeling relieved.

"But you said last week we weren't going to have sex," he says.

"That was last week." A hundred things have changed since then. (Emotionally. In my head.)

"Okay, but why today?" Alex has rolled off me entirely now and is lying by my side, which isn't filling me with confidence.

"Why not today? Let's get it done."

He laughs, sounding nervous. "You're making it seem like . . ."

"Like what?"

"Like a chore."

"No, I'm not. I just want to get the first time out of the way." I am saying "the first time" so he might think I mean the first time between us, but I am quite sure he knows I've never had sex before and that what I really mean is "my first time ever."

"*Out of the way?*"

"Over with."

"That's worse."

"You know what I mean." (I'm starting to think maybe he doesn't.)

"You're freaking me out," he says, sitting up and rubbing his temples.

"Just the first time might be not great. After that we can get better at it. Go beyond the basics," I say, trying to sound as up-beat as possible, and also hoping he won't ask me what I think the basics are.

"Your expectations of me are terrifyingly low."

"Isn't it better to exceed expectations than fail to meet them?" I honestly go into every situation with the lowest expectations possible, and it always surprises me when I find out that other people don't think that way.

"This conversation is very stressful." He gets up off the bed and starts to pace.

"Well, I don't want to make things worse, but I have something else to ask you," I say.

"What?" he says, looking pained.

"How many people have you had sex with?" I ask. The question has been on my mind ever since he wouldn't answer it that night in Queenscliff, and I figure, as things are already going badly, I may as well head in this direction. It would really help me to know.

"Wow. You definitely made it worse," he says.

"Is it more than ten?" Ten is a number that represents enormous experience. I might realistically never sleep with ten people in my whole life. If Alex has already had sex with ten people, I don't think I can be with him. I don't think I can be *around* him. The gulf between us is too wide.

"Two."

"That's not true."

"Why wouldn't that be true?"

"Zach told me it was more."

"Zach has no idea how many people I've slept with."

"So how many?"

"Two."

"I'm not that naive. You're cute, and you worked in a bar. It's more than two."

"I'm short, hairy, and I worked in the kitchen of a pub. I spent most nights sweaty and covered in food stains."

I let a long silence hang between us.

He puts his hands behind his head and lets out a long breath.

"Fine. *Fine.* Six people. And that's the truth! I have slept with six girls in my life. One was a girlfriend, two were kind of on-and-off casual things, and the other three were one-nighters."

"How many times with each?"

"Natalie, I am not answering that. I don't even think I *could* answer that. I don't keep a tally of all the times I've had sex."

"I'm looking for ballpark figures, nothing exact. Like with Vanessa—"

"I don't want to talk about Vanessa."

That means Vanessa was great in bed.

"How many of them did you meet on Tinder?"

"What? None!"

"I know you're on Tinder," I say, in my most I-am-very-relaxed-about-this-information-and-it-doesn't-scare-me-at-all voice.

"I'm not, actually."

He throws his phone on the bed. "Go ahead and check."

I've made him surrender his phone for me to look through like a police officer. This doesn't seem *ideal*. I nudge the phone back to him.

"I'm not looking at your phone."

"Then you'll have to trust me." The scariest words in the world.

Now that I've opened the floodgates and I know he has had sex with six different people, all I can think is: *You have to ask him about diseases, you have to ask him about diseases.* If I'm not mature enough to ask, I'm not mature enough for sex. (That's the mantra we learned at school.)

"Have you ever had an STI check?" I say. There, I did it. And probably no one ever actually asks this question, and I can see why, because the moment after asking is terrible.

"Yes. Once."

"And?"

"It was fine. Nothing. Negative."

"How many people have you slept with since then?" Maybe there is some secret way to have this conversation and still keep the mood light and flirty, but my approach definitely leans more toward a cross-examination. Maybe I should be massaging his shoulders or something. No, I think that would be weirder.

"Two."

"Did you use protection?"

"Yes."

"Every time?"

"Yes."

"Okay."

So he might have something, he might not. I don't really know what to do with this information. They never gave us an explanation of what to do with the answer, especially if the answer was like this one. Or if they did, I can't remember. Should I ask for paperwork? Make him go back to the doctor? That sounds like something a teacher would suggest and no one would ever do in real life. I've had the HPV vaccine, so that's something, at least.

"Are you running out of questions?" He looks hopeful.

"I will probably never run out of questions," I say. He should at least know this about me.

"Can I ask a question?"

"Yes."

"Why do we need to have sex today?"

"You don't want to?"

"I'm worried that you don't actually want to."

"It's my idea. Of course I want to."

"We could wait and just let things happen. You know, decide in the moment."

"That's how people get pregnant."

The idea of treating sex as something that might just *happen* is not an idea I can get on board with. It would be like getting in a car and just driving aimlessly. I always like to know where I'm going. I need to know before I start something where I'm going to stop.

"I mean, be prepared, obviously, but see how we feel. Maybe we have sex today. Maybe we do something else. Maybe we do it next week, or the week after, or at some unspecified date in the future."

I don't know how to tell if he's being a good guy, or patronizing, or if he doesn't want to have sex with me at all (which wouldn't be surprising after all my questions). I want to say, *I am perfectly capable of knowing when I want to have sex, thank you very much.*

"Okay. Well, I have these," I say instead. I take the packet of condoms out of the drawer and sit them on the bedside table with a flourish. Usually it's covered in books, tissues, earrings, and mugs with a little bit of cold tea in the bottom, but I've cleared everything else away, which was a mistake, because now the condoms are alone, and I may as well have installed a blinking neon light that says SEX, SEX, SEX.

The box itself is still wrapped in plastic, and I'm worried we'll have to spend too long trying to unwrap it in the throes of passion. (To be honest, I don't even know what the word *throes* means but I guess it means we'll be thrashing around in pleasure. *Thrashing* might be a worse word than *throes*.) Maybe I should get some scissors. I'm not even sure when exactly the condom-putting-on moment is supposed to occur, or how fast it happens, if you can take your time or if you need to be rushing.

I think I'm visibly sweating now. I need a tissue to pat down my forehead.

Alex sits back down on the bed.

"How many people have you slept with?" he asks. The question I was hoping we could skim past.

"Um, not many." I know I just demanded a lot of answers from him, and it's very hypocritical, but I'd really rather remain a bit mysterious on this topic. I'm certain he suspects I'm a virgin, but I'd feel a lot better if we could just keep it as vague information circling in our minds rather than spelling it out.

"How many is not many?"

"A very, very small amount."

"How small?"

"A statistically insignificant number."

"Natalie."

"None."

"Okay." He rubs his palms on his jeans. I think he's sweating too.

"Is that a problem?" I ask.

"Of course not," he says, but he looks worried.

"Your face says otherwise."

"My face is normal."

"It's not."

"It is."

"You look like someone who just got told bad news."

"No, I don't."

"Don't worry, I'm not someone who has any romantic fantasies about their first time."

"Clearly. You've already told me how bad you think it's going to be."

"Not bad. I never said *bad*. Just not good."

"Right. You brought me over here to get the *not good* sex out of the way."

"So we can get to the good sex. You're leaving that part out."

Alex lies back on the bed and covers his face with his hands. His T-shirt rides up, exposing his stomach a little. I resist the urge to lay my palm against his skin, to press my face against it.

"You're killing me," he says.

"Forget everything I've said today. Let's start over."

"I can't. It's all burned into my brain."

"Well, unburn it."

"I'm trying."

"Would it help if I said something sexy?" I don't know why I suggest this, because I've legitimately never said anything sexy in my life, but I need to turn things around somehow.

"No."

"Why not?"

"It would make us both feel awkward, I think."

"Let's try it. It might reset the mood."

"I really don't think—"

"You look great in that T-shirt."

He sits up a little, dropping his hands from his face.

"You know what, I didn't hate that."

"See? Now you try."

"Your hair looks really good today."

"That was a nice compliment, but it wasn't sexy."

"Okay, you look great in that top."

"You're just repeating me."

"Yes, but you look great for a different reason," he says, and his cheeks are a little bit pink. (I'm wearing my best-fitting bra with the Boob Top, so I know immediately what he means.)

"We're not bad at this," I say.

He slides over and kisses me, and it feels good to have his body covering mine again.

After a while I pause. "We're not going to have sex today," I say.

"I know," he says.

"You don't care that I keep changing my mind?" I say.

"No," he says.

28

NOT THE RESULT
WE WERE HOPING FOR

This is it, the life-changing moment, the what-will-I-be-for-the-rest-of-my-life reveal. Or, more accurately, the what-will-I-be-doing-for-the-next-three-years reveal.

I have read the articles and heard from the career counselors that no one has a career for life anymore, and we'll all change jobs two hundred times and end up working in tech industries that don't exist yet, and then robots will replace those jobs, and we'll end up floating heads in glass cases buying things through our AI companions as the seas rise up to slowly consume us (Zach and I started co-writing a sci-fi novel based on this premise a year ago—it was going to be the first in a nine-book series, until we argued for a week over what to name the main character and then got distracted and forgot about it), and none of this really matters, except this moment right here, this am-I-getting-into-university-and-if-I-am-what-university-will-it-be-and-what-course-will-I-be-studying moment. This feels like it does matter, it really, really matters.

University offers are announced online at 2 p.m. It's 1:57 p.m. I have spent the past hour and forty-three minutes freaking out: deep-breathing, pacing, chewing five pieces of gum at once until my jaw aches, blocking social media on my phone so I don't have to see reactions from other people, regretting the blocking and trying to delete the social-media blocking app. An irrational feeling of dread settled on me this morning, that maybe I actually misread my score last year, that maybe it was all a mistake, that maybe it's not good enough and I won't be offered anything, anywhere.

At least this is an improvement on how I behaved before our final results were announced, when I got up at six a.m. and sat in my closet for an hour, refusing to speak to Mum and Dad.

The clock ticks over. I log in, and the page loads very, very slowly. And then there it is. The degree I wanted, bachelor of arts, at the university I wanted, the University of Melbourne.

There. I did it.

Everything as expected. My choice has been made.

It feels . . . anticlimactic.

I thought I would be filled with relief and happiness, and I am, sort of. A slice of my future is now hard and concrete. But still, for the hours and hours of study I went through in year twelve, I thought I would feel something . . . more. I want to jump around the room and scream and cry with happiness. Instead I'm already thinking about how big and scary the university is, and how I have no idea what I want to major in. And what does an arts degree get you anyway? Why didn't I apply for a law degree or a business degree or something vaguely useful? Or, on the other hand, why didn't I apply for something risky and creative and interesting? Why am I even going to university? I should be traveling, experiencing *real life*. Nothing I've ever done has felt like *real life* to me.

I call Mum, then Dad, and they're both filled with excitement and pride, which should make me feel better, but somehow makes me feel worse, partly because I have to have pretty much the same conversation twice.

I think maybe I am very bad at being happy for myself.

I text Lucy, and she doesn't respond, which is strange. I want to text Zach, but I can't, because we're still fighting, or, at least, I'm still furious at him and he hasn't apologized and I don't know where we stand with each other, and the fact that our friendship is a mess right now is one of the main factors contributing to my unease about everything.

Then my phone rings, and Lucy's name appears on the screen.

"Hi," I say.

"I'm outside."

"My house?"

"Yes."

"Well, come in."

I go to the front door, and Lucy is standing there, looking upset. "What's wrong?" I say.

"I didn't get in."

"Oh, Luce."

I hug her, and lead her into the lounge room. I fill the kettle, putting a bag of Lucy's favorite herbal tea into the most soothing mug we own, which is so big that it is more bowl than cup.

Lucy starts pacing in my lounge room. "Okay, first tell me what you got into," she says to me.

"Arts at Melbourne."

"Good. Okay. That makes me feel a bit better," she says.

"So you didn't get into commerce at Melbourne?" That was her first preference plan. Do a commerce degree, and then postgrad law.

"No."

"Did you get into law?" Her second, third, and fourth preferences were undergrad law at other universities.

"No."

"At any uni?"

"Nope."

"How is that possible?" Lucy got great marks. Her mother bought her a monogrammed leather satchel as a graduation gift for doing so well.

Now Lucy's face crumples a little, and she doesn't meet my eye. She sits down on the couch and puts her head into her hands. "I don't know how to say it," she says.

The kettle pings then, and I leave her for a moment to make the tea and bring it back in. I put it on the coffee table in front of her.

"Careful, it's hot," I say, like she's a little kid.

She still doesn't raise her head from her hands. I take the cup back to the kitchen and put some cold water in, because I'm worried she's too distracted to listen to what I'm saying and she'll take a big mouthful and burn herself.

"Okay, I'm just going to say it," she says, when I put the cup down a second time.

"Good."

"On the count of three."

"Okay."

"Can you do the count?"

"One, two, three."

"That was too fast. I wasn't ready."

"One . . . two . . . three."

Lucy takes a huge breath in and lets it out. Her hands are shaking a little. "One more time."

"Luce. Come on." She's starting to scare me.

"Just do it one more time."

"One one thousand. Two one thousand. Three one thousand."

"Okay. Okay. Here it is. I lied about my score."

"You *what*?"

"You and Zach got such great marks, and I saw them, and I just . . . pretended I got that mark too."

The morning our results were announced, the three of us had our usual group chat. Zach posted his mark first, then I wrote mine, and now that I think about it, there was definitely a pause before Lucy posted hers. At the time it had seemed miraculous and yet completely right that we all got marks so close. We all worked so hard. We were all brought up to be overachievers. We studied together. It made sense. But maybe it didn't.

"Oh, Lucy."

"My score isn't even that bad! It's fine. Average, maybe. It just isn't amazing like yours. It wasn't good enough for law. Or anything at Melbourne Uni. I don't know why I lied. There's something wrong with me, probably."

"There's nothing wrong with you."

"Yes, there is."

"Lucy, did you get into anything?"

"Yes."

"Good."

"Teaching."

"Teaching?"

"Yes."

"Since when did you want to be a teacher?"

"When I got my marks, I added teaching to my course preferences because . . . because it was something I might get into, something I might be good at. I don't know. I don't know what I want to be."

"You always said you wanted to be a lawyer."

"That's what I said, yes."

"But it wasn't true?"

"I thought it was true. It's what my parents want. They are so mad at me right now. But I don't think I ever wanted to be a lawyer. Especially after I did work experience at that law firm. Do you know what a lawyer does all day? Reads really detailed, boring contracts, mostly, and sits in meetings and has conference calls. And they do this for, like, ten or twelve hours a day."

"That does sound boring." All office jobs sound boring, when you really think about it. I did work experience at the office of my local council, and people seemed to spend their time reading emails, complaining about emails, worrying about finding space in the fridge for their lunch, and getting excited about coffee.

"And you have to wear a suit. Suit jackets look ridiculous on me," Lucy continues. Neither of us has ever worn a suit jacket, not that I know of, but I nod anyway.

"It's because you've got very delicate shoulders."

"I like little kids. And I'm small, so I won't be intimidating to them."

"That's important," I say. I have exactly zero idea about what is important. When I first started school, every teacher looked like a giant to me.

"Oh god, I have no idea what I'm doing," Lucy says.

"I mean, we're young. We should have no idea what we want to do."

"Well, I'm going to study teaching now, so I hope I know."

"You do. You know. I'm the one who doesn't."

I hug her, and she whimpers a little into my shoulder. I feel slightly dizzy, trying to comprehend the fact that Lucy, who never lies, lied about this. That she is going to be a teacher. I had already planned the gift I was going to give her when she graduated as a lawyer. I had planned our futures around the idea that she would have much more money than me. I was going to be the creative one, the one struggling for money and living in the spare room of her beautiful house, and she was going to be the rich, cutthroat corporate sellout who paid for our taxis and takeaway food, and was secretly jealous of my artistic struggles. Now the picture looks different. Now she's going to inspire children and be deeply fulfilled, and I'll just be directionless and unemployable.

"I'm psycho. You'll never trust me again after this," she says.

I can feel her shaking. I want to hug her forever. "I still trust you," I say.

"You shouldn't."

"I'll always, always, always trust you."

"What if I keep lying? What if I can't stop?"

"Then we'll find a way to make you stop."

"I haven't told Zach."

"We'll tell him together."

"No, no, I have to do it on my own."

"We'll make a plan of how to do it. Look, I'll get a pen right now and we'll write down what you can say. We'll role-play it. You know I do a good Zach impression."

"He'll break up with me."

"Don't be ridiculous. He'll never break up with you. He loves you."

"I knew I had to tell you both. I was going to do it on New Year's Eve. But I couldn't."

"Lucy, it's okay. It's none of our business what score you got, anyway."

"Yes, it is. I *lied* to you. That is unforgivable."

"Lucy, everything is going to be fine. Drink your tea. You'll feel better."

Lucy holds the mug in her hands, half-heartedly raising it to her lips and pretending to drink, and I sit cross-legged on the floor in front of her, smiling encouragingly like I know how to fix everything.

29

SHINY HAPPY PARTY PEOPLE

I'm at a fluro party.

Alex is wearing a neon-yellow singlet and neon-yellow sunglasses and he's carrying a bright green water pistol and has neon-yellow zinc stripes over his cheeks. Most of the girls are wearing hyper-colored bikini tops, teeny-tiny denim shorts, and wild eye makeup, with colored hair spray and glitter and armfuls of fluro bracelets and glow-in-the-dark nail polish. Music is pumping, everyone looks drunk or high or overwhelmingly *bright*. It's basically a rave party in somebody's very expensive three-story house, and I'm perched on the couch self-consciously yanking up my mother's hot-pink exercise top (the closest thing I could find to something fluro in my house) to stop my bra from showing.

"Want me to zinc your face?" Alex asks, holding up a stick of orange sunscreen.

"Sure." I close my eyes and let him draw a stripe across each cheek. My skin will break out after this—it freaks out at unscented moisturizer, let alone thick, colored sludgy balm that has touched who knows how many other faces. This is the first concession I will make toward having fun tonight.

"And your arms?" he asks.

I hold them out and he writes a word down my left arm and then my right one.

I twist my head to look at them. On my left arm, GOOD. On my right arm, BAD. Lucy and I could spend weeks analyzing what this means. I almost text her, but decide not to, because I've been texting her nonstop since she left my house this afternoon, and I think she needs a little bit of space. (I think this because she texted me and said, *I appreciate you worrying about me, but I'm okay and I just need some space right now.*)

"Now me," Alex says, and I pause and then write LOVER and HATER on his arms.

"We should get tattoos like this," Alex says, squirting his water pistol at a guy walking past, who sticks his finger up without missing a beat.

I really hope he's joking about the tattoos.

I study Alex out of the corner of my eye. Maybe he's on something. I need to stand directly in front of him and see if his pupils are dilated. Is he sweating? Yes, but it's hot in here and pretty much everyone is sweating. Is his jaw moving strangely? I can't tell from this angle.

I'm not sure how I feel if he is. Mostly nervous, because if he's high, he won't be a very good safety net for me, and there's no way I am surviving this party without a safety net. The other party was a Beginners party, maybe an Intermediate. This one is Advanced. I'm not ready for Advanced. I'll never be ready for Advanced.

"Let's go upstairs," Alex says, and I follow him up a grand staircase. This is a rich person's home, which adds to my discomfort. The music is much louder on the next floor, and all the furniture has been pushed to the sides so the big space in the middle can be used as a dance floor. The floor is polished concrete, and a huge rug has been rolled up and propped on its end in the corner. That rug is probably worth thousands of dollars. Maybe tens of thousands. I feel anxious just looking at it. I want to drape a sheet over it.

People are shouting and jumping up and down in time to the music. The bass is turned up so loud you can hardly hear the music itself, just the deep, thrumming pounding, which is inside my chest immediately. One guy, covered in stripes of yellow zinc and pink glitter, is lying on the floor in the corner, banging his hands in time to the beat.

I am in my own personal rainbow-colored hell.

I wish Zach and Lucy were here.

"Let's dance," Alex says. His water pistol has a strap and it's hanging off his shoulder like he's some weird neon action hero.

The party was Alex's idea, obviously. He said we needed to celebrate me getting into uni, into my first preference. I said sure, imagining an evening picnic. Maybe he would make food. Buy me a bunch of flowers. Get me a journal for taking notes during class. Create a special Spotify playlist of celebratory songs. Go on a long drive down the coast and stand on a cliff together, talking about our futures and looking at the sunset. In the space of about ten seconds, I had quite a romantic fantasy going.

Instead, he'd said, "Come to my friend's party, we'll have fun." I said, "Okay, sure, sounds good," which means, *I absolutely don't want to and I am annoyed you are even suggesting it*. He doesn't know me well enough to read that subtext.

Then he said it's a fluro party, as if that would mean something to me. I laughed, and then I panicked and googled "fluro party" and then I pulled every single piece of clothing out of my wardrobe and onto the floor in a state of near hysteria. I wanted to call Lucy and beg her for help, but at that point she had already asked me for space and her crisis felt a little bigger than mine.

And now here we are. Alex keeps introducing me to people, and I keep smiling and nodding and struggling to think of things to say. Alex is in a strange mood. He seems buoyant and happy in a false way, like he's trying too hard. I thought going to a party with him would be easier than going to one alone, but it turns out it's much harder, because now everything I do feels like it's a reflection on him.

My face must be betraying my anxiety, because Alex takes a step closer and tucks a strand of my hair behind my ear.

"It's not really dancing. It's jumping. It's fun, trust me."

Oh, jumping. Cool. We large-breasted girls love jumping.

There are neon-yellow and green jelly shots on a platter, and Alex sucks down two in a row before heading to the heaving mass of jumping bodies. I hover over the jelly shots before also grabbing one and sucking it down. It tastes like jelly with a burn. It's much better than actually drinking alcohol, at least. It might be the only good thing about this party. That, and the cupcakes with fluro icing I saw downstairs.

I'm ignoring the fact that my ears are already ringing from the music, and now that I'm in the crush of bodies, I feel overwhelmingly claustrophobic. The sound of the music gets into my mouth and rattles my teeth.

This is fun, this is fun, this is fun, this is fun.
This is how people have fun.

I jump in time to the beat and close my eyes, which gives me a not entirely awful out-of-body-and-time experience, and for a moment I understand the appeal of letting your body go and thinking of absolutely nothing. The jelly shot is helping.

I bump into someone who is very, very sweaty. Their sweat is on me now. That's okay, I can handle that. Everything is hot and sticky in this room. I can feel the zinc running down my face. I probably have sweat marks on my top. I need to get to a bathroom and reapply my concealer at some point.

Someone puts their hands on my waist from behind, and I know it's not Alex because I can see him in front of me, bopping around, grinning, spraying people with his water gun, having the time of his life. I twist around and try to see who is holding me, but before I can, the person is lifting me in the air, up and down, like I weigh nothing. (I do not weigh nothing.)

I wriggle free, turning to see that it's Owen Sinclair.

"*Wooooooo!*" he yells, waving his hands in the air. His eyes are wobbly and unfocused, and his hair is slick with sweat. This is the most unattractive he's ever looked.

I am filled with a deep sense that I do not want to be here. I definitely do not want Owen Sinclair lifting me up and down like I'm a toy.

Then Alex appears.

"Are you okay?" he mouths—the music is too loud to hear words properly.

"Not really," I mouth back.

Alex leans closer to me. "What's wrong?"

I want to calmly give him a clear and detailed explanation of how I'm feeling, but that's not quite what happens.

"I hate this!" I shout.

"What?"

"This whole thing."

I wave my hands vaguely and take a second to glare at Owen Sinclair, who gives me a thumbs-up in return.

"What happened?" Alex says.

My heart is racing, and I feel like I might cry, which would give me a 100 percent cry rate at parties.

"I'm leaving," I say in return. I walk down the stairs and out into the backyard. I find a chair to sit on and take in big gulps of air. My heart is still going a million miles an hour. Maybe it was the jelly shot. Maybe my body is having a reaction to alcohol.

I hunch over, close my eyes, and count to ten—one-two-three-four-five-six-seven-eight-nine-ten—and I feel a bit better, so I do it again. One-two-three-four—

"What's going on?" Alex says, squatting next to me.

I open my eyes. "I shouldn't have come," I say.

"Why not?"

"Because I knew it would be like this."

"Like what?" He looks impatient.

"Like this. All these awful people. I hate everyone here." I don't even care that they're his friends.

"I shouldn't have invited you," Alex says, in a tone that pisses me off.

"No, you shouldn't have. I thought this was supposed to be about celebrating me getting into uni."

"I thought it would be fun for both of us," he says.

"Well, haven't you heard, I'm not a fun person."

"Natalie." He sounds tired. Like I'm an exhausting, annoying toddler that he has to babysit.

"Don't treat me like I'm a burden," I say. My panic from before has turned into a hot anger.

"Don't treat me like I'm torturing you!" he says, standing up.

"Well, I hate every second of being here," I say. I stand up as well, because I don't like the feeling of him looking down at me.

"Then go," Alex says.

"Maybe this whole thing is a mistake," I say, because I'm not finished being angry.

"Maybe it is," he says.

"By 'whole thing,' I mean us. Being together." There I am, being like Dad, unable to stop myself from hammering the point home.

"I know what you mean," Alex says.

We are staring at each other, both of us breathing hard. Arguing with my parents, or even with Zach and Lucy, I know what direction they'll go in, what they're likely to say, the buttons they'll push, the zigs and zags they'll take. But Alex is different. The ways I am vulnerable are different, and I can't predict what he might say.

Also, even now, even when I'm super-mad at him, I find him attractive. Which makes me even madder.

I turn and start walking away.

"Wait," he says, and I'll give him credit for saying that, because it's vitally important to my sense of self that when I storm away from a boy I like, he says, "Wait."

"No," I say, not turning around, which is what I always pictured myself doing in this scenario, and I'm proud of myself for not even looking over my shoulder.

30

MELTDOWN

I am holding my phone in my hand, about to call an Uber—on the verge of tears but too angry to be upset (that stage will come later, when I'm safe in bed)—when Lucy's name pops up on my screen, calling me. Thank god. She's exactly the person I need to talk to.

"Natalie." Her voice is wobbly. It sounds strange.

"Luce?"

"Can you come and get me?" She's drunk. She's slurring almost every word. I've seen Lucy drunk before, but the way she sounds now—it sends a little cold shiver down my spine.

"Where are you?"

"I don't know."

"Are you with Zach? Where's Zach?"

"I was with him. But I don't know where he is now." She gives a small, pitiful sob. "Please, come and get me."

"I will."

"Please. I need you!"

"I will, Lucy. Just tell me where you are and what's going on."

"I don't know where I am." (Snuffling crying noises.)

"Can you go to Google Maps on your phone and see your current location?"

"No!" (Tearful hiccup.)

"Lucy, please just do this one thing. The app is right there on your home screen. Just the suburb, even."

"All right, all right."

There's the sound of scrabbling around. A long silence. A clattering sound and some swearing. Then more silence. Finally, Lucy is back on the phone.

"Brunswick."

"Okay, good. That's a great start."

"Please come and get me." Every word is stretched a little bit too long.

"Where in Brunswick?"

"On a street."

"You need to give me a bit more."

"Come and get me, please!" She's yelling now, and I'm so panicked I almost drop the phone, but then she starts laughing.

"What's so funny?"

"I've lost my shoes!"

"Okay, I'm coming. Lucy, I'm hanging up, but I'll call you back soon, okay?"

"I found my shoes!"

"Great. Lucy? When you see me calling you, answer, okay?"

"I love you."

"I love you too."

I hang up and call Zach. It goes straight to voice mail. I call twice more, to be sure. I think about calling my mum, but it feels like a betrayal of Lucy to let a parent see her in this state. I'll have to get a cab or an Uber, but I might need to drive around the streets looking for her. I cringe at the thought of how expensive it could get.

I'm walking through the front yard of the fluro party house, deep in thought, and don't notice until it's too late that I'm about to walk into someone. I slam into their back, getting a mouthful of shiny black hair.

"Ow." The person turns around and it's Vanessa. Of course it's Vanessa.

"Sorry, sorry." I duck my head and keep going. I must look distraught, because Vanessa walks beside me as I hurry on.

"Hey, are you okay?"

"Yes. I'm fine."

"I know you," she says.

"No, you don't."

"Yeah, I do. You're Alex's new girlfriend."

Now I look at her. "Who told you that?"

She grins at me. "Oh, everyone's talking about it."

I feel like my eyes might bug out of my head. "Everyone?"

"Well, okay, not *everyone*. A few people. I'm his ex. People like to keep me informed."

"Well, their information is not accurate."

"Where are you going in such a hurry?"

"Brunswick."

"Need a lift?"

I look at her, to see if she's being serious. "Can you drive?"

"I wouldn't be offering if I couldn't."

"No, I mean, have you been drinking?"

"Not a drop. I don't drink."

"What, at all?"

"Not at the moment."

"Do you take . . . anything else?"

"I am currently one hundred percent sober in every way and offering you a ride to Brunswick. Take it or leave it."

I have a million anxieties about being in an enclosed space

with Vanessa, but my desire to get to Lucy as fast as possible overrides all of them.

"Yes. I'll take it. Thank you."

She smiles. "Great. This party sucks and I was so ready to leave. Owen is off his head and I can't stand to be around him a second longer."

Every negative thought I might have ever had about Vanessa evaporates in that moment.

She's wearing a neon-colored flower crown, hot-pink lipstick, and a white dress that is breathtakingly short, almost see-through, and I want to buy one immediately even though I would never wear it.

I follow her as she walks toward an old station wagon.

"Do you need to tell anyone you're leaving?" I say.

"Nope."

She unlocks the door and I get into the passenger seat. Her car is messy, really messy, but she doesn't seem to care.

"Just push all that stuff out of your way," she says. I lift clothes, papers, and a bike helmet and put them on the backseat. There is dog hair all over everything.

"My dog sheds. A lot. Hope you're not allergic."

"No, all good."

She has a dog. She is everything I have ever dreamed of being. I am one step away from wanting to steal her identity.

As we pull away, I see Alex out of the corner of my eye, on the street, watching us drive away, his zinc-smeared face looking confused.

My phone starts ringing and his name flashes on my screen. I don't answer, and seconds later a text appears.

—Did I just see you in Vanessa's car??????

It's thrilling to not reply and leave him wondering. I am a woman of mystery—he cannot fathom my layers.

"Where are we going?" Vanessa asks.

"Brunswick."

"I know, but where in Brunswick?"

"I don't know yet. A street in Brunswick."

She gives me a look I pretend not to see. I dial Lucy's number, but it rings out. "Shit."

"What?"

"She's not answering."

"Who are we talking about?"

"Lucy. My friend. She called me, really drunk, and asked me to come get her. I know she's somewhere in Brunswick, but that's it."

"Don't worry, finding drunk people is my specialty."

Vanessa is a very calming presence, I decide.

"She's probably in a pub or something and it's really loud," Vanessa continues.

"She was outside when I spoke to her before."

"We'll find her."

"What if she's passed out somewhere?"

"We'll find her," she says again. Her voice is firm. I believe her.

I call Lucy again and again. She doesn't answer, and I try to stay calm. Her phone is always on silent, she probably hasn't even noticed it ringing.

"So, where's Alex?" Vanessa asks.

"Back at the party."

"I mean, why isn't he with us?"

She's playing the role of my knight in shining armor tonight, so the least I can do is give her some gossip on her ex. "We had a fight."

"A bad one?"

"Pretty bad."

"Breakup bad?"

I look at her. My trust in her is suddenly wavering. I have no idea if Alex and I have broken up. Possibly. Probably. The word *breakup* might not be applicable if the words *boyfriend* and *girlfriend* haven't yet been spoken. Whatever is a step down from breakup could be what's happened. No longer seeing each other. Ending things. Stopping contact. Withdrawing one's affections. Calling time.

"Don't make that face at me. I'm not trying to steal him back," she says.

"Why did you and Alex break up?" I ask. I know I shouldn't. I'm breaking a rule. I haven't even asked Alex this question, and I'm trying to get the story from his ex.

"Oh, lots of reasons. I had a really hard time in years eleven and twelve. I went off the rails a bit, and I would push him away and then expect him to pick up the pieces when I did stupid things. We broke up and got back together so many times. And we were never going to survive once we finished school."

She sounds more experienced at life than I'll be at thirty.

"But you still hang out all the time."

"We've been hanging out a bit this summer, because everyone has regressed to our high school group. But we didn't see each other for months this year."

"Do you miss him?"

"Sometimes. Yeah." She shrugs.

We sit in silence. I want to ask about the cheating. I need to ask about the cheating. I shouldn't ask about the cheating. The cheating is none of my business.

"Did Alex cheat on you?" I say, rushing the words out of my mouth so fast I am worried she won't understand me.

But Vanessa turns her head as soon as I say it, and the car veers a little.

"Who told you that?" she says, sounding surprised.

"He did."

"*Alex* told you that?"

"Well, Alex confirmed it, after his brother told me."

"Huh. Yes, he did cheat on me."

She pauses, changes lanes, curses a little under her breath at another car, and I wait.

"But look. It was one kiss at a party, after a fight when I told him . . . when I said some pretty terrible things to him. Alex isn't perfect, that's for sure, but I wouldn't want the cheating thing to be the only takeaway from our relationship."

"What else should I know?"

"This is a weird conversation."

"Agreed. But what else should I know?"

"Okay, he's a good listener. He'll always respect your opinion. And look after you if you drink too much. He's fun. He's kind. Even with the cheating thing, which broke my heart at the time, I think he's a good person," she says.

"A good person and a good boyfriend are different things, though."

"Yes," she says.

We look at each other.

"I probably shouldn't have told you all of that," she says.

"I shouldn't have asked."

"Let's agree that this conversation is in the vault."

"For sure."

It takes about fifteen minutes to get to Brunswick and we're almost there when I call Lucy again, and finally, finally, she answers.

"Lucy." I am so relieved she is alive, I could cry.

"Natalie." She sounds like she *is* crying.

"What's wrong? Are you okay?"

"I threw up. In the gutter."

"I'll be there soon. Where are you?"

"I want to go home."

"I'm coming to take you home."

"Hurry."

"Tell me what street you are on."

"I can't."

"Yes, you can."

"It's too dark. I can't see anything. I'm all alone."

"Just walk to the nearest street sign and tell me what it says."

"I can't. I can't! I'm lying down. On the grass. I can't get up."

"Yes, you can. I know you can."

There's a long silence when I can hear nothing but her breathing, loud and rattling and uneven, and then she says, "Wilson Street."

"Great! Stay there. Don't move."

"I'm going to hide behind a car."

"Okay, do that. Stay on the phone."

"I can't, I can't." She sounds near-hysterical.

"Okay. Don't worry. We'll be there soon."

She hangs up then, and Vanessa looks at me.

"She's on Wilson Street," I say.

"Great."

I don't mention the throwing up, because I need Vanessa to let Lucy in her car.

I call Zach again, but there's nothing but his voice mail. I leave a very short message, telling him to meet me at my house. I don't think I've ever left a voice mail message for Zach before. No one I know even listens to their voice mail, but I figure I should do it in this case.

We turn onto Wilson Street and I call Lucy, but her phone is dead now and goes to voice mail.

Vanessa slows to a crawl and I roll down my window.

"Lucy," I shout out the window at every car.

"Oh, everyone who lives on this street is going to love us," Vanessa says, as I shout at three or four more cars.

"Natalie!" Lucy's head appears from behind a red Astra. Her makeup is smeared and she looks disheveled.

Vanessa brakes, and I throw open the door and leap out of the car before it has completely stopped. I run to Lucy, and she immediately starts crying and lies down on the footpath. Her feet are bare.

"I feel so horrible," she says. Tears are sliding down her cheeks.

I stroke her hair. "Can you stand up?"

"No."

"Come on. Get in the car and we'll take you home."

"I can't go home."

"My house, then. Or Zach's."

She makes an anguished little noise at the sound of Zach's name.

"Where is Zach?" I ask her.

"I don't know. We had a fight."

"Alex and I had a fight too."

"And you and Zach are fighting. And Mum and I are fighting. And your parents are divorcing. Everyone in the world is fighting. I want to die."

More tears.

"*We're* not fighting, though," I say, patting her head.

Vanessa appears beside us and squats down.

"Hi Lucy, I'm Vanessa." She is using the same kind of voice I would use when introducing myself to a toddler.

"I'm not going to be a lawyer," Lucy says in response to this introduction, and then she turns her head and retches a little.

I can't look at Vanessa, in case she says that Lucy can't be put in her car.

"Lucy, can you stand up?" Vanessa asks, now using a firm, no-nonsense voice.

"No, no, no, no," Lucy says in response, rolling her head from side to side.

I lean down, take hold of her arms, and try to haul her up, but she yelps and flops back onto the ground.

"Let's carry her," Vanessa says. "She's pretty small. You take her shoulders, I'll grab her legs."

"No, no, no, no," Lucy moans again, as we attempt to lift her. I cradle her head and shoulders as best I can, but her bum drags along the ground as we start moving.

"She's dragging," I pant.

"She'll be fine," Vanessa says, trying to get a better grip on Lucy's legs.

This must be what it feels like to move a dead body. Vanessa would be a pretty good partner-in-crime. Maybe she has moved a dead body before. Maybe she and Alex accidentally killed someone and they had to hide the evidence, and now—

We hit the gutter and Lucy yelps as her bum whacks on the concrete.

"Lift, lift, lift," Vanessa says, hauling Lucy's legs higher. I grit my teeth and hold her shoulders up as high as I can as we stagger-walk her to the car.

Vanessa puts Lucy's legs on the ground, opens the back door, picks them up again, and we haul her up and stuff her in as gently as we can. Vanessa goes to her trunk, grabs a bucket, and shoves it into my hands. (Who has a bucket in their car? Vanessa must really be experienced with transporting drunk friends.)

"Sit with her in the back and if she pukes, make sure she pukes in that."

I really, really don't want to, but I recognize this as my Best Friend Duty.

Vanessa gets in the driver's seat and turns around to Lucy. "You'll be home soon, you poor thing." The compassion in Vanessa's eyes shames me, because I'm sitting as far from Lucy as I can and leaning over to hold the bucket in her vicinity. I shuffle across into the middle, and let Lucy snuggle up against me. I stroke her hair and she leans her head over the bucket, muttering to herself and weeping. "I'm so stupid. I'm so stupid."

"Shhhhhh," I say. Her hair is damp at the sides from all the tears.

"Teachers aren't supposed to get drunk like this," she cries.

"You're not a teacher yet, and I'm sure teachers get drunk all the time," I say.

"I want to be an inspiration," Lucy says, and then she throws up into the bucket.

31

SHOW ME YOUR WOUNDS

"Look who's here," Vanessa says, as she pulls up to my house.

Lucy has fallen asleep in my lap, and I shift her head a little to turn and look out the window.

Zach and Alex are sitting on the porch steps, side by side. On any other night, the sight of the two of them waiting for me would warm my heart. Tonight, it makes me tired. I don't have the energy for either of them.

"Oh god," I say.

"Well, you can't hide. They've seen us," says Vanessa.

They are looking at us, their faces upturned at the same angle. In the shine of Vanessa's headlights, they look so similar: that hair, those eyebrows, Zach's face a softer, clean-shaven mirror of Alex's.

"Is your mum home?" Vanessa asks.

"She's out." I suspect she's on a date with Eric and not telling me. *My mother might be on a date.* Those words will never not sound weird to me.

Zach stands up and walks toward the car, leaving Alex on

the porch steps. Vanessa gets out and folds her arms like a security guard.

"Wait," she says, as Zach gets closer. She holds up a hand.

"Where's Lucy?" he says.

"In the car. But wait. Are you here to help, or to upset her further?" Vanessa asks.

Vanessa is like a superhero. It's the three of us against the world.

Zach shakes his head.

"I'm not going to upset anyone. I just want to see her."

He pokes his head in the car window. Lucy nestles her head farther into my lap.

"Natalie."

"Zachary."

We stare at each other for a moment. I lean down and pick up the vomit bucket, and I hand it to him.

"Gross," he says.

"Can you empty it and rinse it out with the hose so I can give it back to Vanessa?"

"What about Lucy?"

"Then we'll get her out."

He reaches his hand in and touches Lucy's shoulder for a second, his face tender. Then he walks into my front yard and tips out the bucket and looks around for the hose, while Vanessa leans against the car and Alex remains sitting on the porch. It's too dark to see Alex's face, except for the glow of the zinc that is still all over his cheeks.

Zach comes back with the bucket and hands it to Vanessa, who throws it into the passenger seat of her car. She really is very relaxed about mess.

Zach sticks his head back into the backseat. "Now what?"

he asks. He seems to have accepted that Vanessa and I are in charge of the situation.

"Now we get her inside," I say.

Lucy is awake, or sort of awake. I saw her eyes flutter open and then shut again, and I can feel some tension in her body, but she's pretending to still be asleep as Zach, Vanessa, and I maneuver her out of the car.

"We have to carry her," I say. Vanessa and I line up to take a leg each, but Zach scoops Lucy up in his arms in one quick movement.

"You're okay," Zach whispers to her, kissing her forehead, and it feels so intimate that I look away. Zach carries her toward my front door.

Alex stands up, looking alarmed. "Is she okay?" he asks.

"She's fine," I say.

"Why are you carrying her?" Alex says to Zach.

"She's tired. And drunk. And a little bit sick." I keep answering the questions even though Alex is asking Zach.

I unlock the front door, and Zach goes in first with Lucy, followed by Vanessa. Alex hesitates at the door, glancing at me, waiting until I give him a small nod, then walks through. He's still holding his water pistol.

Zach has put Lucy down on my bed, and we all stand around her. She looks like a little drunk angel curled on her side, and I think she has properly fallen asleep, because she is making small snoring noises. I pull my blanket over her, feeling very motherly.

Zach walks into the lounge room, and Vanessa and Alex follow him, and suddenly I'm hosting a very awkward gathering.

"Would you like something to drink?" I say. I'm mostly speaking to Vanessa, since I'm still possibly fighting with both Alex and Zach, but no one answers me anyway. I go into the kitchen and they all follow.

"I have, um, water?" I say, staring into our fridge, which has three cartons of expired milk and nothing else, because Mum keeps forgetting that Dad was the one who drank all the milk and we don't need as much anymore. I can feel all three of them behind me, silently judging the contents of our fridge, so I shut it and usher them back into the lounge room.

"What about tea? I'll make everyone a cup of tea," I say, because I need to fill the silence and also have something to do. Probably I should kick them all out. I don't even know how Alex and Zach got here, or what they're planning to do now.

I know how Zach drinks his tea, and Vanessa requests a green tea. Alex says nothing. I have no idea of his tea preference, and I don't want to ask him, because I don't want Vanessa and Zach to know that I don't know. (It feels important somehow, this basic fact about each other—*of course* we weren't going to work out if we didn't even know how to make each other a cup of tea.)

So I just bring Alex a cup of white tea in a mug. He says thanks, and sips it, and I suspect he does not like tea at all, but I appreciate he's also hiding how little we know about each other from the others.

Then I rummage in the cupboards until I find Mum's emergency chocolate, and I snap the block into little squares. Zach grabs piece after piece. He doesn't even like fruit and nut chocolate. He's stress-eating.

"What happened?" I ask him.

"Lucy and I went out to a friend's house—"

"Which friend?"

"Braydon."

"I hate Braydon," I say. Braydon is one of those people who says *just to play devil's advocate* when he really means *just to be an asshole.*

"I know."

"Why would you take her to Braydon's when she's feeling vulnerable?" I ask. Vanessa raises her eyebrows, and Alex continues to make a show of drinking his tea.

"In hindsight, it was a mistake," Zach says, grabbing another piece of chocolate.

"And what happened?" I ask.

"She got really drunk and we had a fight."

"She told you about the . . . the thing?" I say, not wanting to expose Lucy's secret in front of Alex and Vanessa.

"Yes."

"Were you mad?"

"No! Sort of. I don't know." He rubs a hand over his face.

"Why was your phone dead?" I feel irrationally angry about this.

"Because I lost my charger."

"How do you lose a charger?"

"Why are you acting like I'm the bad guy?" Zach says.

"Because you are!"

"Right. Everything is my fault."

"Not everything. But some things. Most things, actually."

"That's not fair."

I can see Vanessa and Alex exchanging uncomfortable this-is-awkward looks, but I don't care.

"Why were you fighting?" I ask.

"Because."

"Because why?"

Zach doesn't answer.

"Because Zach has something else to tell you," Alex says.

"What do you mean?"

Zach glares at Alex, and then he turns to me. "What I haven't told you yet is that as well as getting into science at

Melbourne, I got an offer from interstate. Medicine at the University of Adelaide."

"Oh my god. Oh my god. You got into medicine? Zach! This is huge."

"I know. I think I'm going to take it."

"Of course you should take it."

"But I'll have to move to Adelaide."

"I didn't even know you had applied to Adelaide." I feel like crying, suddenly. *We were all supposed to go to uni together,* I want to scream. *What about The Plan?* First my parents, then Lucy, now Zach. I want a ban on all secrets going forward. Everyone has to sign a contract stating they'll clear every decision with me for the rest of their lives, and I don't even care if that makes me sound like a dictator, because it's a small price to pay to be in control of everyone and everything.

"I told you I applied all over the country. But I didn't think I would get in anywhere," Zach says.

"But you did." I am so happy for him, and so furious at him.

"But I did."

"I think I should leave," Vanessa says suddenly.

"Me too," Alex says, but he looks at me as he says it, with a question in his eyes.

"You should," I say, because I'm still mad at him. Or, I still want him to think I am mad at him.

"Do you want a lift home?" Vanessa says to Alex, and then she looks at me, uncertain, regretful, and mouths, *Is that okay?* I nod.

Alex hesitates and looks at me again. He came here and sat on my veranda and waited for me. He must have something to say to me. If he leaves, in this moment, it feels like it will be the end of us.

"Are you sure you want me to go?" he says. I have the urge to get a tissue and wipe all the zinc off his face.

No, I am not sure. I want you to stay. Here. In my bed. I want you to do that nice thing where you stroke my arm again, and I want you to apologize first.

"Yes," I say, because if there is one thing I know for certain about myself, it is my unfailing ability to ruin my own happiness.

I walk them both to the door. I feel like I should hug Vanessa, even though I'm not a hugger, because we've been through a lot tonight, but if I hug her, I might have to hug Alex as well.

I will cry if I hug him.

"Thank you," I say to Vanessa.

"That's okay," she says.

We smile at each other, and I kind of half pat her shoulder, which is weird, but she seems to accept it as a gesture of thanks.

She walks out to her car and gets in, and leaves Alex and me alone together on the doorstep.

"What did you come here for?" I ask him. We're standing close to one another.

"To check that you got home okay," he says, looking at his feet and then up at me. I meet his eyes for a second before looking away.

"Well, I did," I say.

He starts to say something else, but stops, and turns like he's going to walk away. Then he turns back.

"I told my parents today. About losing my job," he says quietly.

"How did they take it?" I say.

"They were okay. Sort of. On the surface supportive, but underneath I think they're panicking. Zach is going to be a doctor, and their firstborn is a failure and all that."

"You're not a failure," I say. I really do want to hug him, but I don't. I lean a little toward him, but he's not looking at me, and I think he might be fighting back tears.

He fiddles with the water pistol for a second, and takes a deep breath. "'Bye," he says, and starts to walk away, and maybe he wants me to yell, *Wait,* after him, but I don't, because being the person who yells wait is vulnerable and desperate in a way I can't afford to be, ever, even if it ruins everything.

It hurts more than I thought it would, watching him walk toward Vanessa's car. Probably they're going to have a big deep and meaningful conversation now, and all their old feelings will resurface, and it will all be my own fault, and I can't even think about that.

Alex gets in the passenger side without hesitating, and that hurts too, because even though I refuse to run after him, I thought maybe he would run back to me and make a big romantic declaration. I want him to roll down the window and shout, *I'm in love with you.* (No, I don't, a public I-love-you at high volume would be mortifying.)

Instead, there's nothing, and I have no idea what to do.

32

A LIKABLE FACE

When I walk back to the lounge room, Zach isn't there. I look in at my bedroom and see him curled up beside Lucy. His eyes are open, and we stare at each other for a few seconds.

"You should have told us you were applying interstate," I whisper, so as not to wake Lucy, who is definitely snoring now and looks so firmly asleep she probably wouldn't wake up if I blared a horn in her ear.

"I *did* tell you," Zach says, at almost normal volume.

Lucy doesn't stir.

"But you implied that you had no chance, that you didn't have the right marks. You never made it seem like something that would ever actually happen."

"Well, that's what I thought. Anyway, *you* should have told me about Alex," he says.

"Not the same."

"How is it not the same?"

"The Alex thing just happened. I didn't plan it. I didn't even have *time* to tell you."

"And I didn't think I would get into medicine anywhere. I didn't want to think about it because I knew if I got in, I probably wouldn't go because it would be too hard to leave Lucy. And you. And my family."

"But you are leaving," I say, and I sit down on the end of the bed.

"Yes. I think so. I am."

"So it's not that hard, after all." I can't resist the urge to be mean.

"That's not fair." He closes his eyes.

I sigh. "You're right. I take it back." I crawl up the bed and squeeze next to him, staring at the ceiling.

"I'm proud of you," I say eventually.

"Thank you."

"Leaving is brave."

"It's scary."

"But exciting."

"It feels like I'm choosing a career over my relationship and friendships and family. I don't even know if I want to be a doctor enough to give up all the things I have here."

"We're not going anywhere."

"It won't be the same. Especially for me and Lucy. What are we going to do, be in a long-distance relationship for *six years*?"

"Well, it's only an hour-and-a-half flight, you could see each other every month, maybe even more than that, and on holidays . . ." It's my job to show Zach how this can work, even though in my heart of hearts I'm not sure it can.

"And we just keep doing that for years on end?" he says.

"Maybe Lucy could transfer to a uni in Adelaide."

"I don't want her to have to do that. I don't want to hold her back from her life here. We can't live in limbo for years."

"Well . . ." I don't know any more options. "It might not work out, then." I feel sick, like I am betraying both of them by saying it out loud.

"I don't want to break up with her. Ever," he says.

"But you want to be a doctor."

"Yeah."

"And you've accepted the offer, haven't you?"

"Yes."

"Then you've made your decision."

"I don't know if it's the right thing to do."

"It is," I say.

"How do you know?"

"Because it's what you want."

He looks at me, and I elbow him gently. "We'll survive without you," I say.

"How could you possibly survive without me?"

"We'll carry a cardboard cutout of your face around with us."

"And get tattoos of my name."

"Of course."

He sighs and puts both hands over his face. I think for a second he's crying, but then he takes them away and looks at me, and he's dry-eyed.

"I thought Lucy and I would move in together in a couple of years. Like, when we were twenty. And then I thought we'd run off and get married when we were, like, twenty-two or twenty-three, and everyone would think we were reckless for getting married so young, but we'd be happy, and we'd travel the world, and have all these adventures together."

"I kind of thought that would happen too. Except in my version, I'm part of your wedding, and your roommate, and I'm having adventures with you both."

"Oh yeah, you're there in my version of this. You're our witness when we get married, and we need you to live in our spare bedroom to help pay the rent."

In Zach's mind, I'm in the supporting role of the movie of his life, which makes sense from his point of view, but it only occurs to me in this moment that I've also cast myself in the role. I'm not even the lead of my own movie.

"You and Lucy might still get married one day. We might still all travel together and live together."

"Maybe," he says, and suddenly I feel very sure that it won't happen like that, that Zach and Lucy's story is ending, not beginning, and that the movie of our lives is going to be about something else entirely.

We lie in silence for a little while, listening to Lucy's snuffling snores.

"I'm sorry," I say, breaking the silence. "I should have told you about Alex as soon as it happened. But I didn't know what was going on. I still don't, really."

"What's going on is he likes you."

"I don't know why."

"Don't fish for compliments."

"I'm not."

"You're always at our house, so it was bound to happen."

"Oh god, that's it, isn't it? I was there and it was convenient."

"I meant, he was bound to notice how smart, funny, and interesting you are. Yes, *interesting*. You need to stop second-guessing people and thinking the worst."

"I don't think the worst."

"Yes, you do."

"Well, so do you. The whole fuss you made over Alex and me getting together was based on you thinking the worst."

"That's true. But I don't think the worst of you. Or Lucy."

"Maybe not, but you did yell at me."

"I'm sorry for that. I was completely overreacting." Zach turns on his side to look at me as he says this. His expression changes to what I think of as his serious listening face. "So you and Alex had a fight."

"Yes. A bad one."

"He wouldn't tell me much, but I got the gist."

"You two are talking now?"

"I apologized to him."

"Wow. This is a big day for you. I don't think I've ever seen you say sorry to him before."

"Well, I'm not normally wrong."

"Zachary Russo: the Boy Who Is Never Wrong."

"I'm obnoxious. I know. Lucy told me that many times after the movie."

"Why were you being *so* obnoxious about this, though?"

"I don't know. I just felt really angry. Like Alex was stealing you from me. No, *stealing* is the wrong word. That's gross. I don't own you. God, I'm saying this all wrong. I just . . . I don't trust him to be the kind of guy that's right for you."

"What kind of guy is that?"

"Someone who gets your jokes, and knows you hate really loud music, and that you want every text message to have an emoji in it. Someone who will recommend great books, and listen to your fan theories, and bring you cups of tea when you're stressed out."

Everything he just listed is the stuff he and Lucy do for me. "What I want in a guy is . . . well, I don't quite know yet, I'm still figuring it out, which is the point. You can't know who is right or wrong for me if I don't know."

I don't know how to put into words what it is I like about Alex. Part of it is something that feels too shameful to say: that Alex makes me feel special, wanted, desired, *seen* for the first time in my life. Which is problematic, because I'm supposed to love and accept myself without the help of anyone else. I know that, I have absorbed that message via every possible channel. Alex can't be the hero who saves me from my low self-esteem. It goes against every feminist narrative I've ever read, every lesson I learned at my progressive all-girls school, every positive, healthy, empowering message I've ever seen someone share on Instagram. *A woman saves herself. Be the hero of your own story. Be Katniss, not Bella.* Even though I always related to Bella's angst more than Katniss's trauma.

But when people say you've got to love yourself first, they never explain how, exactly, you get past people screaming, "Gross bitch," how you get past feeling like your best days are only your best days because you're managing to hide the bad bits, how you feel desirable if no one has ever desired you.

It's something I haven't managed to figure out on my own, and Alex makes me feel like I'm a little bit closer.

Also, he has great hair.

"Look, I'm sorry. I suck," Zach says.

"I accept your apology," I say. I stopped being mad at him at least fifteen minutes ago.

"I think I was jealous, in a weird way," Zach says. "You're supposed to be *my* friend, not his, and all that."

"Well, I'm sorry too. For not caring enough about your feelings."

"Arguing with you is one of my favorite things, but fighting with you is one of the very worst," he says.

"Let's argue forever and never fight again," I say, and we smile at each other. He turns back to look at the ceiling.

We lie there and listen to Lucy snoring.

"You should tell Alex," Zach says after a while.

"Tell him what?"

"Whatever it is you are feeling. Whatever it is you want from him."

"I don't know what I feel or what I want."

"Yes, you do."

"No, I don't."

"Natalie, you know exactly what you want, all the time, but you hide it under all these layers of bullshit, and you make it impossible for anyone else to figure out."

"No, I don't."

"You're doing it right now."

"No, I'm not." Okay, yes, I am, but he's making something very complicated sound very simple, and I resent that.

"Just go to Alex and be honest with him."

"I'll try."

"Don't try, just do."

"Okay, I'll do."

"Also . . ." Zach says.

"What?"

"Also, I just wanted to say that I'm scared about leaving, I'm really scared."

"Don't be scared. You're going to do so great, wherever you are. You have a very likable face."

"That's what you've always said."

"It's true. Plus, you'll have us, no matter what."

"I know."

I close my eyes and start drifting into sleep. In this moment, I can believe the three of us will be friends forever, even though Zach is going away and I don't know if he and Lucy will stay together, and if they don't stay together, then I don't know if the friendship can survive their breakup, and it feels like we're on the precipice of so much change that it seems impossible we'll all hold ourselves together as we are now.

Lucy, suddenly, sits up, groaning. "I feel awful," she says, squinting at us groggily.

"Shhhh. Lie back down," Zach says.

"Where am I?" she asks.

"In Natalie's bed. You're with us," Zach says.

"Both of us," I say.

"Good, good," Lucy says, lying down again, closing her eyes, and falling straight back to sleep.

33

BERT AND ERNIE

I knock on the door, feeling oddly formal. I've never been inside Alex's bedroom. I've walked past it countless times, I've looked into it, I've avoided looking into it, and I've mostly not thought about it until now, this very moment, when it feels like the scariest place in the world.

"Who is it?" Alex sounds gruff.

"Me."

He doesn't answer.

"Natalie," I say, as the door opens.

"I know who 'me' is," he says. He looks sleepy and rumpled, like I've just woken him.

"Can we talk?" I say.

He nods and takes a step back and I walk into the room. I can't make any small talk because I've been rehearsing what I'm going to say to Alex in my head all morning, and if I say anything else, I'll forget the stuff I need to say.

"How's Lucy?" he asks, leaning against his desk.

"She's good," I say, hovering near the door. This isn't true.

She's hungover, still fighting with her parents, and her future with Zach is looking very shaky.

"That's good."

I take a step forward and stand in the middle of his room. It's surprisingly less messy than mine; in fact, it's hardly messy at all. It's clean and organized, and he didn't even know I was coming over. Which means I need to completely reevaluate everything I think about us both as individuals and if we are a couple. Maybe he's the Bert and I'm actually the Ernie.

He's looking at me expectantly.

"Okay, so, what I wanted to say is . . . about us . . . is that we should . . ."

Not even a sentence in, and I'm prattling nonsensically. The monologue I had in my head pops like a bubble, gone in seconds. Alex raises his eyebrows. I clear my throat. "This is hard for me. You've done it all before, but it's all new for me," I say.

"Done what before?"

"This. All of this. Relationships, dating, whatever."

"Uh, no. I've never done *this* before."

"Yes, you have."

"I've never been on a double date before."

"Well—"

"And I've never brought someone to a party before either. Not like that, where it's all my friends and you don't know anyone."

"Okay—"

"I've never liked my brother's friend before."

"Sure, but—"

"I've never had this conversation before."

"Well, you've probably—"

"And the way I feel about you. It's different from how I've liked other people. It's a new feeling."

"A new feeling?" This is definitely something we need to dig into a lot more deeply.

"You think I'm some kind of expert, and I'm really, really not. I'm bad at this. *Really* bad. Maybe a disaster."

"I don't think you're that bad."

"What bits am I good at?"

Kissing, I want to say. *You're really good at all the kissing bits.* "You're good at the bits when it's just you and me."

"I'm trying to be better at the other parts," he says, and he looks so earnest and hopeful I want to squish his face.

"Well, it's hard for you, because I'm really bad at them too," I say.

"So what are you trying to say?"

I hear Zach's voice in my head. *You know what you want. Just tell him.*

I take a deep breath. "I like you. I want us to be together. Officially, no confusion, together. I'm the kind of person who needs to know where she stands on things. I like labels, I like structure, I like things to be clear, otherwise I just obsess over things. So, what I'm saying is, I want you to be my boyfriend."

He opens his mouth to speak but I keep going, because I can't let the words "I want you to be my boyfriend" be the last thing I say.

"I know I'm hard work. Like the way I freaked out at the party. And the beach. That stuff is going to keep happening, probably. I'm not going to have some kind of epiphany where I realize I'm a completely different person. So you'd need to figure out a way to deal with that. And, I'm not sure if you can even be my boyfriend when we haven't had sex or anything yet, so I know I'm probably overstepping things. Also, I've never been in a bar and don't like being drunk and I'm thinking about becoming a vegetarian, which would be a deal-breaker for some chefs—"

"Wait, wait, wait," he says. "Go back to the boyfriend part."

Now I feel shy. "What about it?"

"Say that bit again."

"Well, I like labels and definitions—"

"No, the boyfriend bit."

Saying it a second time takes as much courage as the first time. "I want you to be my boyfriend."

He smiles and steps forward, putting his arms around me. "That's the only part you need to say," he says.

I lean in to him for a second, and then pull back. "Wait, I want to tell you one more thing."

He looks at me expectantly.

"I used to have bad skin." I rush the words out, fast, because they are the scariest words I've ever said out loud. *Here is the thing I am most ashamed of: take it, take it.*

"And . . . ?" he says.

"And, what?"

"You had bad skin, and . . . ?" He looks like he's waiting for me to add something else, like this is not enough of the story. I don't know how to possibly convey to him what I actually mean. To say, *This thing that you're practically shrugging off is what has defined my life to this moment. To really know me, you need to know this.*

"And it was really hard for me. And I have lots of scars on my back, that you might see one day."

"Show me," he says.

We just look at each other for a long moment. I swim through a thousand excuses in my mind and tell myself, *Be brave, be braver than you've ever been,* and I turn away from him, and hold the bottom of my T-shirt in my hands and then lift it up, all the way, so it's around my neck and he can see all of my back and shoulders, all of the marks, indents, and lumps. All of the brutal ugliness. I stand like that for a second, maybe two, maybe three, listening to him breathing behind me, and then lower my T-shirt back down. I turn around to face him, and my hands are shaking so badly that I want to shove them in my pockets.

He takes my shaking hands in his, folds them up, presses my fingers to his lips.

"Do you know why I was afraid to kiss you at Benny's party?" he says.

"No."

"And why I've been kind of freaking out ever since?"

"I didn't know you were freaking out."

"Because I'm this guy who's not at uni, who doesn't even have a *job* anymore, who has no idea what he's doing. And you, you're so smart—you just got into one of the best universities in the country—and you're funny, you're gorgeous, you're *beautiful*. I don't give a shit about those scars. I knew everyone would tell you that I wasn't right for you, and what they would really mean is, you can do better. I thought they would say, *Gee, it's a shame she couldn't be with someone more like Zach.*"

He's talking so fast, I can hardly catch all his words. I want to tell him, *Go back and say it all again, slowly, really slowly, then let me go away for an hour to process everything.*

I also want to hug him and tell him a thousand nice things to make him feel better about himself. It's shocking to me, the thought that I could do that, that I might do that one day, that he might *need* me to do that. I'm so used to being the broken one.

"Okay. So now what?" I say.

"Now I'm your boyfriend," he says, smiling a little.

"I guess you are," I say, leaning forward and kissing him.

Probably everything will be terrible and we'll never last, but right now, right this second, it feels like it could be something wonderful.

34

A NEW PLAN

"That's not going to fit," Zach says.

"That's not going to fit," Dad yells.

"It'll fit," Mum and Alex yell back in unison.

Lucy and I are watching the four of them grappling with a very old sagging-in-the-middle couch we bought online and haggled the owner into delivering for free.

Lucy and I are moving in together.

The thought of Mum and me sharing an apartment, while she may or may not be dating, while she may or may not be *having sex,* possibly with *Eric,* was too much for me. The same goes for Dad. The plan of me living at home only worked with them together, I realized. It only worked in our house, with everything as it was before. Now they're out there forging new lives for themselves, and I have to try to as well.

Mum and Dad are helping me with rent, but I need to find a part-time job. If I can't earn enough money to cover my expenses, then I'll have no choice but to move in with one of them. I have two interviews at cafés lined up for next week. My dream is to transition from waitress to retail worker to bookseller over the next three years, while I study. That's my plan. My new plan.

I still can't really think about university, even though it's looming right around the corner. Picturing myself walking into a lecture theater, on my own, for my first lecture, is so scary it makes my palms sweaty. But no one has ever died from sitting alone in a room full of people. That's what I keep telling myself.

Lucy has deferred uni for a year. She is going to work full-time and take the year to figure out what she wants, and hopefully save up enough money to go backpacking around South America for a month. Maybe with Zach. Maybe not.

Lucy and I are renting a run-down house that has an ancient oven that possibly hasn't been cleaned in a decade, a back door that lets in the slightest draft, a bathroom with a sink and mirror that are far too small for anyone with needs beyond brushing their teeth, and a permanent dank smell in the laundry area. We have another roommate, a girl our age called Samira who described herself over email as quiet and mature, wanting to focus on her studies, but greeted us with a scream when we first met her. She runs an Instagram account featuring her girlfriend's pug dog, and she owns what appears to be more than fifty pairs of shoes. I already mostly love her.

Zach leaves in a week, and he and Lucy still don't know what they're going to do. Possibly try long-distance, but they might break up, or take a break, or something between the two that they've both tried to explain to me and I can't make sense of. ("We'll still be together emotionally," Lucy keeps saying, and I keep nodding.)

Alex is very excited that I've moved out.

"How many nights a week should I come over?" he asked as soon as we found a place. He's been my boyfriend for five weeks and two days, and I think things are going pretty well. He got a new job last week, which has made him so much happier, even though the chef in his new kitchen also yells a lot, but Alex says it's a different kind of yelling, the funny kind, the tolerable kind.

I am still getting used to the idea that we're together. Sometimes I'll just think of him, of us being together, and I want to shout with happiness. Other times, it feels like my life would be so much easier if I didn't have to be vulnerable in this new way.

Alex can be annoyingly slow to respond to text messages, he wears his shoes indoors constantly, and we have opposite taste in music, but the other night he leaned over to me and said, "Look at this," with a big goofy grin on his face, and held up his phone with a picture of someone's pet rabbit wearing a bow tie and top hat at their wedding, and I looked at him and thought, *I might love this guy.*

Now everything is unpacked in our house and we've officially moved in, but Mum and Dad are reluctant to leave.

"I don't think the couch fits right," Mum says.

"It does," I say.

"It's better where it was before," she says.

"Then we'll move it back. Later. Tonight. After Samira has seen everything."

"Are you sure you have enough food?"

"Are you kidding? You've given me a week's worth of meals to freeze. The freezer doesn't even have that much space."

I steer them both to the front door and out toward their respective cars.

"Well, this is it, kiddo," Dad says.

Mum has tears in her eyes.

"I don't think I did a great job of teaching you how to cook," she says. This is true, she has taught me nothing about cooking, mostly because she herself knows very little.

"Mum, I'm going out with an apprentice chef."

"Yes, but you need to know how to make stuff for yourself."

"That's what the internet is for."

"I didn't think you'd be moving out so soon," she says.

"Well, you guys shouldn't have broken up."

That was a test, to see how sensitive they are to a pending-divorce-themed joke, and they both look upset, and I feel bad. But not that bad, because I'm still not over it, the ten-month lie and the destruction of our family. It's like a little hard ball inside me, which I can ignore, which I can live with, but it's still always *there*.

"I'm kidding," I say. "This is good. This is a big step. One that we didn't think was going to happen until I was at least thirty."

"You can still come home."

"I plan to."

"I mean, if it doesn't work out."

"Yes, I know. I'll have no other choice."

"Call us both every night," Dad says.

"That's excessive."

"Just for the first two weeks."

"I'll try."

"And visit both of us every weekend."

"I will," I say. (I absolutely will not.)

This is it. There's nothing else left to say. I open my arms, and we hug, all three of us, for a long time.

Then I turn and go inside, where Zach, Lucy, and Alex are waiting for me. Where the beginning of a whole new life is waiting for me.

ACKNOWLEDGMENTS

Thank you to Text Publishing for believing in my book, and for investing in young adult and children's books through the Text Prize. Winning the Text Prize has been life changing for me, and I am so grateful that such an opportunity exists.

A huge thank-you to my editors, Jane Pearson from Text and Sarah Barley from Flatiron Books, for their ongoing support, brilliant editorial guidance, and for making my book the best it could be.

Thank you also to Michael Heyward, Penny Hueston, Shalini Kunahlan, Patti Patcha, Kate Lloyd, Jamila Khodja, Khadija Caffoor, and Anne Beilby for their enthusiasm, encouragement, and championing of my work.

Thank you to cover designer Philip Pascuzzo and art director Keith Hayes for creating the book's gorgeous cover design.

To my first readers, Bronte Coates and Emily Gale. This book would not have been written without your encouragement, weekly emails, invaluable feedback, good humor, and gossip. I'm forever thankful for our writers' group. Thank you to booksellers all over Australia for your passion, hard work, and dedication, especially those who were early readers of this book in manuscript.

An extra-special thank-you to all my colleagues at Readings. Working with you has been a joy every day and has inspired me as a writer more than I ever could have thought.

I became a writer by being a reader, so I am indebted to the thousands of talented authors whose worlds I have visited throughout my life, especially the YA authors.

Thank you to Mum and Dad, who have encouraged my reading and writing at every point in my life, and supported me in every way possible, including surrounding me with books from as early as I can remember.

I couldn't have written the family dynamics of this book without my sister, Carla, and brother, John. Thank you for providing me with many years of laughter, arguments, and fun.

I am incredibly glad for my wonderful circle of friends and family, whose ongoing excitement about the impending publication of this book has been a constant source of joy. A special shout-out to Aleixandria McGearey, who was by my side at writing camp when we were awkward fifteen-year-olds and I was first dreaming of becoming an author.

To Dan, my partner and best friend. Thank you for supporting and believing in me, and for being more excited, proud, and delighted than I could have imagined when we found out my words were going to become a book, and for sharing so genuinely and happily in every moment along the way. I'm so glad we chose each other.

Finally, I am writing these acknowledgments while pregnant with my daughter. I can't wait to meet you, little one, and I look forward to us reading many books together.

ABOUT THE AUTHOR

Nina Kenwood is the marketing manager at Readings bookshop in Melbourne, Australia. She has worked in the book industry for ten years, but has been writing, secretly, for much longer. Find her book recommendations on Twitter at @NinaKenwood and on her website at www.ninakenwood.com. She is available to sort you into a Hogwarts house upon request.